M
Brown

Brown, Rita Mae.
Murder, she meowed.

DATE			

Mynderse Library

Seneca Falls, New York

Murder, She Meowed

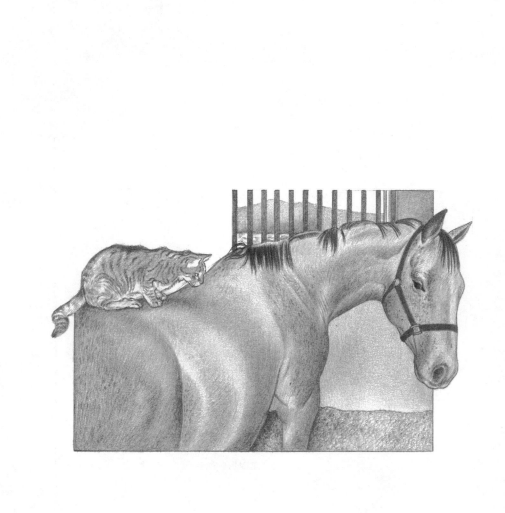

Murder, She Meowed

RITA MAE BROWN
& SNEAKY PIE BROWN

ILLUSTRATIONS BY WENDY WRAY

BANTAM BOOKS   NEW YORK • TORONTO • LONDON • SYDNEY • AUCKLAND

M U R D E R ,   S H E   M E O W E D
A Bantam Book / December 1996

Library of Congress Cataloging-in-Publication Data

Brown, Rita Mae.
Murder, she meowed / Rita Mae Brown & Sneaky Pie Brown; illustrations by Wendy Wray.
p.   cm.
ISBN-0-553-09604-4
1. Montpelier Hunt Races, Montpelier Station, Va.—Fiction.   2. Haristeen, Harry (Fictitious
character)—Fiction.   3. Murphy, Mrs. (Fictitious character)—Fiction.   4. Women detectives—
Virginia—Fiction.   5. Women cat owners—Virginia—Fiction.   6. Cats—Fiction.   I. Title.
PS3552.R698M89   1996

813'.54—dc20   96-20727
                                                                                                     CIP

Published simultaneously in the United States and Canada

Bantam Books are published by Bantam Books, a division of Bantam Doubleday Dell Publishing Group, Inc.
Its trademark, consisting of the words "Bantam Books" and the portrayal of a rooster, is Registered in U.S.
Patent and Trademark Office and in other countries. Marca Registrada. Bantam Books, 1540 Broadway,
New York, New York 10036.

P R I N T E D   I N   T H E   U N I T E D   S T A T E S   O F   A M E R I C A
BVG   10 9   8   7   6   5   4   3   2   1

Dedicated to Pooh Bear and Coye
who love and guard Mrs. William O. Moss

Cast of Characters

Mary Minor Haristeen (Harry), the young postmistress of Crozet, whose curiosity almost kills the cat and herself

Mrs. Murphy, Harry's gray tiger cat, who bears an uncanny resemblance to authoress Sneaky Pie and who is wonderfully intelligent!

Tee Tucker, Harry's Welsh corgi. Mrs. Murphy's friend and confidante; a buoyant soul

Pharamond Haristeen (Fair), veterinarian, formerly married to Harry

Mrs. George Hogendobber (Miranda), a widow who thumps her own Bible!

Market Shiflett, owner of Shiflett's Market, next to the post office

Pewter, Market's fat gray cat, who, when need be, can be pulled away from the food bowl

Susan Tucker, Harry's best friend, who doesn't take life too seriously until her neighbors get murdered

Big Marilyn Sanburne (Mim), queen of Crozet

Rick Shaw, Albemarle sheriff

Cynthia Cooper, police officer

Herbert C. Jones, Pastor of Crozet Lutheran Church, a kindly, ecumenical soul who has been known to share his sermons with his two cats, Lucy Fur and Elocution

Arthur Tetrick, distinguished steeplechase officer and lawyer

Charles Valiant (Chark), young to be a steeplechase trainer but quite talented

Adelia Valiant (Addie), she turns twenty-one in November, catapulting her and Chark into their inheritance. She's a jockey—headstrong and impulsive

Marylou Valiant, Chark and Addie's mother, who disappeared five years ago

Mickey Townsend, a trainer much loved by Addie and much deplored by Chark

Nigel Danforth, recently arrived from England, he rides for Mickey Townsend

Coty Lamont, the best steeplechase jockey of the decade

Linda Forloines, vicious lying white trash whose highest value is the dollar

Will Forloines, on the same ethical level as his wife but perching on a lower intelligence rung

Bazooka, a hot 'chaser owned by Mim Sanburne

Orion, Mim's hunter, who displays an equine sense of humor

Rodger Dodger, Mim's aging ginger barn cat, newly rejuvenated by his girlfriend, Pusskin. Rodger likes to do things by the book

Pusskin, a beautiful tortoiseshell cat, she dotes on Rodger and irritates Mrs. Murphy

Dear Reader:

Thank you for your letters. While I try to answer every one I can answer some of the more frequent questions here.

Do I use a typewriter? No. Mother does. I use a Toshiba laptop that costs as much as a used Toyota. I like the mouse.

Do I write every day? Only when the real mousing is bad.

Do I live with other cats and dogs? Yes, and horses, too, but I'm not giving them any free advertising. After all, I'm the one who writes the books therefore I deserve the lion's share of the attention.

Is Pewter really fat? Well, parts of her have their own zip code. And I just saw her eat a mushroom not ten minutes ago. A mushroom is a fungus. What self-respecting cat eats fungus? She drinks beer, too.

Is Mother fun? Most times. She slides into the slough of despond when she has to pay bills. She had a lot to pay this year because floods washed out part of our road and bridge. The insurance didn't cover it but I could have told her that. She's been working very hard and while I sympathize it does keep her out of my fur.

Am I a Dixiecat? Well, I was born in the great state of Virginia so I believe we're not here for a long time but we're here for a good time. I sure hope you're having as good a time as I am!

Love,

SNEAKY PIE

Murder, She Meowed

1

The entrance to Montpelier, once the home of James and Dolley Madison, is marked by two ivy-covered pillars. An eagle, wings outstretched, perches atop each pillar. This first Saturday in November, Mary Minor Haristeen—"Harry"—drove through the elegant, understated entrance as she had done for thirty-four years. Her parents had brought her to Montpelier's 2,700 acres in the first year of her life, and she had not missed a race meet since. Like Thanksgiving, her birthday, Christmas, and Easter, the steeplechase races held at the Madisons' estate four miles west of Orange, Virginia, marked her life. A touchstone.

As she rolled past the pillars, she glanced at the eagles but gave them little thought. The eagle is a raptor, a bird of prey, capturing its victims in sharp talons, swooping out of the air with deadly accuracy. Nature divides into victor and victim. Humankind attempts to soften such clarity. It's not that humans don't recognize that there are victors and victims in life but that they prefer to cast their experiences in such terms as good or evil, not feaster and feast. However she chose to look at it, Harry would remember this crisp, azure day, and what would return to her mind would be the eagles . . . how she had driven past those sentinels so many times yet missed their significance.

One thing was for sure—neither she nor any of the fifteen thousand spectators would ever forget this particular Montpelier meet.

Mrs. Miranda Hogendobber, Harry's older friend and partner at work, rode with her in Harry's battered pickup truck, of slightly younger vintage than Mrs. Hogendobber's ancient Ford Falcon. Since Harry had promised Arthur Tetrick, the race director, that she'd be a fence judge, she needed to arrive early.

They passed through the gates, clambering onto the bridge arching over the Southern Railroad tracks and through the spate of hardwoods, thence emerging onto the emerald expanse of the racecourse circling the 100-acre center field. Brush and timber jumps dotted the track bound by white rails that determined the width of the difficult course. On her right, raised above the road, was the dirt flat track, which the late Mrs. Marion duPont Scott had built in 1929 to exercise her Thoroughbreds. Currently rented, the track remained in use and, along with the estate, had passed to the National Historic Trust upon Mrs. Scott's death in the fall of 1983.

Straight ahead through more pillared gates loomed Montpelier itself, a peach-colored house shining like a chunk of soft sunrise that had fallen from the heavens to lodge in the foothills of the Southwest Range of the Blue Ridge Mountains. Harry thought to herself that Montpelier, built while America labored under the punitive taxes of King George III, was a kind of sunrise, a peep over the horizon of a new political force, a nation made up of people from everywhere united by a vision of democracy. That the vision had darkened or become distorted didn't lessen the glory of its birth, and Harry, not an especially political person, believed passionately that Americans had to hold on to the concepts of their forefathers and foremothers.

One such concept was enjoying a cracking good time. James and Dolley Madison adored a good horse race and agreed that the supreme horseman of their time had been George Washington. Even before James was born in 1752, the colonists wagered on, argued over, and loved fine horses. Virginians, mindful of their history, continued the pastime.

Tee Tucker, Harry's corgi, sat in her lap staring out the window. She, too, loved horses, but she was especially thrilled today because her best friend and fiercest competitor, Mrs. Murphy, a tiger cat of formidable intelligence, was forced to stay home. Mrs. Murphy had screeched "dirty pool" at the top of her kitty lungs, but it had done no good because Harry had told her the crowd would upset her and she'd either run into the truck and pout or, worse, make the rounds of everyone's tailgates. Murphy had no control when it came to fresh roasted chicken, and there'd be plenty of that today. Truth be told, Tucker had no self-control either when it came to savoring meat dishes, but she couldn't jump up into the food the way the cat could.

Oh, the savage pleasure of pressing her wet, cold nose to the window as the truck pulled out of the farm's driveway and watching Mrs. Murphy standing on her hind legs at the kitchen window. Tucker was certain that when they returned early in the evening Murphy would have shredded the fringes on the old couch, torn the curtains, and chewed the phone cord, for starters. Then the cat would be in even more trouble while Tucker, the usual scapegoat, would polish her halo. If she had a tail, she'd wag it, she was so happy. Instead she wiggled.

"Tucker, sit still, we're almost there," Harry chided her.

"There's Mim." Mrs. Hogendobber waved to Marilyn

Sanburne, whose combination of money and bossiness made her the queen of Crozet. "Boiled wool, I see. She's going Bavarian."

"I like the pheasant feather in her cap myself." Harry smiled and waved too.

"How many horses does she have running today?"

"Three. She's having a good year with Bazooka, her big gelding. The other two are green and coming along." Harry used the term that described a young animal gaining experience. "It's wonderful that she's giving the Valiants a chance to train her horses. Having good stock makes all the difference, but then Mim would know."

Harry pulled into her parking space. She fished her gloves out of her pocket. At ten in the morning the temperature was forty-five degrees. By 12:30 and the first race, it might nudge into the high fifties, a perfect temperature for early November.

"Don't forget your badge." Mrs. Hogendobber, a good deal older than Harry, was inclined to mother her.

"I won't." Harry pinned on her badge, a green ribbon with OFFICIAL stamped in gold down the length of it. "I've even got one for Tucker." She tied a ribbon on the dog's leather collar.

The Hepworths, Harry's mother's family, had attended the first running of the Montpelier Hunt Races in 1928 when it was run over a cross-country course. It was always the "Hepworth space" until a few years ago when it became simply number 175.

Harry and Tucker hopped out of the car, ducked under the white rail, sprinted across the soft, perfect turf, and joined the other officials in the paddock area graced by large oak trees, their leaves still splashes of orange and yellow. In the center sat a small green building and a tent where jockeys changed into their silks and picked up their saddle pad numbers. Large striped tents were set up alongside the paddock in a restricted area for patrons of the event. Harry could smell the ham cooking in one tent and hoped she'd have time to scoot in for fresh ham biscuits and a cup of hot tea. Although it was sunny, a light wind chilled her face.

"Harry!" Fair Haristeen, her ex-husband and the race veterinarian, was striding over to her, looking like Thor himself.

"Hi, honey. I'm ready for anything."

Before the blond giant could answer, Chark Valiant and his sister, Adelia, walked over.

Chark, so-called because he was the sixth Charles Valiant, hugged Harry. "It's good to see you, Harry. Great day for 'chasing."

"Sure is."

"Oh, look at Tucker." Addie knelt down to pet her. "I'd trust your judgment anytime."

"A corgi official or an Official Corgi?" Chark asked, his tone arch.

"*The best corgi,*" the little dog answered, smiling.

"You ready?" Harry peered at Addie, soon to be twenty-one, who'd followed her older brother into the steeplechasing world. He was the trainer, she was the jockey, a gifted and gutsy one.

"This is our Montpelier." She beamed, her youthful face already creased by sun and wind.

"Mim's the nervous one." Chark laughed because Mim Sanburne, who owned more horses than she could count, paced more than the horses did before the races.

"We passed her on the way in. Looked like she was heading up to the big house." Harry was referring to Montpelier.

"I don't know how she keeps up with her dozens of committees. I thought Monticello was her favorite cause." Fair rubbed his hands through his hair, then put his lad's cap back on.

"It is, but she promised to help give elected officials a tour, and the Montpelier staff is on overload." Harry did not need to explain that in this election year, anyone running for public office, even dogcatcher, would die before they'd miss the races and miss having a photo of themselves at the Madison house run in the local newspaper.

"Well, I'm heading back to the stable." Chark touched Harry on the shoulder. "Find me when the races are over. I hope we'll have something to celebrate."

"Sure."

Fair, called away by Colbert Mason, director of the National Hunt and Steeplechase Association, winked and left Harry and Addie.

"Adelia!" Arthur Tetrick called, then noticed Harry, and a big smile crossed his angular, distinguished face.

Striding over to chat with "the girls," as he called them, Arthur nodded and waved to people. A lawyer of solid reputation, he was not only acting race director for Montpelier but was often an official at other steeplechases. As executor of Marylou Valiant's will, he was also her two children's guardian—their father being dead—until Adelia turned twenty-one later that month and came into her considerable inheritance. Chark, though older than his sister, would not receive his money, either, until Addie's birthday. His mother had felt that men, being slower to mature, should have their inheritance delayed. She couldn't have been more wrong concerning her own offspring, for Chark was prudent if not parsimonious, whereas Addie's philosophy was the financial equivalent of the Biblical "consider the lilies of the field." But Marylou, who had disappeared five years earlier and was presumed dead, had missed crucial years in the development of her children. She couldn't have known that her theory was backward in their case.

"Don't you look the part." Addie kidded her guardian, taking in his fine English tweed vest and jacket.

"Can't be shabby. Mrs. Scott would come back to haunt me. Harry, we're delighted you're helping us out today."

"Glad to help."

Putting his hand over Addie's slender shoulder, he murmured, "Tomorrow—a little sit-down."

"Oh, Arthur, all you want to do is talk about stocks and bonds and—" she mocked his solemn voice as she intoned, "—NEVER TOUCH THE PRINCIPAL. I can't stand it! Bores me."

With an avuncular air, he chuckled. "Nonetheless, we must review your responsibilities before your birthday."

"Why? We review them once a bloody month."

Arthur shrugged, his bright eyes seeking support from Harry. "Wine, women, and song are the male vices. In your case it's horses, jockeys, and song. You won't have a penny left by the time you're forty." His tone was light but his eyes were intense.

Wary, Addie stepped back. "Don't start on Nigel."

"Nigel Danforth has all the appeal of an investment in Sarajevo."

"I like him." She clamped her lips shut.

Arthur snorted. "Being attracted to irresponsible men is a female vice in your family. Nigel Danforth is not worthy of you and—"

Addie slipped her arm through Harry's while finishing Arthur's sentence for him, "—he's a gold digger, mark my words." Irritated, she sighed. "I've got to get ready. We can fight about this after the races."

"Nothing to fight about. Nothing at all." Arthur's tone softened. "Good riding. Safe races. God bless. See you after the day's run."

"Sure." Addie propelled Harry toward the weigh-in stand as Arthur joined Fair and other jovial officials. "You'll adore Nigel—you haven't met him, have you? Arthur's being an old poop, as usual."

"He worries about you."

"Tough." Addie's face cleared. "Nigel's riding for Mickey Townsend. Just started for him. I warned him to get his money at the end of each day, though. Mickey's got good horses but he's always broke. Nigel's new, you know—he came over from England."

Harry smiled. "Americans don't name their sons Nigel."

"He's got the smoothest voice. Like silk." Addie was ignoring the wry observation.

"How long have you been dating him?"

"Two months. Chark can't stand him but Charles the Sixth can be such a moose sometimes. I wish he and Arthur would stop hovering over me. Just because a few of my boyfriends in the past have turned out to be blister bugs."

Harry laughed. "Hey, you know what they say, you gotta kiss a lot of toads before finding the prince."

"Better than getting a blister."

"Addie, anything is better than a blister bug." She paused. "Except drugs. Does Nigel take them? You can't be too careful." Harry believed in grabbing the bull by the horns.

Quickly, Addie said, "I don't do drugs anymore," then changed the subject. "Hey, is Susan coming today?"

"Later. The Reverend Jones will be here, too. The whole Crozet gang. We've got to root for Bazooka."

Chark waved for his sister to join him.

"Oops. Big Brother is watching me." She dropped Harry's arm. "Harry, I'll see you after the races. I want you to meet Nigel."

"After the races then." Harry walked over to get her fence assignment.

Harry, as usual, had been assigned the east gate jump, so-called because it lay closest to the east gate entrance to the main house. She vaulted over the rail to the patrons' tents, put together a ham biscuit and a cup of tea, turned too fast without looking, and bumped into a slender dark man accompanied by a jockey she recognized.

"I'm sorry," she said.

"Another woman falling over you," Coty Lamont said sarcastically.

"Coty, you aren't using the right cologne. Old manure doesn't attract women." The other man spoke in a light English accent.

Harry, who knew Coty slightly—the best jockey riding at this time—smiled at him. "Smells good to me, Coty."

He recognized her since she occasionally worked other stee-plechase races. "The post office lady."

"Mary Minor Haristeen." She held out her hand.

He shook her hand. He couldn't extend his hand until she offered hers . . . rough as Coty appeared, he had absorbed the minimum of social graces.

"And this here's Nigel Danforth."

"Pleased to meet you Mr. Danforth." Harry shook his hand. "I'm a friend of Addie's."

Their faces relaxed.

"Ah," Nigel said simply, and smiled.

"Then be ready to part-*tee*," Coty said.

"Uh—sure," Harry, a bit confused by their sudden enthusi-asm, said softly.

"See you later." Coty headed for the jockeys' changing tent.

Nigel winked. "Any friend of Addie's . . ." Then he, too, hurried to the tent.

Harry watched the diminutive men walk away from her, struck by how tiny their butts were. She did not know what to make of those two. Their whole demeanor had changed when she mentioned Addie. She felt as if she'd given the password to an exclusive club.

She blinked, sipped some tea, then walked out the east side of the tent area and stepped over the cordon. Tucker ducked un-der it.

"Come on, Tucker, let's check our fence before the hordes arrive."

"*Good idea,*" Tucker said. "*You know how everyone stops to pass and repass. If you don't get over there now you'll never get over.*"

Harry glanced down at the dog. "You've got a lot to say."

"*Yes, but you don't listen.*"

From the east gate jump Harry couldn't see the cars driving in, but she could hear the steady increase in noise. Glad to be alone, she bit into the succulent ham biscuit and noticed Mim walking back through the gates to the big house, toward the races. She thought to herself that the political tour must be over, another reason she was happy to be in the back—no handshaking.

Working in the Crozet post office allowed Harry weekends and a minimum of hassle. The P.O. was open Saturdays from 8 A.M. to noon. Sally Dohner and Liz Beer alternated Saturdays so Harry enjoyed two full days of freedom. Her friends took their work home with them, fretted, burned the midnight oil. Harry locked the door to the small postal building on Crozet's main drag, drove home, and forgot about work until the next morning. If she was going to fret over something, it would be her farm at the base of Yellow Mountain or some problem with a friend. Often accused of lacking ambition, she readily agreed with her critics. Her Smith College classmates, just beginning to nudge forward in their high-powered careers in New York, Boston, Richmond, and far-flung cities in the Midwest and West, reminded her she had graduated in the top 10 percent of her class. They felt she was wasting her life. She felt her life was lived from within. It was a rich life. She used a different measuring stick than they did.

She had one thing they didn't: time. Of course, they had one thing she didn't: money. She never could figure out how you could have both. Well, Marilyn "Mim" Sanburne did, but she had inherited more money than God. In Mim's defense, she used it wisely, often to help others, but to be a beneficiary of her largesse, one had to tolerate her grandeur. Little Marilyn, Harry's age, who glowered in her mother's shadow, was tiring of good works. A flaming romance would take precedence over good deeds, but Little Mim, now divorced, couldn't find Mr. Right, or rather, her mother couldn't find Mr. Right for her.

Harry's mouth curled upward. She had found Mr. Right who'd turned into Mr. Wrong and now wanted to be Mr. Right again. She loved Fair but she didn't know if she could ever again love him in that way.

A roar told her that the Bledsoe/Butler Cup, the first race of the day, one mile on the dirt, $1,000 winner-take-all—had started. Tempted as she was to run up to the flat track and watch, she knew she'd better stay put.

"Tucker, I've been daydreaming about marriage, men"—she sighed—"ex-husbands. The time ran away with me."

Tucker perked up her big ears. *"Fair still loves you. You could marry him all over again."*

Harry peered into the light brown eyes. "Sometimes you seem almost human—as if you know exactly what I'm saying."

"Sometimes you seem almost canine." Tucker stared back at her. *"But you have no nose, Harry."*

"Are you barking at me?" Harry laughed.

"I'm telling you to stop living so much in your mind, that's what I'm saying. Why you think I'm barking is beyond me. I know what you're saying."

Harry reached over, hugged the sturdy dog, and kissed the soft fur on her head. "You really are the most adorable dog."

She heard the announcer begin to call the jockeys for the second race, the first division of the Marion duPont Scott Montpelier Cup, purse $10,000, two miles and one furlong over brush for "maidens" three years old and upward, a maiden being a horse that had never won a race. She could see people walking over the hill. Many race fans, the knowledgeable ones, wanted to get away from the crowds and watch the horses.

A brand-new Land Rover drove at the edge of the course, its midnight blue shining in the November light. Harry couldn't imagine being able to purchase such an expensive vehicle. She was saving her pennies to replace the '78 Ford truck, which despite its age was still chugging along.

Dr. Larry Johnson stuck his head out the Land Rover's passenger window. "Everything shipshape?"

"Yes, sir." Harry saluted.

"Hello, Tucker." Larry spoke to the sweet-eyed dog.

"Hi, Doc."

"We've got about ten minutes." Larry turned to Jim

Sanburne, Mim's husband and the mayor of Crozet, who was driving. "Don't we, Jim?"

"I reckon." Jim leaned toward the passenger window, his huge frame blotting out the light from the driver's side. "Harry, you know that Charles Valiant and Mickey Townsend are fighting like cats and dogs, so pay close attention to those races where they've both got entries."

"What's the buzz?" Harry had heard nothing of the feud.

"Hell, I don't know. These damn trainers are prima donnas."

"Mickey accused Chark of instructing Addie to bump his jockey at the Maryland Hunt Cup last year. His horse faltered at the sixth fence and then just couldn't quite pick it up."

"Mickey's a sore loser," Jim growled to Larry. "He'll break your fingers if you beat him at checkers—especially if there's money bet on the game."

"Goes back further than that." Harry sighed.

"You're right. Charles hated Mickey from the very first date Mickey had with his mother." Jim ran his finger under his belt. "Takes some boys like that. But you know Charles had sense enough to worry that Townsend only wanted her money."

"Chark couldn't understand how Marylou could prefer Mickey to Arthur." Larry Johnson recalled the romance, which had started seven years ago, ending in shock and dismay for everyone. "I guess any woman who compares Arthur to Mickey is bound to favor Mickey. I don't think it had to do with money."

"Off the top of your head, do you know what races—"

Before Harry could finish her question, Jim Sanburne bellowed, "The third, the fifth, and the sixth."

"Nigel Danforth is riding for Townsend," Larry added.

"Addie told me," Harry said.

"You heard about them too." Jim smiled.

"Kinda. I mean, I know that Addie is crazy for him."

"Her brother isn't." Larry folded his arms across his chest.

"Hey, just another day in Virginia." Harry smacked the door of the Land Rover.

"Ain't that the truth," Jim said. "Put two Virginians in a room and you get five opinions."

"No, Jim, put *you* in a room and we get five opinions," Larry tweaked him.

Jim laughed. "I'm just the mayor of a small town reflecting the various opinions of my voters."

"We'll come by after the first race. Need anything? Food? Drink?" Larry asked while Jim was still laughing at himself.

"Thanks, no."

"Okay, Harry, catch you in about a half hour then." Jim rolled up the hill as Larry waved.

Harry put her hands on her hips and thought to herself. Jim, in his sixties, and Larry, in his seventies, had known her since she was born. They knew her inside and out, as she knew them. That was another reason she didn't much feel like being the Queen of Madison Avenue. She belonged here with her people. There was a lot that never needed to be said when you knew people so intimately.

This shorthand form of communication did not apply to Boom Boom Craycroft, creaming over the top of the hill like a clipper in full sail. Since Boom Boom had once enjoyed an affair with Harry's ex-husband, the buxom, tall, and fashionable woman was not Harry's favorite person on earth. Boom Boom reveled in the emotional texture of life. Today she reveled in the intense pleasure of swooping down on Harry, who couldn't move away since she was the fence judge.

"Harry!" Boom Boom cruised over, her square white teeth gleaming, her heavy, expensive red cape moving gently in the breeze.

"Hi, Boom." Harry shortened her nickname, one won in high school because her large bosoms seemed to boom-boom with each step. The boys adored her.

"You're dressed for the job." Boom Boom appraised Harry's pressed jeans and L. L. Bean duck boots—the high-topped ones, which reached only nine inches for women, a fact that infuriated Harry since she could have used twelve inches on the farm; only the men's boots had twelve-inch uppers. Harry also wore a silk undershirt, an ironed flannel tartan plaid, MacLeod, and a goosedown vest, in red. If the day warmed up, she would shed her layers.

"Boom Boom, I'm usually dressed this way."

"I know," came the tart reply from the woman standing there in Versace from head to foot. Her crocodile boots alone cost over a thousand dollars.

"I don't have your budget."

"Even if you did you'd look exactly the same."

"All right, Boom, what's the deal? You come over here to give me your fashion lecture 101, to visit uneasiness upon me, or do you want something from Tucker?"

Tucker squeezed next to her mother. *"She's got on too much perfume, Mom. She's stuffing my nose up."*

Boom Boom leaned over to pat the silky head. "Tucker, very impressive with your official's badge."

"Boom, those fake fingernails have got to go," the dog replied.

"I'm here to visit and to watch the first race from the back."

"Have a fight with Carlos?"

Boom Boom had been dating a wealthy South American who lived in New York City and Buenos Aires.

"He's not here this weekend."

"Trolling, then?" Harry wryly used the term for going around picking up men.

"You can be so snide, Harry. It's not your best feature. I'm here to patch up our relationship."

"We don't have a relationship."

"Oh, yes, we do."

"They're lining up, the starter's tape is up,"—the announcer's voice rang out as he waited for the tape to drop—"and they're off."

"I've got to work this race." Harry moved Boom Boom forcibly back, then took up her stance on the rail dead even with the jump. If a rider went down, she could reach the jockey quickly, as soon as all the other horses were over the fence, while the outriders went after the runaway horse.

The first jumps limbered up the horses and settled the jockeys. By the time they reached Harry's jump, the competition would be fierce. The first race over fences covered a distance of two miles and one furlong; competitors would pass her obstacle only once. This race, and in fact all races but the fifth, the Virginia Hunt Cup, were run over brush, meaning the synthetic Grand National brush fences, which had replaced natural brush some years ago. The reasoning behind the change was that the natural brush varied in density. Because steeplechase horses literally "brushed" through the top of these jumps, any inconsistency in texture or depth or solidity could cause a fall or injury. The Grand National fences provided horses with a safer jump. Timber horses, on the other hand, had to jump cleanly over the whole obstacle, although the top timbers were notched on the back so they would give way if rapped hard enough. Even so, the last thing a timber trainer or jockey wanted was for one of their horses to "brush" through a timber fence.

Harry heard the crowd. Then in the distance she heard the thunder. The earth shook. The sensation sent chills up her spine, and in an instant the horses turned the distant corner, a kaleidoscope of finely conditioned bays, chestnuts, and seal browns, hooves reaching out as they lengthened their stride. She recognized the purple silks of Mim Sanburne as well as Addie's determined gaze. The Urquharts, Mim's family, had registered the first year that the Jockey Club was organized, 1894, so their horses ran in solid color silks. Harry also saw the other silks: emerald green with a red hoop around the chest, blue with yellow dots, yellow with a diagonal black sash, the colors intense, rippling with the wind, heightening the sensation of speed, beauty, and power.

The first three horses cleared the brush, their hooves tipping the top of the synthetic cedar, making an odd swishing sound, then she heard the reassuring thump-thump as those front hooves reached the earth followed by the hind. The three leaders pulled away, and the remainder of the pack cleared the jump, a Degas painting come to life.

She breathed a sigh of relief. No one went down at her fence. No fouls. As the hoofbeats died away, moving back up the hill toward the last several jumps and the homestretch, the crowd screamed while the announcer called out the positions of the horses.

"Closing hard, Ransom Mine, but Devil Fox hanging on to the lead, and here they come down the stretch, and Ransom Mine is two strides out, but oh, what a burst of speed, it's Devil Fox under the wire!"

"Hurray for Mim!" Harry whispered. "A strong second."

Boom Boom drew alongside her. "She didn't expect much from Ransom Mine, did she?"

"She's only had him about six months. Picked him up in Maryland, I think."

"Changing trainers helped," Boom Boom said, "Chark is working out really well for her."

"Will and Linda Forloines are still going around telling horror stories about how much they did for Mim, and how vile she was to fire them." Harry shook her head, recalling Mim's former trainer and his wife, a jockey. "Will couldn't find his ass with both hands."

"No, but he sure found the checkbook," Boom Boom said. "And I don't think Will has a clue as to how much Linda makes selling cocaine or how much she takes herself."

"They're lucky Big Mim didn't prosecute them, padding the stable budget the way they did."

"She'd spend thousands of dollars in court and still never see a penny back. They've squandered all of it. Her revenge will be watching them blow out. Mim's too smart to directly cross druggies. She'll let them kill themselves—or take the cure. Thank God Addie took the cure."

"Yes," Harry said succinctly. She hated people who took advantage of others and justified it by saying the people they were stealing from were rich. If she remembered her Ten Commandments, one said, *Thou Shalt Not Steal*. It didn't say, *Thou Shalt Not Steal Except When the Employer is Wealthy*. Will and Linda Forloines still hung around the edges of the steeplechase world. The previous year Will had been reduced to working in a convenience store outside of Middleburg. Finally they had latched on to a rich doctor who moved down from New Jersey and who wanted to "get into horses." Poor man.

"They're here."

"Here?" Harry said. Boom Boom's deep voice could lull one, it was so lovely, she thought.

"You'd think they'd have the sense not to show their faces."

"Will never was the brightest bulb on the Christmas tree." Harry peeled off her down vest as Boom Boom changed the subject.

"I'm here to tell you that I'm sorry I had a fling with Fair, but it *was* after your divorce. He's a sweet man, but we weren't the right two people. I hadn't dated anyone seriously since Kelly died, and I needed to put my toes in the water."

Harry didn't think it was Boom Boom's toes that had fascinated Fair, but she resisted the urge to make a comment. Also, she didn't believe for one minute that the relationship had magically started right after the divorce. "Can you understand how it would upset me?"

"No. You divorced him."

"That didn't mean I was over him, dammit." Harry decided not to try to pinpoint the exact date of Boom Boom's liaison with Fair. At least they hadn't appeared in public until after the divorce.

"Why take it out on me? Take it out on him."

"I did, sorta."

"Well, Harry, what about the women, uh, while you were married? Those were your enemies, not me."

"Did I ever say I was emotionally mature?" Harry crossed her arms over her chest as Tucker followed the conversation closely.

"No."

"So."

"So what?"

"So, I could see you. I couldn't see those affairettes he was having while we were married. I got mad at you for all of them, I guess. I never said I was right to get mad at you but I did."

"You're still mad at me."

"No, I'm not." Harry half lied.

"You certainly never go out of your way to be nice to me."

"I'm cordial."

"Harry, we're both born and raised in Virginia. You know exactly what I mean." And Boom Boom was right. One could be correct but cool. Virginians practiced cutting one another with precise elegance.

"Yeah, well, since we were both raised in Virginia, we know how to avoid subjects like this, Boom Boom. I have no desire to explore my emotions with you or anybody."

"Exactly!"

Harry squinted at the triumphant face. "Don't start with me."

"We've got to grow beyond our conditioning. We've got to cast aside or break through our repression. You can't hold your emotions in, they'll eat away at you until you become ill or dry up like some people I could mention."

"I'm very healthy."

"You're also not twenty anymore. You've been holding these emotions in for too long."

"Now, look." Harry's voice oozed reasonableness. "What

you call repressed, I call disciplined. I am not teetering on the brink of self-annihilation. I don't drink. I don't take drugs. I don't even smoke. I like my life. I'd like a little more money maybe, but I like my life."

"You're in denial."

"Denial is a river in Egypt."

"Harry," her voice lowered, "that joke's got gray hairs. You don't fool me with your quips. I want you to come with me to Lifeline. It's changed my life, absolutely. Six months ago I would never have been able to approach you, I would have held on to my own anger, but now I want to reach out. I want us to be friends. Lifeline teaches you to take responsibility for yourself. For your own emotions. It's a structured process, and I know you like structure. You can learn these things, learn new ways to be with people in a group that will encourage you. You'll feel safe. Trust me, Harry, it will make you happy."

Trusting Boom Boom was the last thing Harry would ever do. "I'm not the type."

"I'll even pay for it."

"*What?*"

"I mean it. I'll pay for it. I feel so bad that you're still mad at me. I want us to be friends. Please consider my offer."

"I—" Harry, caught off guard, stuttered, "I, I—Jesus, Boom Boom."

"Think about it. I know you'll find a thousand reasons not to do this, but why don't you take out a pad of paper and list the pros and cons? You might find more reasons to engage in Lifeline than you know."

"Uh—I'll think about it."

"One other little thing."

"Oh, God."

"Think about the fact that you're still in love with Fair."

"I am not! I love him but I'm not in love with him."

"Lifeline." Boom Boom smiled seraphically, moving off.

Harry breathed deeply, conscious of her heart pounding. Jim Sanburne's midnight-blue Land Rover hove into view. She collected herself.

"News?" Larry inquired.

"Clean as a whistle," Harry said.

"Are you all right?" the doctor asked, observing her flushed face and rapid breathing.

"I'm fine. How long till the next race?"

"Half hour. Just about," Jim answered her.

"I need a co—cola."

"You need something," Larry joked. "You're breathing like a freight train. Why don't you come to my office Monday? How long's it been since you had a checkup?"

"Larry, I'm fine. I had a little tête-à-tête with Boom Boom."

"Say no more." He smiled and as the two men drove off, Jim said, "Did she say tit a tat?"

"No." Larry laughed loudly. "Jim, you're just a redneck with money."

Jim grunted. "Sounded like body parts to me, good buddy."

2

"Mom, I'm hungry."

"Tucker, stop yapping, you're getting on my nerves."

"You've had a ham biscuit and I haven't had anything since breakfast." The aroma from the food tents drove Tucker to distraction.

Harry checked her watch. Twenty minutes. She dashed into a tent, grabbed fried chicken, a small container of coleslaw, another one of beans, one cold Coke, and a big cup of hot tea with a plastic cover on it.

As Harry threaded her way through the crowd, she passed the jockeys' tent. A commotion stopped her. The flap of the tent opened to reveal colorful silks on hangers dangling from a rope strung across the tent. Ace bandages, caps, and socks were tossed on low benches.

Nigel, close-cropped black hair gleaming in the sun, charged out. Chark Valiant charged out after him.

"Leave him alone," Addie called after her brother. She opened the tent flap, sticking her head through. She hadn't finished changing and couldn't come all the way out.

"Shut up, Adelia." Chark pushed her head back behind the flaps, then twirled on the young man. "You flaming phony—you don't fool me. If my sister weren't a Valiant, you wouldn't give her the time of day."

Addie popped her head back out of the tent as a florid Mickey Townsend bore down on the scene from one direction.

Arthur Tetrick leaned out of the top of the two-story finish-line tower. "Mickey, don't—" He shut up, realizing he'd cause a bigger scene.

The jockey kept walking away from Chark, who grabbed him by the right shoulder, spinning him around.

"Stop it." Nigel's voice was clipped and furious.

"You stay away from my sister."

"She's old enough to make her own decisions."

Chark shook his finger in Nigel's face. "You want her money, you lying sack of shit."

"Bugger off," Nigel growled.

Chark hauled off to hit him but Mickey Townsend grabbed Chark from behind, pulling him back. "Settle this later."

Chark twisted his head to see Mickey as Nigel returned to Addie, who'd stuck her head out of the tent again. He slipped into the tent with her as three other jockeys slipped out.

"Takes one gold digger to know another." Chark struggled.

Mickey, square-built and powerful, continued dragging him away. "Shove it."

Arthur, who had hurried down from the tower, approached the two men. "Mickey, I'll take over from here."

"Suit yourself." Mickey unleashed his iron grip on the young man.

"Thank you for defusing an embarrassing situation." Arthur grabbed Chark's elbow.

"Yeah, sure." Mickey inclined his handsome, crew-cut head, then ambled back to the paddock.

"Charles, this will not do," Arthur sternly admonished him. "I'll kill that creep."

Arthur rolled his eyes heavenward. "The more resistance you offer, the more irresistible he becomes. Besides, Adelia's a baby. She's not going to date men you find attractive."

"I don't find men attractive," Chark sassed back.

"A slip of the tongue. You know what I mean." Arthur draped his arm over Chark's shoulder. "Calm down. Ignore this absurd romance. If you do, it will die of its own accord." The horses were now in the paddock. "Tell you what, after the races I have to fax in the paperwork to National from the big house. Take everyone maybe an hour. How about if I meet you at the Keswick Club for a drink? We can talk this over then. Okay? Then we'll look in on Mim's party or she'll banish us to Siberia."

"Okay," Chark replied, trying to settle his churning emotions. "But I just don't get it."

Arthur chuckled. "That's what makes the world go 'round. They don't think like we do—"

Chark interrupted. "They don't think."

"Be that as it may, men and women see the world quite differently. I've got to climb back up to my perch. Keswick Club at eight."

"Yeah." Chark smiled at the man who had become his surrogate father, then headed to the paddock where Addie, already up on a rangy bay called Chattanooga Choo, ignored his approach.

Nigel, in orange silks with three royal blue hoops, rode a striking chestnut beside her as they walked the horses around.

Chark sighed deeply, deciding not to give his sister instructions for the third race. She usually ignored them anyway.

Harry jogged back to her position, nodding to friends as she weaved her way through the dense throng. As they spied the official's badge, they waved her on, a few calling that they'd drop by to see her. She wondered what it was about romantic energy or sexual energy that made everybody crazy, producing a scene like the one she had just witnessed.

She returned to the east gate jump, sat down, and opened her tea. A plume of steam spiraled upward.

"*Mother!*" Tucker's voice rose.

"Beggar." Harry tore off a piece of hot chicken which Tucker gobbled. "Fat beggar."

"*I'm not a beggar, but I can't reach the tables and you can. And I'm not fat. Fat is Pewter.*" Tucker aptly described the gray cat who worked at Market Shiflett's convenience store next to the post office in Crozet. Pewter couldn't come to the races either, doubling Tucker's supreme satisfaction.

The announcer called out post time. Harry started eating as fast as Tucker. She hadn't realized how famished she was, but she'd been up since five that morning with only a few bites to sustain her.

Each morning Harry fed her three horses, then turned them out into the pasture. She left marshmallows for the possum who lived in the hayloft. Then she'd feed her pets . . . but sometimes she forgot to feed herself. Mrs. Murphy, apart from a good breakfast, had a huge bowl of crunchies in mixed flavors. Usually Harry left open the animal door that she had installed in her back kitchen door. The screen door off the screened-in porch, which ran the length of the kitchen, was easy for Mrs. Murphy and Tucker to push open. But this morning she had closed up the animal door, deciding she'd keep Mrs. Murphy in the house since the cat had been known to follow the car. By the time she left to fetch Mira, she'd put in three hours of hard work on the farm.

The trumpet call to the third race made Harry eat even faster. She rinsed the food down with tea and Coke.

"Got any left?"

"Tucker, get your nose out of that cup."

"Just curious."

Harry brushed herself off, picked up her debris, and stood at her position.

She heard a crack, then a double shot fired. False start. Those wore on the nerves of riders and horses. The announcer called out the renewed lineup. "Horses in position. They're off!" The third race, the Noel Laing Stakes, two and a half miles over brush, was the second biggest race of the day, with a purse of $30,000—60 percent to the winner.

The crowd yelped in anticipation. The horses charged out of sight and Harry heard the rumble of hooves, the ground shaking like Jell-O. The leader, a bright bay, was way ahead of the others. Every one cleared her fence, although one horse faltered. The jockey pulled up, his green silks with a blue cross already pasted with sweat to his body.

Harry knew this race was two and a half miles long. The horses would be around again in a few minutes. She ran out to the jockey, Coty Lamont.

"You okay?"

"He's come up lame. I'll walk up on the inside rail." Coty dismounted, careful to hold on to the reins as Harry held the horse by the bridle. "Vet's up there."

"Blown tendon, I'm afraid, Coty." Harry hoped she was wrong, because tendon injuries took a long time to heal and the risk of reinjury on a bowed tendon was high.

"Yeah." Coty touched his crop to his cap by way of thanks. He slowly walked the gelding across the course and up the inside rail as Harry raced back to her post.

Seconds later the field came around for another lap. All jumped clean.

As Harry waited for the announcer's report on the victor, she saw Will and Linda Forloines walking down the grassy slope toward her. They had in tow a man all but wrapped in Barbour.

Linda called out, "Hello, Harry."

"Hi." Harry waved to both of them. No reason to be impolite, much as she disliked the couple. She knew instantly the fellow in country drag had to be their soon-to-be-fleeced Yankee employer. She also knew that Will and Linda were making a point of showing him they knew everyone in the steeplechase world. Linda, more cunning than Will, wouldn't stop to talk to many people since she knew they would not warmly welcome her. The New Jersey gentleman wouldn't realize she was not on friendly terms since everyone would be polite. They turned and walked in the other direction as the Land Rover drove toward Harry. Linda ducked her head at the sight of Jim Sanburne.

Jim and Larry pulled up again. This time Mim, in the back-seat, hopped out. She hadn't seen Will and Linda. The men drove on.

"I want to watch the fourth race from here. I can't bear listening to Boom Boom tell me about spiced cream cheese on endive for another second! It's either endives or Lifeline." She twirled her wool cape behind her.

"This fence is too far away for most people to walk." Harry glanced down the rail. "Uh, but not too far for Greg Satterwaite. I see he's working the outside rail. I guess he'll be going to the outside barns next. God forbid he should miss anyone."

"Don't tell me," Mim exclaimed. "Has the good senator seen me?"

"Not yet. He's busy pumping hands and smiling big." Harry pulled a huge fake smile as demonstration.

Mim scurried behind one of the big trees. A telltale whiff of smoke would give her away should anyone be looking. Harry ignored Mim's cheating; she knew Mim wasn't supposed to smoke. Still, she wasn't going to tell Mim what to do or what not to do.

"Hi, there. How are you?" Satterwaite held out his hand, already swollen.

Harry suppressed an evil urge to squeeze it. "Morning, Senator."

"I surely hope I may count on your vote. This is a tough election for me."

"You can," Harry replied with little enthusiasm. She hated politics.

A jet of smoke shot upward from behind the tree.

"Thank you, thank you for your support." He smiled, capped teeth gleaming, then moved on to his next victim.

A few moments later Mim sneaked out from behind the tree. "Whew! Saved. When a politician knows you have money they'll talk until they're blue in the face. Save us from our government!"

"We're supposed to be a democracy. Save us from ourselves." Harry laughed, then noticed the cigarette still in Mim's fingers; it was burning down to a stub.

Mim stomped it into the ground. "Don't tell Jim."

"I won't." But she was surprised to see Mim gambling with her health after her bout with breast cancer.

Harry checked her program. "You've got Royal Danzig in this race. Congratulations on the first division of the Montpelier Cup, by the way. Ransom Mine took this fence with so much daylight he was flying."

"If he stays sound, he'll be one of the great ones, like Victorian Hill." Mim mentioned a wonderful horse, a star in the early '90s.

"Who was the greatest 'chaser you ever saw?"

Mim replied without hesitation. "Battleship, by Man-O'-War out of Quarantine, bred in 1927. To see that horse in Mrs. Scott's pale blue silks with the pink-and-silver cross was something I'll never forget. I was tiny then, but it made such an impression. This place was hopping because Mrs. Scott was in her prime. To have seen Battleship, that was heaven."

"What about Marylou Valiant's Zinger?" Harry remembered the leggy chestnut colt.

"If he hadn't injured his stifle, yes, I think he could have been very fine indeed." She looked up at the sky. "I hope she's up there watching today. People will say I hired Adelia and Charles out of affection. Granted that may have played some small part, but the truth is they're good . . . and getting better. And the difference in the stable since that dreadful couple is gone!" She crossed her arms over her chest. "You know it was a drip-drip like Chinese water torture after Marylou disappeared. The day I admitted to myself she must be dead was one of the darkest days of my life. And I promised to do what I could for her children."

"You more than kept your promise."

"The hard work was done. Marylou and Charley did that. When Chark went to Cornell and Addie to Foxcroft, I saw them at holidays and special school functions. What was hard was knowing when to be firm." She laughed at herself. "Now with Marilyn I never had trouble with that, but . . . well, their loss had been so profound. I sometimes wonder if I should have been tougher, especially with Addie."

Before Harry could say anything, they both heard the shot. Mim moved back. Harry trained her eyes on the roll of the land where she would first see the field.

Again that eerie rumble, and then the horses, packed tightly together, surged into view. Mim's purple silks were in the middle of the pack, a good place for this point in a race of just over two miles. Goggles over her eyes, Addie concentrated on the jump. Harry listened to the grunts and shouts of the jockeys as they cleared the brush, the whap-whap and whoosh as the hind hooves touched the greenery. And then they were gone, raging on, slipping into the dip of the land, and charging uphill again for the next fence.

Mim strained to hear the announcer call out positions. As they cleared Harry's jump, one horse in the rear of the pack took off too early and crashed through the jump, stumbling on the other side but recovering.

Harry watched the horse, which wasn't injured but was tiring badly. "Dammit, why doesn't he pull up?"

"Because it's Linda Forloines. She'll drive a horse to death."

"But I just saw Linda not twenty minutes ago."

"Zack Merchant's jockey got stepped on in the paddock as he was mounting up. Linda scurried right up to Zack, and of course he was desperate. The results speak for themselves."

The crowd noises followed the horses, an odd muffle of congregated voices, and then the field again appeared on the hill, Royal Danzig still safely in the middle.

Harry shook her head. "Linda's a piece of work."

"Precisely." Mim pursed her lips. She was not one to spread negative gossip, but she despised the Forloines to such a degree it took all her formidable discipline not to share her loathing with anyone who would listen.

"Zack Merchant's not exactly a prince among men either." Harry hated the way he treated horses, although to customers and new clients he put on a show of caring for the animals. Other horsemen knew his brutal methods, but as yet there was no way to address abuse inside the racing game. It was a little like telling a man he couldn't beat his wife. You might hate him for it. You might want to smash his face in, but somehow—you just couldn't until you caught him in the act.

The announcer's voice rose in frenzy. "Four lengths and pulling away, this race is all Royal Danzig, Royal Danzig, Royal Danzig, with Isotone crossing the finish line a distant second followed by Hercule and Vitamin Therapy."

"Congratulations!" Harry shook Mim's hand. Mim wasn't a woman designed for a spontaneous hug.

Mim carefully took the proffered hand. Her face flushed. She was wary against her own happiness. After all, the results weren't official yet. "Thank you." She blinked. "I'll find Chark and Addie. Quite a smart race she rode, staying with the pack until the stretch."

"You're having a sensational day." Harry smiled. "And it's not over yet."

"The official results of the Montpelier Cup, second division, are Royal Danzig, Isotone, and Hercule." The announcer's voice crinkled with metallic sound.

Mim relaxed. "Ah—" She couldn't think of anything to say.

"*Congratulations, Mrs. Sanburne.*" Tucker panted with excitement.

Mim said, "Tucker wants something."

"*No, I'm just happy for you,*" Tucker replied.

"Tucker."

"*Why do you always tell me to be quiet when I'm being polite?*" Tucker's ears swept back and forth.

"I'd better head up to the winner's circle. Oh, here comes my knight in shining armor."

Jim Sanburne rolled down in the Land Rover. "Come on, honeybunch."

"Well done, Mim The Magnificent!" Larry laughed.

"Hi, guys." Harry poked her head in the window. "Tell Fair to check on the horse Linda Forloines rode. He looks wrung out."

"Will do," Larry Johnson said as Jim kissed his wife, who was sliding into the front seat.

Larry Johnson moved to the back, and for an instant as Mim swung her attractive legs under her, close together as befits a proper Southern lady, Harry had an intimation of what Mim must have been like when young: graceful, reserved, lovely. The lovely had turned to impeccably groomed once she reached 39.999 and holding . . . as Miranda Hogendobber had put it when she reached sixty herself. However, the graceful and reserved stayed the course. That Mim was a tyrant and always had been was so much the warp and woof of life in these parts that few bothered to comment on it anymore. At least her tyrannies usually were in the service of issues larger than her own ego.

Harry walked to Mim's tree, leaning against the rough bark. Tucker sat at her feet. The temperature climbed to the high fifties, the sky's startling pure blue punctuated with clouds the color of Devonshire cream. Harry felt oddly tired.

Miranda, her brogues giving her firm purchase on the grass, strode straight over the hill, ducked under the inside rail, crossed the course, and ducked under the outside rail. Her tartan skirt held in place with a large brass pin completed an outfit only Miranda could contemplate. The whole look murmured "country life" except for the hunter-green beret, which Miranda insisted on wearing because she couldn't stand for the wind to muss her hair. "No feathers for me," she had announced when Harry had picked her up. Harry's idea of a chapeau was her Smith College baseball cap or an ancient 10X felt cowboy hat with cattleman's crease that her father had worn.

"Tired blood?" Miranda slowly sat down beside her.

"Hmm, my daily sinking spell."

"Mine comes at four, which you know only too well since I collapse on the chair and force you to brew tea." Miranda folded her hands together. "Mayhem up there. I have never seen so many people, and Mim can't take a step forward or backward. This is *her* Montpelier."

"Sure seems to be."

"Isn't it wonderful about the Valiant children?" Miranda still referred to them as children. "They're giving Mim what she wants—winners!"

"Uh-huh."

"When I think of what those two young people endured— well, I can't bear it. The loss of both parents when they were not even out of their teens. It makes me think of the Fortieth Psalm." She launched into her spiritual voice. " 'I waited patiently for the Lord; he inclined to me and heard my cry. He drew me up from the desolate pit, out of the miry bog, and set my feet upon a rock, making my steps secure—' " She caught her breath.

Harry broke in, "Miranda, how do you remember so much? You could recite from the Bible two weeks running."

"Love the Good Book. If you would join me at the Church of the Holy Light, you'd see why I lift up my voice—"

Harry interrupted again; not her style, but a religious discussion held no appeal for her. "I come to your recitals."

Miranda, possessed of a beautiful singing voice, responded, "And so you do. Now don't forget our big songfest the third weekend in November. I do wish you'd come to a regular service."

"Can't. Well, I could, but you know I'm a member of the Reverend Jones's flock."

"Oh, Herbie, the silver-tongued! When he climbs up in the pulpit, I think the angels bend down to listen. Still, the Lutheran Church contains many flaws that"—she tried to sound large-minded about it—"are bound to creep in over the centuries."

"Miranda, you know how I am." Harry's tone grew firm. "For some reason I must be today's target. Boom Boom appeared to force a heart-to-heart on me. Large ugh. Then Senator Satterwaite came over, but I didn't give him a chance to turn on the tapedeck under his tongue. And now you."

Miranda squinted. "You get out on the wrong side of bed today?"

"No."

"You shouldn't let Boom Boom control your mood."

"I don't," fired back Harry, who suspected it might be true.

"Uh-huh." This was drenched with meaning. Miranda crossed her arms over her chest.

Harry changed the subject. "You're right, the Valiants have been through a lot. These victories must be sweet."

"What would torment me is not knowing where my mother's body was. We all know she's dead. You can only hope but so long, and it's been five years since Marylou disappeared. But when you don't know how someone died, or where, you can't put it to rest. I can go out and visit my George anytime I want. I like to put flowers on his grave. It helps." George, Miranda's husband, had been dead for nine years. He had been the postmaster at Crozet before Harry took over his job.

"Maybe they don't think about it. They don't talk about it— at least, I've never heard them, but I only know them socially."

"It's there—underneath."

"I don't guess we'll ever know what happened to Marylou. Remember when Mim offered the ten-thousand-dollar reward for any information leading to Marylou's discovery?"

"Everyone played detective. Poor Rick." Miranda thought of the Albemarle County sheriff, Rick Shaw, who had been besieged with crackpot theories.

"After Charley died, Marylou kept company with some unimpressive men. She loved Charles Valiant, and I don't think any man measured up for a long time. Then too, he was only thirty-eight when he died. A massive heart attack. Charley was dead before he hit the ground." Miranda held up her hands, palms outward. "Now I am not sitting in judgment. A woman in her late thirties sliding into her early forties, suddenly alone, is vulnerable, indeed. You may not remember, but she dated that fading movie star, Brandon Miles. He wanted her to bankroll his comeback film. She went through men like popcorn . . . until Mickey Townsend, that is."

"Next race!" Harry got up suddenly. The timber jump was alongside the brush jump.

The fifth race, the $40,000 Virginia Hunt Cup, the final leg of the Virginia Fall Timber Championship Series, provided no problems apart from two riders separating company from their mounts, which served to improve the odds for those still in the saddle. Mickey Townsend and Charles Valiant evidenced no antagonism. Their horses and jockeys were so far apart in the four-mile race that neither could cry foul about the other.

As for Linda Forloines, she had picked up Zack Merchant's other horses and had come in third in the Virginia Hunt Cup.

She'd take home a little change in her pocket, 10 percent of the $4,400 third-prize money.

The sixth race, the first division of the Battleship, named in memory of Mrs. Scott's famous horse, was two miles and one furlong over brush and carried a $6,000 purse. Miranda, weary of the crowd, stayed with Harry. The tension swept over the hill. They could feel the anticipation. Back on the rail, Mim, wound tighter than a piano wire, tried to keep calm. The jockeys circled the paddock. Addie, perched atop Mim's Bazooka, a 16.3-hand gray, would blaze fast and strong if she could keep him focused. She still avoided Chark. Nigel, wearing Mickey Townsend's red silks with the blue sash, joked with her. Both riders looked up when the low gate was opened so they could enter the grassy track. Linda Forloines, in the brown-and-yellow silks of Zack Merchant, spoke to no one. The sixth race would be difficult enough for those jockeys who knew their horses; she didn't. Coty Lamont exuded confidence, smiling to the crowd as he trotted onto the turf.

The gun fired. "They're off!"

It seemed only seconds before the field rounded toward Harry, soared over the east gate fence, and then pounded away.

"Fast pace," Harry remarked to Miranda.

The crowd noise rolled away over the hill, then rose again as the horses appeared where the largest number of spectators waited. Again the noise died away as the field went up the hill and around the far side of the flat track; only the announcer's voice cut through the tension, calling out the positions and the jumps.

Again the rhythm of hoofbeats electrified Harry, and the field flew around the turn, maintaining a scorching pace.

Bazooka, in splendid condition, held steady at fourth. Harry knew from Mim that Addie's strategy, worked out well in advance with Chark, would call for her to make her move at the next to last fence.

As the horses rushed toward her obstacle, she saw Linda Forloines bump Nigel hard. He lurched to the side as his horse stepped off balance.

"Bloody hell!" he shouted.

Linda laughed. Nigel, on a better horse, pulled alongside her, then began to pull away. In front of the fence Harry saw Linda lash out with her left arm and catch Nigel across the face with her whip. Bloody-lipped, Nigel cleared the fence. Linda cleared a split second behind him. She whipped Nigel again, but this time he was ready for her. He'd transferred his whip from his left to his right hand, and he backhanded her across the face, giving her a dose of her own. Linda screamed. Harry and Miranda watched in astonishment as the two jockeys beat at each other away and up the hill.

"Harry, what do you do?"

"Nothing until after the race. Then I'll have to hurry to the tower and file my report. But unless one of them protests, not a thing will happen. If either one does—what a row!"

"Vicious!"

"Linda Forloines?"

"Oh—well, yes, but the other one was almost as bad."

"Yes, but he was in the unenviable position of having to do something or she'd get worse. People like Linda don't understand fair play. They interpret it as weakness. You need to hit them harder than they hit you."

"In a race?" Miranda puffed up the hill behind Harry as the winner was being announced—Adelia Valiant on Bazooka. Tucker, ears back, scampered on ahead.

"In the best of all possible worlds, no, but that's when people like Linda go after you. When they think you can't or won't fight back. I'd have killed her myself."

They reached the tower, Mrs. Hogendobber panting.

"Miranda, climb up here. You're a witness, too."

Miranda stomped up the three flights of stairs to the tower

top where the announcer, Arthur Tetrick, and Colbert Mason, national race director, held sway. Tucker stayed at the foot of the steps.

The horses, cooling down, galloped in front of the stand.

"Harry," Arthur Tetrick said, offering her a drink, "thank you so much for all you've done today. Oh, sorry, Mrs. Hogendobber, I didn't see you."

"Arthur." Harry nodded to Colbert Mason. "Colbert. I'm sorry to report there was a dangerous and unsportsmanlike incident at the east gate jump. Linda Forloines bumped Nigel Danforth. It could have been an accident—"

"These things happen." Colbert, in a genial mood, interrupted, for he wanted to rush down to congratulate Mim Sanburne on the stupendous display of winning two races and placing second in another, all in one day. He was especially pleased that Mim had won the Virginia Hunt Cup.

"But wait, Colbert. Then she struck him across the face with her whip. After the jump they flailed at each other like two boxers. Mrs. Hogendobber witnessed it also."

"Miranda?" Arthur's sandy eyebrows were poised above his tortoise-shell glasses.

"Someone could have been seriously injured out there, or worse," Miranda confirmed.

"I see." Arthur leaned over the desk, shouting down to the second level to the race secretary. "Paul, any protest on this race?"

"No, sir."

Just then Colbert leaned over the stand. "I say . . ." Now he could see the welts on Nigel's face and his bloody lip as the jockey rode by to the paddock. A look at Linda's face confirmed a battle.

Arthur leaned over to see also. "Good Lord." He shouted, "Nigel Danforth, come here for a moment. Linda Forloines, a word, please."

The two jockeys, neither looking at the other, rode to the

bottom of the tower as their trainers and grooms hurried out to grab the bridles of their horses.

"Have you anything to report on the unusual condition of your faces?" Arthur bellowed.

"No, sir," came the Englishman's reply.

"Linda?" Arthur asked.

She shook her head, saying nothing.

"All right, then." Arthur dismissed them as Mim, floating on a cloud, entered the winner's circle. "Harry, there's nothing I can do under the circumstances, but I have a bad feeling that this isn't over yet. If you'll excuse me, I'm due in the winner's circle. I have the check." He patted his chest pocket. "See you ladies at Mim's party."

As the crowd slowly dispersed, the grooms, jockeys, trainers, and owners went about their tasks, until finally only the race officials remained. Even the political candidates had evaporated. One horse van after another rumbled out of the Madison estate.

Harry, Mrs. Hogendobber, and Tucker hopped into the truck as the sun slipped behind the Blue Ridge Mountains. Darkness folded around them as they slowly cruised down the lane.

"Lights are still on in the big barn," Harry noted. "There's so much to do." The horses required a lot of attention after a race—cold-hosing their legs, checking medications, feeding them, and finally cleaning the tack.

"All done," Miranda sang out.

"Huh?"

"The lights just went out."

"Oh." Harry smiled. "Well, good, someone got to go home early."

An hour later the phone jingled up at Montpelier where Arthur and Colbert had repaired for a bit of warmth, then to collate and fax the day's results to the national office in Elkton, Maryland.

"Hello." Arthur's expression changed so dramatically that Colbert stood to assist him if necessary. "We'll be right over." Arthur carefully replaced the receiver in the cradle.

He ran out to his car with Colbert next to him, headed for the big stable.

3

"Where is he?" Harry grumbled. "You'd think I'd be used to it by now. He's never been on time. Even his own mother admitted he was a week late being born."

"Last time I saw Fair he was checking over that horse with the bowed tendon," Addie said as yet another person came up to congratulate her. "Wherever he is, Nigel's probably with him. He's never on time either."

Mim, champagne glass in hand, raised it. "To the best trainer and jockey in the game, Hip, hip, hooray!"

The assemblage ripped out, "Hip, hip, hooray!"

Chark lifted his glass in response. "To the best owner."

More cheers ricocheted off the tasteful walls of Mim Sanburne's Georgian mansion just northwest of Crozet.

Her husband, Jim, jovially mixed with the guests as servants in livery provided champagne—Louis Roederer Cristal, caviar, sliced chicken, smoked turkey, delicately cured hams, succotash, spoon bread, and desserts that packed a megaton calorie blast.

Many of the serving staff were University of Virginia students. Even with her vast wealth Mim ran a tight ship, and given Social Security, withholding taxes, workers' compensation, and health insurance to pay, she wasn't about to bloat her budget with lots of salaries. She hired for occasions like this, the rest of the time making do with a cook, a butler, and a maid. A farm manager and two full-time laborers rounded out the payroll.

Charles and Adelia Valiant trained her horses, but they trained other people's as well. Once a month Mim received an itemized bill. Since they enjoyed the use of her facilities for half the year, Mim was granted a deep discount. The other half of the year the Valiants wintered and trained in Aiken, South Carolina.

Mim called steeplechasers slow gypsies since they stayed for four to six months and then moved on.

The Reverend Herbert Jones, tinkling ice cubes in his glass, joined Harry as Addie was pulled away by another celebrant.

"Beautiful day. 'Course, you never know with Montpelier. I've stood in the snow, the rain, and I've basked in seventy-four degrees and sunshine. Today was one of the best."

"Pretty good." Harry smiled.

Herb watched Boom Boom Craycroft out of the corner of his eye. She worked the room, moving in a semicircle toward Harry. "Boom Boom's tacking your way." He lowered his gravelly voice.

"Not again."

"Oh?" His eyebrows shot upward.

"She freely shared her innermost feelings with me between the first and second races. Forgiveness and redemption are just around the corner if I'll join Lifeline."

"I thought forgiveness and redemption were mine to dispense." The Reverend Jones laughed at himself. "Well, now, let her ramble. Who knows, maybe this Lifeline really has helped her in some way. I prefer prayer myself."

In the background the phone rang. Rick Shaw, the Sheriff of Albemarle County, was summoned to it.

"He never gets a break. Coop neither," Harry observed. Shaw's deputy was Cynthia Cooper.

"Lots of drunks on the road after Montpelier."

"They don't need the races for an excuse. I figure they IV the stuff."

Rick hung up the phone, whispered something to Mim, and left the party. Mim's face registered shock. Then she quickly regained her social mask.

4

Sheriff Rick Shaw, penlight in hand, pulled back an eyelid. Nothing. He continued carefully examining the body before him, with Dr. Larry Johnson observing. Shaw didn't want the corpse moved yet.

Nigel Danforth sat exactly as Fair Haristeen had found him—upright on a tack trunk, wearing his red silks with the blue sash. A knife was plunged through his heart.

Although the murder appeared to have taken place in Orange County and Rick Shaw was sheriff of the adjoining county, Orange's sheriff, Frank Yancey, had called him in. Rick had handled more murders than he had, and this one was a puzzle, especially since the knife had been plunged through a playing card, the Queen of Clubs, which was placed over Nigel's heart.

Fair, arms crossed, watched, his face still chalky white.

"His body was *exactly* like this when you found him?" Rick asked the lanky vet.

"Yes."

"See anything, anyone?"

"No, I walked in through the north doors and turned on the lights. All the horses should have been removed by then but I thought I'd double-check. He was sitting there. I didn't know anything was wrong, although I thought it was peculiar that he'd sit in the dark. I called to him, and he didn't answer. When I drew closer, I saw the knife sticking out of his chest. I felt his pulse. Goner."

"What about his body temperature when you touched him?"

"Still warm, Larry. Maybe he had been dead an hour. His extremities hadn't started to fill with fluid. He really looked as though he was just sitting there."

"No sign of anybody—anything?" Rick sighed. He'd known Fair for years, respected him as a vet and therefore as a scientific man. Fair's recollections counted heavily in Rick's book.

"None in the barn. A few big vans pulled out across the road. Their noise could have covered someone running away. I checked the stalls, I climbed into the hayloft, tack room. Nothing, Sheriff."

"The card's a neat trick." Frank Yancey shook his head. "Maybe it's a payback for a gambling debt."

"Helluva payback," Larry Johnson said.

"Helluva debt?" Frank gestured, his hands held upward.

"Frank, you've got the photos and prints you need?" Rick continued when Frank nodded in the affirmative, "Well, let's remove the body then. Do you mind if Larry sits in on the autopsy?"

"No, no, I'd be glad to have him there."

"Guess I can't keep this out of the papers." George Miller, Orange's mayor, unconsciously wrung his hands. He had arrived minutes after Yancey's call. "Colbert Mason and Arthur Tetrick were horrified, but they turned cagey pretty fast. They especially didn't want a photo of the body to get into the papers."

"One murder in the steeplechase world doesn't mean it's seething with corruption," Larry remarked sensibly.

"Five years ago there was another murder." Fair's deep baritone sounded sepulchral in the barn.

"What are you talking about?" Frank leaned forward.

"Marylou Valiant."

"Never found her, did they?" Frank Yancey blinked, remembering.

"No," Rick answered. "We know of no connection to steeplechasing other than that she owned a good string of horses. That's not a motive for murder. There are some who think she's not dead. She just walked away from her life."

"They say that about Elvis, too," Fair replied. "Anyone told Adelia Valiant?"

"Why?" Frank and George said simultaneously.

"She was dating Danforth . . . pretty serious, I think."

Frank eyed the big man. "Well—can you tell her?"

Rick and Fair glanced at each other, then at Larry.

"I'll tell her," the old doctor said gently. "But I'd like you fellows with me. And Rick, don't jump right in, okay?"

The sheriff grimaced. He tried to be sensitive, but the drive to catch a murderer could override his efforts. "Yeah, yeah."

Two ambulance attendants rolled the gurney into the barn from the south doors as Fair, Larry, and Rick left through the north.

Rick turned to Fair. "Was he a good jockey?"

"Not bad."

5

Will Forloines's face fell longer and longer. His color deepened. He couldn't hold it in any longer. "That was a damn fool thing you did to Nigel."

"Bullshit."

"Don't cuss at me, Linda. I can still kick your ass into next week."

"I love it when you get mad." She sarcastically parodied old movies.

He shifted his eyes from the road to her. "You're lucky he didn't file a complaint."

"Had him by the short hairs."

"Oh—and what if he'd nailed you? You didn't know he wouldn't file against you."

"Will, let me do the thinking."

The wheel of the brand-new Nissan dropped off the road. Will quickly returned his gaze to the road. "You take too many chances. One of these days it will backfire."

"Wimp." While she insulted him, she took the precaution of dropping her hand into his lap.

"Things are going good right now. I don't want them screwed up."

"Will, relax. Drive. And listen." She exhaled through her nose. "Nigel Danforth has bought a shitload of cocaine over the last two months. He can't squeal."

"The hell he can't. He can finger us as the dealers."

"Better to be mad at me over one race than lose his connection. And if he blew the whistle on us, he'd be blowing it on himself—and his girlfriend. All that money isn't coming from race purses."

Will drove a few minutes. "Yeah, but you're cutting it close."

"Paid for this truck." She moved closer to him.

"Linda, you"—he sputtered—"you take too many risks."

"The risk is the rush."

"Not for me, Babe. The money is the rush."

"And we're sitting in the middle of it. Dr. D'Angelo's loaded, and he's dumb as a post."

"No, he's not," Will contradicted her. "He's dumb about horses. He's not dumb about his job or he wouldn't have made all that money. Sooner or later he'll figure things out if you try to sell him too many horses at once. Take it slow. I'd like to live in one place for a couple of years."

She waited a moment. "Sure."

As this was said with no conviction, Will, irritated, shot back, "I like where we live."

She whispered in his ear, enjoying her disagreement with him just so she could "win" the argument, get him under her control. She might have loved her husband, but she truly needed him. He was so easy to manipulate that it made her feel powerful and smart. "We'll make so much money we can buy our own farm."

"Yeah . . ." His voice trailed off.

She smiled. "Nigel will forget all about it. I guarantee it. He owes me for a kilo. He's coming up tomorrow to pay off the rest of it. I got part of the money today before the race." She laughed, "Bet he couldn't believe it when I whipped him. He'll forget though. He'll be so full of toot, I'll be his best friend."

6

When Fair Haristeen walked through the door of Mim's party, Harry determined to pay no attention to him. However, she couldn't help noticing his jaw muscles tightening, which she recognized as a sign of distress. Dr. Larry Johnson and Sheriff Rick Shaw flanked him, and Larry headed straight for Addie Valiant. Fair turned to follow them.

"Doom and gloom," Susan Tucker observed.

"Hope someone didn't lose a horse," Harry said.

"I know. It was such an unusual Montpelier. The worst was that bowed tendon, pretty fabulous when you consider some of the accidents in the past. But maybe it's because the course is so difficult. People are careful."

"Huh?"

"Harry, are you paying attention?" her best friend said.

"Yes, but I was thinking I'd have to head home before too long. Miranda closes up shop by nine, you know." Harry referred to Miranda's lifelong habit of early retirement and early rising.

"Well, as I was saying before you drifted off, because the course is demanding jockeys stay focused. Sometimes when it's a bit easy they get sloppy."

"Mom, I'm hungry," Tucker pleaded.

Susan dropped a piece of cake for the dog.

"Susan, you spoil Tucker worse than I do." It was Susan who had bred the corgi. Harry noticed Larry taking Addie by the elbow and Rick whispering in Mim's ear. "Something's going on. Damn, I hope it's not some kind of late protest. I wouldn't put anything past Mickey Townsend. He hates to lose."

Five minutes passed before a howl of pain sounded from the library. All conversation stopped. Mim, holding her husband's hand, put her other hand on Chark's shoulder, guiding him to the library. Larry had wanted to inform Addie before bringing her brother into it. The confusion and concern on Chark's face upon hearing his sister's cry alerted even the thickest person in the room to impending sorrow.

Mim shut the library doors behind her. All eyes were now on her. She walked over to the three-sash window and collected herself. Then, her husband at her side, she addressed the gathering.

"I regret to inform you that there appears to have been a"—she cleared her throat—"murder at Montpelier." A gasp went up from the crowd. "Nigel Danforth, the English jockey riding for Mickey Townsend, was found dead this evening in the main stable. Sheriff Shaw says they know very little at this time. He asks for your patience and cooperation over the next few days as he will be calling upon some of us. I'm afraid the party is over, but I want to thank you for celebrating what has been a joyous day—until now." She opened her hands as if in benediction.

Little Marilyn, unable to conceal her agitation, called out. "Mummy, how was he killed?"

"Stabbed through the heart."

"Good God!" Herbie Jones exclaimed, and after that the noise was deafening as everyone talked at once.

"That explains it," Susan said to Harry, who understood she was referring to Fair's miserable countenance. "How about we pay our respects to our hostess and leave?"

Miranda bustled over. "My word, how awful, and how awful for Mim, too. It certainly casts a pall on her triumph. Harry, Herbie's offered to escort me home so I'm leaving with him."

"Fine. I'll see you on Monday."

"Good, then I'll ride with you." Susan piped up then called to her teenaged son, Danny, "One dent in that car and you are toast."

On the way home Harry, Susan, and Tee Tucker wondered why a jockey would be killed after the races. They ran through the usual causes of death in America: money, love, drugs, and gambling. Since they knew little about Nigel, they soon dropped the speculation.

"Another body blow for Addie." Harry cupped her hand under her chin and stared out the window into the sheltering darkness.

"Ever notice how some people are plagued with bad luck and tragedy?"

"*King Lear?*" Harry quipped, not meaning to sound flippant. "Sorry."

"I'm not sure I will ever understand how your mind works," Susan wryly said to her friend.

"There are days when it doesn't work at all."

"Tell me about it. Especially after you have children. What's left of your mind flies out the window." As a mother of two teenagers, Susan both endured and enjoyed her offspring. She pulled down the long driveway to Harry's farm.

"Bet you Boom Boom makes a beeline for Addie once she emerges from the library," Harry grumbled.

"Mim will shoo her out first."

"Ha!" Harry said derisively. "Boom Boom will volunteer to clean up after the party, the sneak. Bet you she pounces on Addie with an invitation to join her at Lifeline. Bloodsucker."

"She does seem to draw sustenance from other people's problems." Susan inhaled. "But then again this program of self-exposure or whatever it is has calmed her down."

"I don't believe it."

"You wouldn't." Susan stopped at the screened door at the back of the house. Mrs. Murphy was visible in the window and then disappeared. "A pussycat is anxious to see you."

"Come on in. She wants to see you, too. I'll feed her, then carry you home."

"Good. Then I can look for my black sweater. I know I left it here."

"Susan, I swear I've searched for it. It's not here."

"You won't believe what happened," Tucker called out, eager to tell her friend everything and also eager to watch Mrs. Murphy fume because she'd missed it.

"Tucker, hush." Harry opened the door and ushered Susan inside.

The temperature was in the forties and dropping, and the chill nipped at Harry's heels, so she hurried along behind her friend. The kitchen, deceptively calm, lured her into comfort.

"Here, kitty, kitty."

"I hate you," Mrs. Murphy called from the bedroom.

Harry walked into the living room followed by Tucker and Susan.

"Uh-oh." Tucker laid her ears flat.

Susan gasped, "Berlin, 1945!"

The arm of the sofa had been shredded, methodically destroyed. Lamps smashed to the ground bore witness to the tiger

cat's fury. She had also had the presence of mind to scratch, tear, and bite magazines, the newspapers, and a forlorn novel that rested on Harry's wing chair. The pièce de résistance was one curtain, yanked full force, dangling half on and half off the rod.

Harry's mouth dangled almost in imitation of the curtain. She slapped her hands together in outrage.

"Mrs. Murphy, you come out here."

"*In a pig's eye.*" The cat's voice was shrill.

"I know where you're hiding. You aren't that original, you little shit!" Harry tore into her bedroom, clicked on the light, dropped to her knees, and lifted up the dust ruffles. Sure enough, a pair of gleaming green eyes at the furthest recesses of the bed stared back at her.

"I will skin you alive!" Harry exploded.

"*You're in deep doo-doo,*" Tucker whined.

"*She'll forget it by morning,*" came the saucy reply.

"I don't think so. You've wrecked the house."

"*I know nothing about it.*"

7

Since Harry had closed off the animal door, Mrs. Murphy stayed inside. She would have preferred to go out to the barn just in case Harry woke up mad. As it was she prudently waited until she heard the cat food can being opened before she tiptoed into the kitchen.

"You're impossible." Harry, good humor restored by a sound night's sleep, scratched the cat at the base of her tail.

"I hate it when you leave me."

As Harry dished out shrimp and cod into a bowl upon which was prophetically written UPHOLSTERY DESTROYER, Tucker circled her mother's legs.

"Why do you feed her first? Especially after what she's done."

"I'll get to you."

"She feeds me first because I'm so fascinating."

"*Gag me.*" Tucker remembered that the cat knew nothing of yesterday's bizarre event. She forgot her irritation as she settled into the pleasure of tormenting Mrs. Murphy. "*Beautiful day at the races.*"

"*Shut up.*"

"*Boom Boom swept down on Mom, though.*"

Mrs. Murphy, on the counter, turned her head from her food bowl. "*Oh, did Mom cuss her out?*"

"*Nah.*" Tucker jammed her long nose into the canned beef food mixed into crunchies.

Harry brewed tea and rummaged around for odds and ends to toss into an omelet while the animals chatted. Tucker finished her food so quickly it barely impeded her conversational abilities.

The tiger, delicate in her eating habits, paused between mouthfuls, gently brushing her whiskers in case some food was on them. She surveyed the damage in the living room without a twinge of guilt. "*How'd Mim do?*"

"*Second in the second race, won the fourth race, and she won the big one.*"

"*Wow.*" She swatted her food bowl, angry all over again at being left out. "*I grew up with horses. I don't know why Mother thinks I won't behave myself at Montpelier. As if I've never seen a crowd before.*"

"*You haven't. Not that big.*" Tucker licked her lips, relishing her breakfast and the cat's discomfort.

"*I can handle it!*" She glared down at the dog. "*I ride in cars better than you do. I don't bark. I don't ask to be fed every fifteen minutes, and I don't whine to go to the bathroom.*"

"*No, you just do it under the seat.*"

Mrs. Murphy spit, her white fangs quite impressive. "*No fair. I was sick and we were on our way to the vet.*"

"*Yeah, yeah. Tapeworms. I'm tired of that excuse.*"

The pretty feline shuddered. "*I hate those tapeworm shots, but they do work. Haven't had a bit of trouble since. Of course, flea season is over.*"

She had heard the vet explain that some fleas carry the tapeworm larvae. When animals bite the spot where a flea has bitten them, they occasionally ingest an infected flea, starting the cycle wherein the parasite winds up in their intestines. Both cat and dog understood the problem, but when a flea bites, it's hard not to bite back.

Harry sat down to her hot omelet. Mrs. Murphy kept her company on the other side of the plate.

"I am not giving you any, Murphy. In fact, I'm not forking over one more morsel of food for days—not until I clean up the wreckage of this house. I've half a mind to leave you home from work tomorrow, but you'd run another demolition derby."

"Damn right."

Tucker, annoyed at not being able to sit on the table, plopped under Harry's chair, then rose again to sit by her mother's knee. *"Oh, Murph, one little thing . . . a jockey was murdered last night at the Montpelier stable, the big old one."*

The green eyes grew larger, and the animal leaned over the table. *"What?"*

"Mrs. Murphy, control yourself." Harry reached over to pet the cat, who fluffed her fur.

"A jockey, Nigel somebody or other—we don't really know him although Adelia Valiant does—he was stabbed. Right through the heart." Tucker savored this last detail.

"You waited all this time to tell me?" Murphy unleashed her claws, then retracted them.

Tucker smiled. *"Next time you tell me cats are smarter than dogs, just remember I know some things you don't."*

Murphy jumped down from the table, put her face right up into Tucker's, and growled. *"Don't mess with me, buster. You get to go with Mom to the races. You come home and tell me nothing until now. I would have told you straightaway."*

The little dog held her ground. *"Maybe you would and maybe you wouldn't."*

"When have I withheld important news from you?"

"The time you and Pewter stole roast beef from the store."

"That was different. Besides, you know Pewter is obsessed with food. If I hadn't helped her steal that roast beef, I wouldn't have gotten one measly bite of

it. *She would have stolen it herself, but she's too fat to squeeze into the case. That's different.*"

"No, it isn't."

Harry observed the Mexican standoff. "What's got into you two this morning?"

"*Nothing.*" Murphy stalked out of the room, taking a swipe at Tucker's rear end when the dog's head was turned.

Harry prudently reached down and grabbed Tucker's collar. "Ignore her."

"*With pleasure.*"

The phone rang. Harry answered it.

"Sorry to call you so early on a Sunday morning," Deputy Cynthia Cooper apologized. "Boss wants me to ask you some questions about the races yesterday."

"Sure. Want to come out here?"

"Wish I could. You ready?"

"Yes."

"What do you know about Nigel Danforth?"

"Not much, Coop. He's a new jockey on the circuit, not attached to a particular stable. What we call a pickup rider or a catch rider. I met him briefly yesterday."

Hearing this, Mrs. Murphy sourly returned to the kitchen. She didn't so much as glance at Tucker when she passed the dog, also eavesdropping.

"*Crab.*"

"*Selfish,*" the cat shot back.

"Did you ever speak to Nigel?"

"Just a 'pleased to meet you.' "

"Do you know anything about his relationship with Addie?"

"She told me yesterday morning that she liked him." Harry thought a minute. "She intimated that she might be falling in love with him, and she wanted us to get together after the races at the party."

"Did you?"

"Well, I was at Mim's party. Addie was there, too." She

added, "First, though, I waited on standby at the tower after the last race to see if Arthur Tetrick or Mr. Mason wanted me to file a report. There was a nasty incident at my fence, the east gate fence, between Nigel Danforth and Linda Forloines."

"I'm all ears."

Harry could hear Cooper scribbling as she described the incident.

"That's quite serious, isn't it? I mean, couldn't they get suspended?"

"Yes. I told Arthur and Colbert Mason, he's the national director, but I guess you know that by now. Neither of the jockeys lodged a protest, though. Without a protest there's nothing the officials can do."

"Who has the authority in a situation like that?"

"The race director. In this case, Arthur."

"Why wouldn't Arthur Tetrick haul both their asses in?"

"That's a good question, Coop." Harry sipped her tea. "But I can give you an opinion—not an answer, just an opinion."

"*We want to hear it*," the cat and dog said, too.

"Shoot."

"Well, all sports have umpires, referees, judges to see that mayhem is kept to a minimum. But sometimes you have to let the antagonists settle it themselves. Rough justice."

"Expand."

"If an official steps in, it can reach a point where Jockey A is being protected too much. I mean, Coop, if you're going to go out there, then you've got to take your lumps, and part of it is that some riders are down and dirty. If they think no one is looking, they'll foul you."

"But you were looking."

"I don't understand that." Harry recalled the brazenness of the situation.

"Is Linda dumb?"

"Far from it. She's a low-rent, lying, cunning bitch."

"Hey, don't keep your feelings to yourself," Cynthia teased her.

Harry laughed. "There are few people that I despise on this earth, but she's one of them."

"Why?"

"I saw her deliberately lame a horse temporarily, then lie about it to Mim. She took the horse off Mim's hands and sold it at a profit to a trainer out of state. She didn't know that I saw her. I—well, it doesn't matter. You get the point."

"But she's not stupid, so why would she commit a flagrant foul, one that could get her suspended? And right in front of you?"

"It doesn't figure." Harry was stumped.

Coop flipped through her notes. "She can't keep a job, any job, longer than a year. That could mean a lot of things, but one thing it most certainly means is, she can't get along with people over an extended period of time."

"Obviously, she couldn't get along with Nigel Danforth." Harry sipped her tea again.

"Do you have any idea, I don't care how *crazy* it sounds, why Linda Forloines would hit Nigel in the face?"

Harry played with the long cord of the phone. "I don't have any idea, unless they were enemies—apart from being competitors, I mean. The only other thing I can tell you—just popped into my head—is that people say Linda deals drugs. No one's ever pinned it on her though."

"Heard that, too," Cooper replied. "I'll be back at you later. Sorry to intrude on you so early, but I know you're out before sunup most days. Pretty crisp this morning."

"I'll wear my woollies. Let me ask you a question."

"Okay."

"Can everyone account for their whereabouts at the time of the murder?"

"No," Cooper flatly stated. "We've got a good idea when he

died, within a twenty-minute frame, but really—anybody could have had the time to skip in there and kill him. The commotion of the event wears people out, dulls their senses, to say nothing of the drinking.''

"That's the truth. Well, if I think of anything I'll call. I'm glad to help.''

Harry hung up the phone after good-byes. She liked Cynthia, and over the years they'd become friends.

"I couldn't hear what Cynthia was saying. Tell me,'' Murphy demanded.

Harry, cup poised before her lips, put it back down in the saucer. "You know, it doesn't make sense. It doesn't make a bit of sense that Linda Forloines would lay into Nigel Danforth right in front of me.''

"What?'' Mrs. Murphy, beside herself with curiosity, rubbed Harry's arm since she had jumped back on the counter.

"I'll tell you all about that.'' Tucker promised importantly as Harry pulled on an ancient cashmere sweater, slapped the old cowboy hat on her head, and slipped her arms through her down vest.

"Come on, kids, time to rock and roll.'' Harry opened the door. They stepped out into the frosty November morning to start the chores.

┌─────────────┐
│   │
│   8   │
│   │
└─────────────┘

Will Forloines stood up when Linda sauntered out of Sheriff Frank Yancey's office. At first the husband and wife had balked at being questioned individually, but finally they gave in. It would look worse if they didn't cooperate.

Will had been surprised at the blandness of Sheriff Yancey's questions—partly because he was scared the cops might be on to their drug dealing. *Where were you at seven on the night of the murder? How well did you know the deceased?* That sort of thing.

Linda turned and smiled at Frank, who smiled back and shut his door.

Will handed Linda her coat and they opened the door. The day, cool but bright, might warm up a bit.

Not until they were in the truck did they speak.

"What did he ask you?" Will didn't start the motor.

"Nothing much." Her upturned nose in profile resembled a tiny ski jump.

"Well, what?" Will demanded.

"Where was I? I told him in the van with Mickey Townsend. The truth."

"What else?" He cranked the truck.

"He wanted to know why I hit Nigel in the face with my whip before the east gate jump."

"And?" Will, agitated, pressed down so hard on the accelerator he had to brake, which threw them forward. "Sorry."

"I said he bumped me, he'd been bumping me and I was damned sick of it. But not sick enough to kill him for it."

"And?"

"That was it."

"You were in there for half an hour, Linda. There had to be more to it than that. Things don't look so good for us. I told you not to take chances. You're a suspect."

She ignored that. "We passed the time of day. He asked how long I'd been riding. Where did I learn? Nothing to the point. I hit the guy in the face. That doesn't mean I killed him."

"I don't like it."

"Hey, who does?"

Will thought for a moment. "Did he ask anything about drugs? I mean, what if Nigel had coke in his system."

"No, he didn't ask anything like that." She folded her hands and gloated. "I did say that since Fair Haristeen was the person who found Nigel, he ought to be investigated. I hinted that Fair's been doping horses. Just enough of a hint to send him on a wild-goose chase."

Will looked at her out of the corner of his eye. He'd grown accustomed to her habitual lying. "Anyone who knows Fair Haristeen won't believe it."

"Hey, it'll waste some of their time."

"You sure he didn't ask anything tricky?" His voice hardened.

"No, goddammit. Why are you on my case?"

"Because he split us up to see if our stories conflicted."

"I don't have any stories except about Fair. I'll get even with him yet, and Mim, too, the rich bitch."

"I wouldn't worry about them now."

Her eyes narrowed. "She fired you, too."

"Someone fires you, you say you quit. People believe what they want to believe. We make good money now. Revenge takes too much time."

She smirked. "Everyone thinks Mim ran us out of business and that we're broke. Bet their eyes fell out of their heads when we drove into Montpelier in a brand-new truck."

She hadn't reckoned on most people being more involved with the races than with her. Few had noticed their new truck, but then Linda related everything to herself.

"You really didn't tell him anything?" A pleading note crept into his voice.

"NO! If you're getting weak-kneed, then stay out of it. I'll do it. Jesus, Will."

"Okay, okay." They headed up Route 15, north. "Our supplier isn't going to be happy if our names get in the paper. Just makes me nervous."

"The sheriff asked me one weird question." She observed his knuckles whiten as he gripped the steering wheel. "Nothing much. But he asked me if I knew anything about Nigel's green card."

"His immigration card? You mean his right-to-work card?"

"Yeah, the green card." She shrugged. "Said I never saw it. Wonder why he'd ask about that?"

9

Mondays Harry and Mrs. Hogendobber shoveled the mail. Mounds of catalogs, postcards, bills, and letters filled the canvas mail cart and spilled onto the wooden floor, polished by years of use.

Mrs. Murphy, disgruntled because she couldn't snuggle in the mail cart, zipped out via the animal door installed for her convenience at the back. Tucker snored, asleep on her side in the middle of the floor where she could create the greatest obstacle. The cat didn't wake her.

Truth be told, she loved Tucker, but dogs, even Tucker, got on her nerves. They were so straightforward. Mrs. Murphy enjoyed nuance and quiet. Tucker tended to babble.

The door flapped behind her. She sat on the back stoop of the post office surveying the alleyway that divided the row of old business buildings from private backyards. Mrs. Hogendobber's yard sat directly behind the post office. Her garden, mulched and fertilized, usually a source of color, had yielded to winter. She'd clipped off her last blooming of mums.

The cat breathed in that peculiar odor of dying leaves and moist earth. As it was eleven A.M. the frost had melted and the scent of wild animals dissipated with it. Mrs. Murphy loved to hunt in the fall and winter because it was easy to track by scent.

She ruffled out her fur to ward off the chill, then marched over to Market Shiflett's store.

As she approached the back door she hollered, *"Pewter, Pewter, Motor Scooter, come out and play!"*

The animals' door, newly installed at the grocery store, swung open. Pewter rolled out like a gray cannonball.

"Everyone's ass over tit today."

Mrs. Murphy agreed. *"Mondays put humans in a foul mood. Ever notice?"*

"There is that, but the stabbing of that jockey sure has tongues wagging." She lifted her head straight up in the air. *"Let's go root around under Mrs. Hogendobber's porch."*

The two bounded across the alley and ducked under Miranda's porch.

"He was here again last night." Pewter's pupils grew large.

Mrs. Murphy sniffed. *"Like a skunk only, umm, sweeter."* She stepped forward and caught her whiskers in cobwebs. *"I hate spiders!"* She shot out from under the porch.

"Ha, ha." Pewter followed her, highly amused at the cobwebs draped over her friend's whiskers and face. *"You look like a ghost."*

"Least I'm not fat."

Pewter, nonplussed, replied, *"I'm not fat, just round."* She moseyed over to the garden. *"Bet Mrs. H. would have a major hissy if she knew a fox visited her nightly."*

"Pickings must be good."

"I wouldn't want to be undomesticated," Pewter, fond of cooked foods, revealed.

"*You sit in that store and dream on. I've never once thought of that.*"

"*Know what else I've thought about?*" Pewter didn't wait for a reply. "*Sushi. What Crozet needs is a good sushi bar. Imagine fresh tuna every day. Now I enjoy tuna from the can, I prefer it packed lightly, not in heavy oil, mind you. But fresh tuna . . . heaven.*"

The tiger licked the side of her right paw and swept it up over her ears. "*Would we have to use chopsticks?*"

"*Very funny. I bet I could steal sushi from a pair of chopsticks on their way to some dope's mouth.*" She imitated her stealing motion, one swift swipe of the paw, claws extended. She shuddered with delight at the thought of it.

"*Hey, look.*" Mrs. Murphy intruded on Pewter's reverie.

Both cats watched Addie Valiant drive up and park behind the post office. She closed the door of her blue Subaru station wagon, the back jammed with tack, wraps, saddle pads, and other equine odds and ends. Turning up the collar of her heavy shirt, she knocked on the back door of the post office, listened, then opened the door.

"*Let's go.*" Murphy ran across the yard.

"*What for?*" Pewter didn't budge.

"*The dead jockey was her boyfriend.*"

"*Oh.*" Pewter hurried to catch up. Both cats hit the animal door simultaneously, spit at one another, then Murphy slipped in first, a disgruntled Pewter literally on her tail.

Murphy had washed only half her face; the other half was resplendent with cobwebs.

Addie pulled her mail from the back of her mailbox.

Harry checked through the magazine pile to see if anything was there for her.

"Now, honey, you let me know if there's anything we can do. Anything at all." Miranda handed Addie a bun with an orange glaze. An excellent baker, she made a little money on the side by baking for Market Shiflett's store.

"I'm not hungry, thank you."

"*I am*," Pewter purred.

Tucker, awake now, scrambled to her feet. "*Me, too.*" She noticed Mrs. Murphy's face. "*Halloween's over.*"

Harry noticed at the same time. "Where have you been?"

"*Under Miranda's porch.*"

Harry scooped up the pretty cat, grabbed a paper towel, and wiped off the cobwebs, not as simple as she thought since they were sticky.

Addie dropped into a chair. "Mind if I sit a minute? I'm tired."

"Shocks will do that to you." Miranda patted her on the back.

"Yeah—I know. I guess I didn't think there were any left for me."

"Life has a funny way of being loaded with surprises, good and bad," the kindly woman said.

"*Is anyone going to eat that orange bun?*" Pewter asked.

"Chatty Cathy." Harry scratched the gray cat behind the ears.

Miranda pulled little pieces of the bun apart and munched on them.

Pewter let out a wail. "*Give me some!*"

Miranda ignored this so Pewter scrambled onto a chair and thence onto the small table in the back where the buns rested enticingly on a white plate. She licked off the icing while the humans, deep in conversation, never noticed. Mrs. Murphy, not to be outdone, joined her friend.

Tucker complained bitterly. Murphy batted a hardened bit of icing off the table to the dog to shut her up. If she kept up her racket, the humans might notice their uninvited snack.

"They asked me so many questions they made me dizzy." The young woman's hands fluttered to her face. "I couldn't an-swer half of them. I wasn't much help. They pumped Chark pretty hard, too."

"Rick Shaw said that Frank Yancey's an okay guy, so he was just asking what he had to, I guess." Harry wanted to be helpful, but she didn't know what to do or say.

Addie's big blue eyes misted over. "I was just getting to know him so—"

"Of course, of course." Miranda patted her hand this time.

"How long had you known him?"

"Two months, give or take a week. I met him at the Fair Hill races and whammo!" She smacked her hands together.

"Happens that way sometimes." Harry smiled.

"We had so much in common. Horses. Horses and horses," Addie said. "He taught me a lot. You know how some people keep what they know to themselves? Won't share anything. Not Nigel. He was happy to teach me, and he was just as happy to learn from me too."

"Sounds like a lovely young man," Miranda, ever the romantic, replied soothingly.

Harry, far less romantic, nonetheless wanted to be supportive, but her inquiring nature couldn't be suppressed for long. "Do you think he had enemies?"

"Harry, you sound like Frank Yancey." Addie crossed one leg over the other, then winced.

"What'd you do?" Miranda solicitously inquired.

"Knees. They take a beating out there, you know." She turned back to Harry. "As far as I know he didn't have enemies. No one knew him long enough, and besides, he was fun, a real positive person." She paused. "Everyone's got some enemies though."

"His poor parents in England." Miranda shook her head.

"Hadn't thought of that," Harry said. "Do you have any idea why this happened?" Her curiosity had surged.

"No." Addie got up. "Everyone is asking me that."

"I'm sorry. But it's natural."

"I hope whoever killed him rots in hell!" Addie flared, then wiped away the unexpected tears.

" 'Whoever sheds the blood of man, by man shall his blood be shed; for God made man in His own image,' " Mrs. Hogendobber quoted from Genesis.

"I'll happily shed blood." Addie clamped down her lips.

"What do you mean?" Harry asked.

"I mean, if I find the killer first . . ."

"Don't say that," Miranda blurted out.

"Yeah, don't." Harry seconded her older friend's feeling.

"I don't give a damn. If the killer is caught, he'll go to trial. Lots of money will get spent, and the system is so corrupt that he probably won't get convicted, and if he does he'll be out on parole in no time. It's a farce."

Much as Harry tended to agree, she didn't want to encourage Addie to murder. "You know, the scary part is, what if you do find the killer, or get close? What if he turns on you, Addie? Stay out of it. You liked this guy, but you didn't know him well enough to die for him."

"Harry, you can fall in love in an instant. I did."

"Oh, Addie . . ." Harry's voice trailed off.

Miranda draped her arm over Addie's thin shoulder. "Harry's not trying to argue with you or upset you, honey. She doesn't want you to do something impulsive that could ruin your life. And I agree. Neither one of us wants you to expose yourself to danger. After all, no one knows why Nigel was killed. It's not just the who, it's the why, you see. That's where the danger lies."

Addie cried again. "You're right. I know you're right."

Both women comforted her as best they could. When Addie left the post office, she passed the now empty white plate. The cats had fallen asleep next to the scene of their crime.

10

Work continued despite the personal sorrow Adelia Valiant had to absorb. Horses needed to be fed, watered, exercised, groomed, turned out, and talked to over a stall door. The routine, oddly consoling, numbed her mind.

Mim told her to take time off if she needed it, but Addie kept riding. After all, she and her brother had other clients to serve, and when people pay you money, they expect results.

The Valiant fortune, some eighteen million and growing due to good investments directed by Arthur Tetrick, should have ensured that Adelia and Charles Valiant need never labor for their bread and butter.

But Marylou had witnessed the dismal effects of wrapping children in wads of money to soften the hard knocks of life. She didn't want her children to become the weak, petty tyrants she had often observed. She wanted to give them grit.

Enough was drawn annually from the trust fund to pay for lodging, cars, clothes, the necessities. This forced her children to work if they wanted more. If they turned into gilded turnips after Adelia's maturity, so be it.

As it happened, both sister and brother loved their work. There was no doubt in either of their minds that they'd continue working once the inheritance was theirs. They might build a good stable of their own, but they'd continue to train and ride.

Addie's past drug problems had more to do with her personality than with her background. Plenty of poor kids ran aground on drugs too. And plenty of poor kids spent their money as soon as they picked up their paycheck. Addie's impulsiveness and desire for a good time had little to do with class.

Addie wiped down the last horse of the day, a leggy gray, as the white Southern States delivery truck rolled down the drive.

"Feed man."

Chark, at the other end of the barn, called out, "I'll attend to it. You finish up what you're doing."

As Addie rubbed blue mineral ice on the gray's legs, she could hear the metal door clang up on the truck, the dolly clunk when it hit the ground, and the grunts of her brother and the delivery man as they loaded fifty-pound sacks of 14 percent protein sweet feed onto the dolly.

After filling up the zinc-lined feed bins—Mim thought of everything in her stable, but still the mice attacked—the delivery man murmured something to Chark and then drove off.

As her brother, a medium-built, well-proportioned man, ambled toward her, Addie asked, "Are we behind on the bill?"

"Up to date—" He smiled. "—for a change."

"What did he want then?"

"Nothing. Said he was sorry to hear about your friend."

The lines around her mouth relaxed. "That was kind of him. People surprise me."

"Yeah." Chark jammed his hands in his jeans. "Sis, I'm sorry that you're sorry, if you know what I mean, but I didn't like Nigel, and you know it, so I can't be a hypocrite now. Not that I wished him dead."

"You never gave him a chance."

"Oil and water." He ground his heel into the macadam aisle.

She led the gray back to his stall. "You don't much like any man I date."

"You don't much have good taste." Chark sounded harsher than he meant to sound. "Oh, hell, I'm sorry. You have to kiss them, I don't." He stopped making circles off his heel. "Nigel was a fake."

"You hate English accents."

"That I do. They smack of superiority, you know, talking through their noses and telling us how they gallop on the downs of Exmoor. This is America, and I'll train my way."

She put her hands on her hips. "Thought we settled that in 1776. You don't like anyone telling you what to do or making a suggestion that you perceive as a veiled criticism."

"I listen to you." His eyes, almond-shaped like his sister's, darkened.

"Sometimes"—she restlessly jammed her hands in her pockets—"you treated Nigel like dirt. And I—I—" She couldn't go on. Tears filled her eyes.

He stood there wanting to comfort her but not willing to give ground on the detested Nigel. Brotherly love won over and he hugged her. "Like I said, I didn't wish him dead. Maybe Linda Forloines did it."

Addie stiffened. "Linda . . . she made a move like a dope fiend." Addie referred to the whipping incident in stable slang.

"That's just it." Chark released his sister. "I'm willing to bet the barn that those two are selling again. Where else would the Forloines get the money for a new truck?''

"Didn't see it.''

"Brand new Nissan. Nice truck.'' He rubbed his hands together. He had arthritis in his fingers, broken years ago, and the chill of the oncoming night made his joints ache.

She shrugged. "Who knows.'' But she did know.

"She's probably doping horses as well as people.''

"I don't know.''

"It wouldn't surprise me if she and Will are—uh, in the mix somehow. A feeling.''

"I don't know,'' she repeated. "But I had my own Twilight Zone episode today.

"Huh?''

"I picked up the mail, and Harry and Mrs. H. were really wonderful except Harry's worse than the sheriff—she asks too many questions. Anyway, I lost my temper and said if I found out who killed Nigel before the law, I'd kill him. They both about jumped down my throat and said, 'Don't even say that.' ''

"They're right. Crazy things happen.''

"What gave me the shivers was their saying that if I got too close to the murderer, maybe he'd turn on me.''

"Damn,'' he whispered.

11

The dagger that killed Nigel Danforth, tagged and numbered, lay on Frank Yancey's desk. Rick Shaw and Cynthia Cooper sat on the other side of the desk.

"That's no cheap piece of hardware." Rick admired the weapon.

Frank touched it with the eraser on his pencil. "The blade is seven and a half inches, and the overall length is twelve and three quarters inches. The blade is double-edged stainless steel, highly polished, as you can see, and the handle is wrapped in wire, kind of like fencing uh—"

"Foils." Cooper found the word for him.

"Right." Frank frowned. "I think this was an impulse killing. Why would someone leave an expensive dagger buried in Nigel's chest?"

"If it was impulse, why the Queen of Clubs?" Rick countered.

Frank stroked the stubble on the side of his jowls. "Well—"

"And another thing, Sheriff Yancey," Cynthia respectfully addressed the older man, "I've been at the computer since this happened. I've talked to Scotland Yard. There is no Nigel Danforth."

"I was afraid of that." Frank grimaced. "Just like I was afraid we'd find no fingerprints. Not a one."

"Well, there are no inland revenue records, no passports, no national health card, no nothing," Cynthia said.

"Who the hell is that on the slab in the morgue?" Frank rhetorically asked.

"About all we can do is get dental impressions and send them over the wires. That will work if the stiff, I mean deceased," Cooper corrected herself, "had a criminal record. Otherwise, your guess is as good as mine."

"I don't like this." Frank smacked his hand on the table. "People want results."

"Don't worry, it's not an election year for you, Frank, and it's not like a serial killer is stalking the streets of Orange. The murder is confined to a small world."

"We hope," Cynthia said.

"I don't like this," Frank repeated. "I'll get Mickey Townsend in here. Why would he hire a man without a green card?"

"Same reason a lot of fruit growers hire Mexicans and don't inquire about their immigration status. They figure they can get the crop in before Immigration busts them. Any American employer whose IQ hovers above his body temperature knows to ask for a green card or go through the bullshit of getting one for the employee." Rick crossed his right leg over his left knee.

"It's the modern version of an indentured servant. You get someone a green card and they owe you for life," Cynthia added.

"Well, we know a few things." Rick folded his hands over

his chest, feeling the Lucky Strikes pack in his pocket and very much wanting a cigarette.

"Sure," Frank said. "We know I'm in deep shit and I have to tell a bunch of reporters we're on a trail colder than a witch's tit."

"No, we also know that the killer likes expensive weapons. Perhaps the dagger has symbolic significance, as does the Queen of Clubs. We also know that Nigel knew his killer."

"No, we don't," Frank said stubbornly.

"I can't prove it, of course, but there are no signs of struggle. He was face-to-face with his killer. He wasn't dragged or we'd have seen the marks on the barn floor."

"The killer could have stabbed him and then carried him to the chair." Cynthia thought out loud.

"That's a possibility, meaning the killer has to be strong enough to lift a—what do you reckon—a hundred-twenty-pound jockey over his shoulder."

"Or her shoulder. A strong woman could lift that." Cynthia scribbled a few notes in her spiral notebook.

"Wish Larry and Hank would call." Frank fidgeted.

"We could go over there, see what they've turned up." Rick stood.

"Bad luck having the county coroner out of town. He's as good as new." Frank, irritated, didn't realize the irony of his remarks.

Just then the phone rang. "Yancey," Frank said.

Hank Cushing's high-pitched voice started spouting out organ weights and stomach contents. "Normal heart and—"

"I don't give a damn about that. Was he stabbed twice or once?" Frank barked into the receiver.

"Twice," Hank responded. "The condition of the liver showed some signs of nascent alcohol damage and—"

"I don't care about that. Send me the report."

"Well, you might want to care about this." Hank, miffed, raised his voice. "He'd put his age down as twenty-six for his jockey application with the National Steeplechase Association, and I estimate his age to be closer to thirty-five. Might be worth sticking that fact in your brain and the fact that he had a serious dose of cocaine in his bloodstream. I'll send the file over as soon as I've written up my report." Miffed, Hank hung up on him.

Frank banged down the phone. "Prick."

"Well—?" Both Rick and Cynthia asked in unison.

"Stabbed twice. Full of coke."

"Makes sense. He'd hardly sit there while someone placed a card over his heart."

"Rick, he would if they'd held a gun to his head."

"Good point, pardner." Rick smiled at Cynthia.

"One other thing, Hank said his age was closer to thirty-five than the twenty-six he wrote down for the steeplechase association."

"Hmm," Rick murmured. "Whoever he was, he was a first-rate liar."

"Not so first-rate," Coop rejoined. "He's dead. Someone caught him out."

"Well, I sure appreciate your help." Frank got to his feet. "I figure the good citizens of Orange can sleep safe in their beds at night."

"That's what I'm doing. Going home to bed." Cynthia felt as if sand was in her eyes from staring at the computer screen for the last two and a half days.

On the way back to Charlottesville in an unmarked car, Rick smoked a cigarette, opening the window a crack first. "Frank's in over his head."

"Yep."

"If we're lucky this will be a revenge killing, and that'll be the end of it. If we're not, this will play out at other steeplechase races or other steeplechase stables, which means the good citizens of Orange and Albemarle counties may not sleep so soundly—not if they've got horses in the barn."

Cynthia stretched her long legs. "Horsey people are obsessed."

"I don't much like them," Rick matter-of-factly said.

"I can't say that, but I can say they fall into two categories."

"What's that?"

"They're either very, very intelligent or dumb as a sack of hammers. No in-between."

Rick laughed, exceeding the speed limit.

12

A sleek BMW 750il, the twelve-cylinder model, cruised by the post office at seven-thirty Tuesday morning. Harry noticed Mickey Townsend behind the wheel as she passed by in her truck.

"Some kind of car."

Mrs. Murphy and Tucker dutifully glanced at the metallic silver automobile but, not being car nuts, they returned their attention to more important matters.

"Hey, Ella!" Mrs. Murphy called to Elocution, Herb Jones's youngest cat, as she sat by the minister's front door.

Since the window was rolled up, Elocution couldn't hear, but Harry sure could.

"You'll split my eardrums."

"Mother, I have to listen to you morning, noon and night."

"Yeah, but she's not screeching for her friends."

"*Tucker, shut up.*" The cat boxed that long, inviting nose. Murphy wondered what cats living with pugs, bulldogs, and chows did since those canines' noses were pushed in. Guess they jumped on their backs and bit their necks.

The lights were already on inside as Harry parked the truck.

"Hey," she called as she opened the back door, the aroma of fresh cinnamon curling into her nostrils.

"Morning." Mrs. Hogendobber put whole coffee beans into a cylindrical electric grinder. The noise terrified Tucker, who cowered underneath the empty mail cart.

"*Chicken.*"

"*I hate that noise,*" the dog whimpered.

Harry heated up water on the hot plate. She couldn't drink much coffee so she made tea. Doughnuts, steam still rising off them, were arranged in concentric circles on the white plate.

"Cinnamon?" Harry said.

"And cake doughnuts too. I'm experimenting with two different doughs." A knock at the back door interrupted her. "Who is it?"

"Attila the Hun."

"Come on in," Mrs. Hogendobber answered.

Susan Tucker, pink-faced from the cold, opened the door. "Good frost this morning. Hi, Tucker." She reached down to pet the dog. "Hello, Mrs. Murphy, I know you're in the mail cart because I can see the bulge underneath."

"*Morning,*" came the sleepy reply.

"Saw Mickey Townsend drive by," Susan said.

"Passed him on the way in. Oh, Susan, I've got a registered letter for you."

"Damn." Susan thought registered letters usually meant some unwanted legal notice or, worse, a dire warning from the IRS.

Harry fished out the letter with the heavy pink paper attached, a copy underneath. "Press hard so your signature shows through."

Ballpoint in hand, Susan peered at the return address. "Plaistow, New Hampshire?" She firmly wrote her name.

Harry carefully tore off the pink label, which she kept, the carbon copy remaining with the envelope.

Susan wedged her forefinger under the sealed flap, opening the letter. "Say, this is pretty nice."

"What?" Harry read over her shoulder.

"State Line Tack exhausted their supply of turnout rugs in red and gold. If I'll accept a navy with a red border, they'll give me a further ten percent discount, and they apologize for the inconvenience. They haven't been able to reach me by phone." She snapped the paper. "Because the damn kids never get off it! What a good business."

"I'll say. You know who else is really great: L. L. Bean."

"The best." Mrs. Hogendobber ate a doughnut. "Mmm. Outdid myself."

Susan folded the letter, returning it to its envelope, and then, as is often the case between old friends, she jumped to another subject with no explanation because she knew Harry would understand the connection: signing for letters. "You must know every signature in Crozet."

"We both do." Mrs. Hogendobber wiped crumbs from her mouth. "We could be expert witnesses in forgery cases. I wish you two would try one of these. My best."

Harry grabbed a cinnamon doughnut even though she had sworn she wouldn't.

"Go on." Mrs. Hogendobber noticed Susan salivating over the plate. "I can't eat them all myself."

"Ned told me I can't gain my five winter pounds this year. He even bought me a NordicTrack." Susan stared at the doughnuts.

"Don't eat lunch." Harry saved her the agony of the decision by handing her one.

Once that fresh smell wafted right under her nose, Susan

popped the doughnut straight in. "Oh, hell." She helped herself to a cup of tea. "Heard some scoop."

"I wait with cinnamon breath—as opposed to bated, that is." Harry untied the first mailbag.

"Nigel Danforth bet a thousand dollars on the fifth race—Mim's horse, not Mickey Townsend's."

Miranda wondered out loud. "Is that bad?"

"A jockey wouldn't bet against himself or the stable he's riding for, plus a jockey isn't supposed to bet at all. That's a fact for all sports. Remember Pete Rose." Susan, suffering the tortures of the damned, grabbed another cinnamon doughnut.

"Wouldn't it mean he's fixing the race?"

"It might, but probably not in this circumstance." Susan continued: "Mickey Townsend's mare didn't have much of a chance. Of course, Nigel placed the bet through a third party. I mean, that's what I've heard."

"Yeah but with steeplechasing—one pileup and a goat could win." Harry leaned over Mrs. Murphy. "Murphy, I need to dump the mail in."

"No."

"Come on, kitty cat."

"No." To prove her point Murphy rolled over on her back, exposing her beautiful beige tummy with its crisp black stripes.

"All right then, smartass." Harry poured a little mail on the cat.

"I'm not moving." Mrs. Murphy rolled over on her side.

"Stubborn." Harry reached in with both hands and plucked her out, placing her in the fleece teepee she'd bought especially for the cat.

Grumbling, Mrs. Murphy circled inside three times, then settled down. She needed her morning nap.

"Doesn't sound cricket to me." Mrs. Hogendobber occasionally used an expression from her youth when, due to World War II, phrases from the British allies were current.

"It's not the most prudent policy." Harry dumped the remainder of the mail from her sack into the cart, then wheeled it over to the post boxes.

"I'd worry less about that and more about where a jockey got one thousand dollars cash." Susan helped with the third-class mail. "Those guys only get paid fifty dollars a race, you know. If they win, place or show they get a percentage of the purse."

"The wages of sin." Harry laughed.

"You know . . ." Susan's voice trailed off.

"We ought to go over to Mim's stable," Harry said, "at lunch. Larry comes in today." Dr. Larry Johnson, partially retired, filled in at lunch so Harry and Mrs. Hogendobber could run errands or relax over a meal at Crozet Pizza.

"Now, girls, just a minute. You heard a rumor, Susan, not a fact. You shouldn't slander someone even though he is dead."

"I'm not slandering him. I only told you, and I don't think it hurts if we sniff about."

"I'll do the sniffing," Tucker told them.

"We should talk to the horses. They know what went down. Too bad there weren't any left in the barn when Nigel was stabbed," Mrs. Murphy drawled from inside her teepee.

"Even if there had been, Murphy, chances are that the horse would have been vanned back to its stable and how would we get there? Especially if it was a Maryland horse?" Tucker lay down in front of the teepee, sticking her nose inside. Mrs. Murphy didn't mind.

The front door opened. The Reverend Herb Jones and Market Shiflett bustled in.

"Got the mail sorted yet?" Market asked.

"Is it eight yet?" Harry tossed mail into boxes.

"No."

"I have yours right here. I did it first because I like you so much," Harry teased him.

As Market blew in the front door, Pewter blew into the back.

"What about me?" Herb asked.

"I like you *so* much, too." Harry laughed, handing him a stack of magazines, bills, letters, and catalogs.

Pewter walked around Tucker and stuck her head into the teepee. Then she squeezed in and curled up next to Mrs. Murphy.

"*Boy, you're fat,*" the tiger grumbled.

"*You always say that,*" Pewter purred, for she liked to snuggle. "*But I keep you warm.*"

"Say, I heard that Linda Forloines bet a thousand dollars on the fifth race against the horse she was riding." Herb Jones flipped unwanted solicitations into the trash.

"See," Miranda triumphantly called as she continued her sorting.

"See what?" he asked.

"Susan said that same thing about Nigel Danforth," Miranda called from behind the post boxes.

"Oh." Herb neatly stacked his mail and put a rubber band around it. "Another rumor for the grist mill."

"Well, someone must have bet one thousand dollars on the fifth race." Susan, chin jutting out, wasn't giving up so easily.

Market leaned over the counter. "You know how these things are. The next thing you'll hear is that the body disappeared."

13

Fair stood in the doorway, looking as serious as a heart attack. Normally Harry would have cussed him out because she hated it when he dropped in on her without calling first. Sometimes he forgot they weren't married, an interesting twist since, when they were married, he'd sometimes forgotten that as well.

The paleness of his lips kept her complaint bottled up.

"*Daddy!*" Tucker scurried forward to shower love on Fair.

"*Brown-noser.*" Mrs. Murphy turned her back on him, and the tip of her tail flicked. She liked Fair but not enough to make a fool of herself rushing to greet him. Also, Murphy, having once endured a philandering husband herself, the handsome black-and-white Paddy, keenly felt for Harry.

"Close the door, Fair. It's cold."

"So it is." He gently shut the door behind him, took off

his heavy green buffalo-plaid shirt, and hung it on a peg by the door.

"I'm down to cheese and crackers tonight because I haven't been to the supermarket in weeks. You're welcome to some."

"No appetite. Got a beer?"

"Yep." She reached into the refrigerator, fishing out a cold Sol, popped the cap, grabbed a glass mug, and handed it to him as he headed for the living room. He sank into the overstuffed chair, a remnant from the forties, which Harry's mom had found at a rummage sale. It could have even been from the thirties. It had been recovered so many times that only bits of the original color, a slate gray with golden stars, straggled on the edges where the upholsterer's nails held a few original threads. The last recovering had occurred seven years ago. Mrs. Murphy, claws at the ready, had exposed the wood underneath the fabric and tufting, which was why you could also see the upholsterer's nails. Her steady application of kitty destructiveness forced Harry to throw a quarter sheet over the chair. Now that she'd gotten used to it, she liked the dark green blanket, edged in gold, used to keep horses' hindquarters warm in bitter weather.

"To what do I owe this pleasure?"

Fair pulled long on the beer. "I am under investigation—"

"For the murder of Nigel Danforth?" Harry blurted out.

"No—for doping horses. Mickey Townsend drove over to tell Mim, and Mim told me, and sure enough Colbert Mason from National confirmed it. He was kind enough to say that no one believed it, but he had to go through the motions."

"Has anyone formally accused you?"

"Not yet."

"It's a crock of shit!"

"My sentiments exactly." The deep lines around his light eyes only added to his masculine appeal. He rubbed his forehead. "Who would do such a thing?"

"Whoever tells you they wouldn't," Harry remarked. "Who has something to gain by doing this to you? Another vet?"

"Harry, you know the other equine vets as well as I do. Not one of them would sink that low. Besides, we cooperate with one another."

Murphy brought in her tiny play mouse covered with rabbit's fur, one of her favorite toys. She hoped she could seduce Harry into throwing it so she could chase it. She jumped on the arm of the chair, dropping it into Harry's lap.

"Murphy, go find a real one."

"*I have cleansed this house of mice. I am the master mouser,*" she bragged.

"*Ha!*" Tucker wedged herself on Harry's foot.

"*You couldn't catch a mouse if your life depended on it.*"

"*Well, you couldn't herd cows if your life depended on it, so there.*"

Harry tossed the mouse behind her shoulder, and the cat launched off the chair, tore across the room, skidded past the mouse because she'd put her brakes on too late, bumped her butt on the wall, slid around, got her paws under her, and pounced on the mouse.

"*Death to vermin!*" She tossed the mouse over her head. She batted it with her paws. She lobbed it in the air, catching it on the way down.

"Wouldn't you love to be like that just once?" Harry admired Mrs. Murphy's wild abandon.

"Freedom." Fair laughed as the tiger, play mouse in jaws, leapt over the corgi.

"*I hate it when you do that,*" Tucker grumbled.

Mrs. Murphy said nothing because she didn't want to drop her mouse, so she careened around and vaulted Tucker from the other direction. Tucker flattened on the rug, ears back.

"*Show-off.*"

The cat ignored her, rushing into the bedroom so she could drop the mouse behind the pillows and then crawl under them to destroy the enemy again.

Harry returned to the subject, "Remember those war philosophy books you used to read? *The Art of War* by Shu Tzu was one.

A passage in there goes, 'Uproar in East, strike in West.' Might be what's going on with you."

"You read those books more carefully than I did."

"Liked von Clausewitz best." She crossed her legs under her. "No one who knows you, no one who has watched you work on a horse could ever believe you would drug horses for gain. Since this complaint came out of the steeplechase set, you know it may not relate to the murder, but then again, it gets folks sidetracked, looking east."

"Yeah—they'll waste time on me," he mumbled.

"Like I said, 'Uproar in East, strike in West.' " She paused. "Did you know Nigel?"

"He didn't talk much so it was a nodding acquaintance." He threw his leg over an arm of the chair. "Want to go to a show?"

"Nah. I'm going to paint the bathroom tonight. I can't stand it another minute.

"You work too much."

"Look who's talking."

"*Isn't anyone going to come in here and play with me?*" Murphy called from the bedroom as she threw a pillow on the floor for dramatic effect.

"She's vocal tonight." Fair finished his beer. "Bring me your mousie."

Seeing a six-foot-four-inch man of steel ask for a cat to bring her mousie never struck Harry as strange. Both she and Fair were so attuned to animals that speaking to them was as natural as speaking to a human. Generally, it produced better results.

Murphy ripped out of the bedroom, mouse in jaws again, and dropped the little gray toy on Fair's boots.

"What a *valuable* mouse. Murphy, you're a big hunter. You need to go on a safari." He threw the mouse into the kitchen, and off ran Murphy.

"*You indulge her.*" Tucker sank her head on her paws.

"Miranda and I were going over to Mim's at lunch to poke

around about the rumors of Nigel betting against himself in the sixth race, or was it the fifth?'' She shrugged. '' 'Course, the same rumor floated around about Linda Forloines.''

''The thousand dollars?''

''Guess it's made the rounds.''

''Yeah. Why didn't you go?''

''Larry relieved us late. Miranda got a call from her church group, some crisis to do with the songfest, so I went over to Crozet Pizza. No point in chasing rumors, which is why I can't believe that Colbert Mason is bothering about this one concerning you. Well, I guess he has to go through the motions.''

''You were always better than I was at figuring out people. I'm not a vet just because I love animals. Don't much like people deep down, I suppose—or maybe I just like a few select ones like you.''

''Don't start,'' Harry swiftly replied.

''Mom, don't be so hard on him.'' Mrs. Murphy deposited her play mouse next to her food bowl.

''Yeah, Mom,'' Tucker chimed in.

''I'm not starting.'' He sighed. ''You know I've repented. I've told you. I'm changing. Hell, maybe I'm even growing up.''

''Mother used to say that men don't grow up, they grow old. Actually, I thought Dad was a mature man, but then again a daughter doesn't see a man the same as a wife does.''

''Are you telling me I can't grow up?''

''No.'' She uncrossed her legs, leaning forward, ''I'm not good at these topics. The conventional wisdom is that women can talk about emotions and men can't. I don't see that I'm good at it, and I don't see any reason to learn. I mean, I know what I feel. Whether I can or want to express it is my deal, right? Anyway, emotions are like mercury, up, down, and if you break the thermometer, the stuff runs out. Poof.''

''Mary Minor, don't be so tough. A little introspection can't hurt.''

''Not the therapy rap again?'' She threw up her hands.

He ignored the comment. "I hated going, but I'd made such a mess of my life it was that or sucking on a gun barrel." He paused. "Actually look forward to those sessions. I'm taking a college course and the subject is me. Guess it means I'm egotistical." He smiled wryly.

"What matters is that for you it's a—" she rummaged around for the right word, "an enlarging experience. You're open to it and getting a lot from it. I'm not. I'm closed. It ain't my deal."

"What's your deal?"

"Hard work. Why do you ask what you already know?"

"Wanted to hear you say it."

"You heard me."

"Harry, it's okay to share emotions."

"Goddammit, I know that. It's also okay not to share them. What good does it do, Fair? And what's the line between sharing and whining?"

"Do I sound like I'm whining?"

"No."

They sat in silence. Mrs. Murphy padded in, leaving her mouse by her food bowl.

"*Go to a movie with him, Mom,*" Tucker advised.

"*Yeah,*" Murphy agreed.

"You know if there's any way I can help you with this inquiry, I'll do it."

"I know." He sat waiting to be asked to stay, yet knowing she wouldn't ask. At last he rose, tossed his long-neck bottle in the trash, and lifted his heavy shirt off the peg. "Thanks for listening."

She joined him in the kitchen. "Things will turn out right. It's a waste of time, but dance to their tune for a while."

"Like singing for my supper? Remember when I was starting out, Mim would give me odd jobs at the stable and then feed me? Funny about Mim. She's tyrannical and snobbish, but underneath she's a good soul. Most people don't see that."

"What I remember is Little Marilyn's first husband driving you bananas."

"That guy." Fair shook his head. "I was glad when she was shuck of him, although I guess it was hard for her. Always is, really. Are you glad to be rid of me?"

"Some days, yes. Some days, no."

"What about today?" His eyes brightened.

"Neutral."

He opened the kitchen door and left. "Bye. Thanks for the beer," he called.

"Yeah." She waved good-bye, feeling that phantom pain in her heart like the phantom pain in an amputated limb.

14

Bazooka, sleek, fit, and full of himself, pranced sideways back to the stable. Addie breezed him but he wanted to fly. He hated standing in his stall, and he envied Mim's foxhunters, who led a more normal life, lounging in the pastures and only coming into their stalls at night.

Like most competitive horses, Bazooka was fed a high protein diet with supplements and encouraged to explode during the race. Mostly he felt like exploding at home. He knew he could win, barring an accident or being boxed in by a cagey opposing jockey. He wanted to win, to cover himself with glory. Bazooka's ego matched his size: big. Unlike most 'chasers at other barns, he also knew that when his competitive days drew to a close, Mim wouldn't sell him off. She would retire him to foxhunting, most likely riding him herself, for Mim was a good rider.

The fact that Mim could ride better than her daughter only deepened Little Marilyn's lifelong sulk. Occasional bursts of filial devotion gusted through the younger Mim's demeanor.

Both mother and daughter watched as Bazooka proudly passed them.

"He's on today," Addie called to them.

"The look of eagles." Mim grinned.

"*I am beautiful!*" Bazooka crowed.

"Mom, I didn't know Harry was coming by." Little Marilyn had grown up with Mary Minor Haristeen, but although she couldn't say she disliked Harry, she couldn't say she liked her either. Personalities, like colors, either look good together or they don't. These two didn't.

Mim, by contrast, found it easy to talk to Harry even though she deplored the younger woman's lack of ambition.

The Superman-blue Ford truck chugged to the parking lot behind the stable. Tucker and Mrs. Murphy appeared before Harry did. They spoke their greetings, then ran into the stable as Harry reached Big Mim and Little Mim, occasionally called Mini-Mim if Harry was feeling venomous.

"What have you got there?" Mim asked, noticing that Harry carried a small box.

"The labels for the wild game dinner invitations. Little Marilyn was printing up the invitations."

"Did you run these off a government computer?" Mim folded her arms across her chest.

"Uh—I did. Aren't you glad your taxes have gone to something productive?"

Little Mim snatched the box from Harry's hands. "Thanks."

"How do the invitations look?" Harry asked.

Little Marilyn squinted at Harry, distorting her manicured good looks. "Haven't picked them up yet." Which translated into: She forgot to order them, and the labels told her she'd better get cracking. "I think I'll go get them right now. Need anything from C-ville, Mum?"

"No. I gave my list to your father."

"Good to see you, Harry." The impeccably dressed young Marilyn hot-footed it to her Range Rover.

No point in either her mother or Harry criticizing her. They knew she hadn't done her job, but she'd do it under pressure. Nor was there any point in discussing it with each other.

Harry walked with Mim into the lovely paneled tack room. The air was nippy even though the sun was high.

"Where's Chark?"

"Other end of the barn. He's finishing up the last set. Bang 'em out early, as he says."

Harry sat down as Mim pointed to a seat covered in a handsome dark plaid. Harry could have lived happily in Mim's tack room, which was prettier than her living room.

"Mim, I know that Mickey Townsend drove over to tell you about the unfounded charges leveled against Fair. Fair dropped by last night. This is outrageous"—her face reddened—"for somebody to smear one of the best vets in practice. Do you have any idea who would pull a stunt like this?"

"No." Mim sat down opposite Harry. "I called Colbert and Arthur first thing this morning and told them the inquiry had better be fast and be quiet or I am going to make life sheer hell for everyone." She held up her hand as if requesting silence from an audience. "I also told them it's a waste of time when they have far more important things to do."

"Well, that's why I'm here. You're one of the most powerful people in the association." Mim murmured denial even as she was pleased to hear it, and Harry continued. "I dropped by Ned Tucker's this morning. Susan filled him in. He said he would represent Fair, no charge. He drafted a letter, which I have right here."

As Mim read, her eyebrows knitted together and then she smiled. "Good show, Ned."

The letter said in exhaustive legalese that Fair had no intention of submitting to an inquiry without a formal accusation. If this was allowed to continue, then every veterinarian, trainer, and jockey could be paralyzed by poisonous gossip. He demanded his accuser come forward, that a formal complaint be filed. Once that was accomplished, he would defend himself.

"What do you think? Rather, what do you think the National Steeplechase Association will think?" Harry took the letter back from Mim's outstretched hand, sporting only her wedding band and engagement diamond today.

"I expect they'll nail the accuser straightaway. But can you get Fair to sign this? You know how he is about honor. Nineteenth century, but then that's what makes him such a splendid man."

"Of course I can't get him to sign it. He thinks people should resolve their differences any way they can before resorting to lawyers. He doesn't understand that America doesn't work that way anymore. The minute we're born we put some lawyer on retainer."

"So what's the solution here?"

"Uh—Mim, what I had hoped is that you would fax this to Colbert. Maybe write a note that Ned Tucker came to you with this because he doesn't want the association further embarrassed. You know, the murder, public relations problems, et cetera. You want to give Colbert and Arthur, too, plenty of warning so they can frame a response should the press jump on this." Harry breathed deeply. She hadn't realized how nervous she was.

Mim sank back in the chair, painted nails tapping the armrests. "Harry, you are far more subtle than I give you credit for— of course I'll do it."

"Oh, thank you. Fair will never know unless Colbert tells him."

"I'll hint in my cover letter that if this can be rapidly resolved, the signed letter will never arrive. Fair will drop legal proceedings."

Harry beamed. "You're so smart."

"No—you are. And you're still in love with him."

"That's what everyone says, but no, I'm not." Harry quickly replied. "I love him. It's different. He's a friend and a good man, and he doesn't deserve this smear job. He'd do the same for me."

"Yes, he would."

As Mim and Harry discussed Fair, love, Jim, Bazooka, Miranda's choir group's fund-raiser for the Church of the Holy Light, as well as the kitchen sink, Mrs. Murphy and Tucker chatted up the barn cat, a strong, large ginger named Rodger Dodger. His tortoiseshell girlfriend, Pusskin, slept in the hayloft, worn out from chasing a chipmunk that morning.

Bazooka, being wiped down in the wash stall, listened disappointedly because the other animals weren't talking about him.

"How's hunting?" Rodger Dodger asked Mrs. Murphy.

"Good."

"Oh, yeah, she kills her play mouse nightly." Tucker giggled.

"Shut up. I account for my share of mice and moles."

"Don't forget the blue jay. That put Mom right over the edge." Tucker gloated.

"I hated that blue jay."

"I hate them, too," Rodger solemnly agreed. "They zoom down from twelve o'clock directly above you and peck you. Then peel out and zoom away. I'd kill every one if I could."

"What's going on around here?" Tucker changed the subject from rodent and fowl kills. Now, if they wanted to discuss how to turn cattle or sheep, she could offer many stories.

Rodger swept his whiskers forward, stepping close to the tiger cat and corgi. "Last night someone took Orion out of his stall, put him in the cross ties, and dug around in the stall, but was interrupted. Whoever it was covered the hole back up and put Orion in the stall."

"Can you smell anything in the stall?"

"Earth." Rodger Dodger rested on his haunches.

"*Let's take a look.*" Mrs. Murphy scampered down the aisle. Since Orion was a hunter, he was playing outside in a field. The animals could go into his stall.

Tucker put her nose to the ground. The cats pawed the wood shavings away. The ground had indeed been freshly turned over.

Mrs. Murphy cautiously investigated the other corners of the stall. Nothing.

"*Doesn't make sense, does it?*" Rodger observed Tucker.

"*I don't know.*" She lifted her head, inhaled fresh air, then put her nose back to the smoothed-over spot. "*If we could get someone to dig here I might find something. If anything was removed, I would smell that.*" She sniffed again. "*Right now it's blank.*"

The three animals sat in the stall.

"*Do you know who it was?*" Tucker asked.

"*No, I was out in the machine shed last night. Good pickings. When Orion made mention of it on his way out this morning, I was too groggy to grill him.*"

"*Let's go ask Orion.*" Mrs. Murphy left the stall just as Bazooka was put into his stall by Chark Valiant.

"*You don't have to ask Orion,*" the steel gray told them. "*I saw who it was. Coty Lamont.*"

"*Coty Lamont!*" Mrs. Murphy exclaimed. Rodger jumped on the tack trunk in front of Bazooka's stall and got on his hind legs to chat with the horse. "*Bazooka, why was he here?*"

"*He didn't say,*" Bazooka sarcastically replied. "*But Mickey Townsend tiptoed in and shut the stall door with Coty in there. Coty tried to get out but Mickey wouldn't let him. He told him to cover it back up, and to come with him.*"

"*Old Kotex hates Mickey.*" Mrs. Murphy used Coty's nickname. "*For that matter, so does Chark Valiant.*"

"*Bet Coty didn't go,*" Tucker said.

"*Oh, but he did.*" Bazooka relished the tale. "*Mickey pulled a gun on him and told him he had to go with him.*"

"*Did he go?*" Tucker's lustrous eyes widened.

"*Sure he did. See, I don't know how he got here. Mickey just tiptoed into* the barn," Bazooka added. "*Anyway, Mickey told him to put his hands behind his head. He unbolted the stall, and Coty walked in front of him.*"

"*Boy, is that weird.*" Rodger Dodger scratched his side with his hind leg.

It was more than weird, because that night at dusk Coty Lamont, the best steeplechase jockey of his generation, was discovered on a dirt road in eastern Albemarle County right off Route 22. He was laid out in the bed of his Ford 350 dually pickup truck painted in his favorite metallic maroon. The Queen of Spades was over his heart, a stiletto driven through it.

15

Rick Shaw lost cigarette lighters the way small children lose gloves. He used disposable lighters because of this. Pulling a see-through lime-green lighter from his coat pocket, he studied the corpse in the truck.

Cynthia Cooper scribbled in her notebook, weakened, and lit up a cigarette herself.

The ambulance crew waited at a distance. Kenny Wheeler, Jr., who had found the body, stayed with the sheriff and his deputy.

"Kenny, I know you've told me this before but tell me again because I need to have the sequence right," Rick softly asked the tall, deep-voiced young man.

"I was checking a fence line. Kinda in a hurry because I was losing light and running behind, you know." He stared down at his boots. "This old road is really on my neighbor's property, but I have use of it, so I thought I'd swing through to get to the back acres. Save a minute or two. Anyway, I saw this truck. Didn't recognize it. And as I drew closer I saw him"—he pointed to the body—"in the bed. I thought maybe the guy fell asleep or something—I mean, until I got closer. Well, I stopped my truck, got out, kinda peeped over the sides. I mean, I knew the man was dead, deader than the Red Sox, but I don't know why I called out, 'Hey.' I stood there for a minute and then I got on the mobile, called you first off, then called Mom and Dad. I described the truck. They didn't know it. Dad wanted to come right out, but I told him to stay put. It's better that I'm the only one involved.

"Well, Dad didn't like that. He's a hands-on guy, as you know, but I said, 'Dad, if you come on out here, then you'll get caught in the red tape, and you have enough to do. I found him, so I'll take care of it.' So he said okay finally, and here I am."

Cynthia closed her notebook. "Rick, do you need Kenny anymore?"

"Yeah, wait one minute." Rick, gloves on, pulled out the registration. "The truck is registered to Coty Lamont. That name mean anything to you?" Rick leaned against the open door of the truck.

"Coty Lamont." Kenny frowned. "A jockey. I'm pretty sure I've heard that name before. We don't race, but . . . that name is familiar."

"Thanks, Kenny. You've been a tremendous help. Go on home. I'll call you if I need you. Give your Mom and Dad my regards. Wife, too." Rick clapped him on the back.

As Kenny turned his truck around and drove out, Rick looked back into the bed of the truck. "Notice anything?"

"Yeah, he was shot in the back for good measure. Probably struggled." Cynthia answered.

"Uh-huh. Anything else?"

"Same M.O. as the last one, pretty much."

"The card, Cynthia, check out the card."

"The Queen of Spades." She whistled. "Lot of blood on this one."

"Spades, Coop—the other card was clubs."

Cynthia rubbed her hands on her upper arms. The sunset over the Southwest Range and the night air chilled to the bone. "Clubs, spades—are you thinking what I'm thinking?"

"Diamonds and hearts to go."

16

The glow from the tip of his cigarette shone through Rick Shaw's hand in the starless night. He cupped it to keep out the wind as he leaned over the railing at Montpelier's flat track.

Barry McMullen, who rented the flat track stable, hunched his shoulders against the biting wind, pulling up his collar.

"There's nothing to this thousand-dollar rumor." Barry pushed his chin out assertively. "I've known Coty Lamont ever since he started out as Mickey Townsend's groom. Then he got his first ride on one of Arthur Tetrick's horses back when Arthur kept twenty horses in training. I just don't think Coty would be suckered into a gambling ring, and I know he would never throw a race."

"Not even for a couple hundred thousand dollars?"

Barry considered that. "No jockey that threw a race—and

it's damned easy to do in 'chasing—would get that much money. The stakes are considerably lower than flat racing, considerably lower.''

"How much?"

"Maybe five thousand. Tops."

"So we're talking about sums, not character."

Barry growled, "Don't put words into my mouth. Coty Lamont possessed an ego three times his size. He was the best, had to be the best, had to stay the best. He wouldn't throw a race. I think this gambling hunch is off the mark—for him. I don't know Jack Shit about the other guy who was killed. That Nigel fella."

"Neither do we." Rick felt hot ashes drop into his hand. He tilted his palm halfway to drop them on the cold ground, stamping them out with his foot.

"Pleasant enough. Asked to ride here. He was a decent hand with a horse, but I didn't have any room for him." He wrapped his scarf tighter around his neck. "Is there a reason we're standing out here in the cold, Rick?"

"Yes. I don't trust anyone in any barn right now."

Barry's light brown eyes widened. "My barn?"

"Any barn. If you repeat my questions there isn't much I can do about it. After all, I'm a public servant and my inquiry must be aboveboard, but it doesn't have to be broadcast. I don't want anyone eavesdropping while mucking a stall or throwing down hay." He shook his head. "I've got a bad feeling about this business."

Barry's jaw hardened. "Jesus, what do you think is going on?"

"What about a ring that sells horses for high prices, then substitutes cheap look-alikes, keeping the high-priced horses for themselves to win races or to be resold again? Possible?"

"In the old days, yes. Today, no. Every Thoroughbred is tattooed on the lip—"

Rick interrupted. "You could duplicate the tattoo."

Slowly Barry replied, "Hard to do but possible. However, why bother? These days we have DNA testing. The Jockey Club demands a small vial of blood before it will register a foal, and it demands one from the mare, too. The system is ninety-nine point ninety-nine percent foolproof."

"Not if someone on the inside substitutes vials of blood."

This floored Barry. "How do you think of things like that?"

"I deal with miscreants, traffic violators, domestic dragons, thieves, and hard-core criminals day in and day out. If I don't think as they do I'll never nail them." The deep creases around Rick's mouth lent authority to his rugged appearance. "It would have to be an inside job. Meaning the seller, the vet, possibly a jockey or a groom, and maybe even someone at the Jockey Club would have to be in on it."

"Not the Jockey Club." Barry vigorously shook his head. "Never. We're talking about *Mecca*. Sheriff, I would bet my life no one at the Jockey Club would ever desecrate the institution even for a large sum of money, and hey, I don't always agree with them. I think they're turned around backward sometimes, but I trust them, I mean, I trust their commitment to Thoroughbreds."

"Well, I hope you're right. If my bait-and-switch hunch isn't right, I'm lost. Two jockeys have been killed within seven days. Unless we're talking about some kind of bizarre sex club here, or irate husbands, then I'm sticking close to gambling or selling horses."

"You'd better put out that weed, Sheriff Rick." Barry smiled, pointing at Rick's hand.

At just that moment the cigarette burned his palm and Rick flapped his hands, dropping the stub. Its fiery nub burned in the dying grass. Rick quickly stepped on it. "Thanks. Got so preoccupied I forgot I was holding the damn thing."

"They'll kill you, you know."

Rick sardonically smiled. "Better this than a stiletto. Anyway, I've got to die of something." What he kept to himself was the fact that he'd tried to quit three times, the pressure of work always pulling him back to that soothing nicotine. "You know what Nigel was doing in this stable?" He nodded in the direction of the imposing flat track stable lying parallel to the track.

"Picking up gear. I think that's what he was doing. Some jockeys stowed their gear here, away from the crowds."

"Where were you immediately after the races?"

"Enjoying Cindy Chandler's tailgate party."

"And after that?"

He put his hands in his pockets. "Ran into Arthur Tetrick and walked with him on his way to the big house. We chatted about Arthur buying a four-year-old I saw in Upperville. Arthur wants back in the game. We walked toward the gate to the house. I left him there and went to check on one last van pulling out from the back stables, not mine." He pointed northeast of his stable in the direction of the smaller stables, well out of sight. "That's when one of Frank Yancey's deputies called me. Pretty dark by then."

"Don't be surprised if Frank asks you all the same questions that I have. I've talked to him, of course."

Barry, although not a native Virginian, had lived in Orange County since the early '70s. He knew Sheriff Yancey well. "Frank's a good man. Not a smart man, but a good man. I'm glad you're on this now."

Rick couldn't cast aspersions on a fellow law enforcement officer. "Frank might be smarter than you know. You see, Barry, it's not what he knows, it's who he knows. I'm going over to roast"—he savored the word—"Mickey Townsend tomorrow. Maybe he'll turn something up for me. You get on with him?"

"Yeah."

Rick started back toward the squad car. "Oh, one other thing. Anyone play cards in this group, the steeplechase people? I don't mean a friendly hand here and there, but impassioned card players?"

"Hell, Mickey Townsend would kill for an inside straight."

17

Dr. Stephen D'Angelo, a pulmonary surgeon, rode toward the stables. He was immaculately dressed in butcher boots, tan breeches, a white shirt, and tweed hacking jacket.

Linda Forloines rode alongside him. "She's a point and shoot."

"Where did you say this horse hunted?"

"Middleburg, Piedmont, and Oak Ridge."

He patted his horse's neck. "How much?"

"Well, they're asking twenty thousand dollars. But let's go over there. If you ride her and like her, I bet I can get that price down."

"Okay. Make an appointment for Thursday afternoon." He stopped outside the stable door, dismounted, and handed the reins to Linda, who had dismounted first.

Time being precious to him, he scheduled his rides at precisely the same time each day. Then he drove to the hospital, changing there.

He had sworn when he moved down from New Jersey that he'd retire, but word of a good doctor gets around. Before he knew it he was again in practice with two mornings' operating time at the hospital.

Like most extremely busy people in high-pressure jobs, he had to trust those around him. Linda kept the stable clean and the horses worked. He couldn't have known that behind his back she made fun of everything about him.

She mocked his riding ability, calling it "death defying." She moaned about his truck and trailer; she wanted a much more expensive one. She lauded her contributions to his farm to all and sundry even as she bit the hand that fed her.

As soon as the horses were untacked and wiped down, she planned to call her friend in Middleburg who was selling the horse Dr. D'Angelo was interested in for someone else. The horse was worth $7,500. If Dr. D'Angelo liked the mare, Linda would "plead" with her friend to plead with her client to drop the price. They'd counter at $15,000. The owner of the horse would indeed get $7,500. Linda and her friend would split and pocket the additional $7,500 without telling anyone. The original owner wouldn't know because they'd cash the check and pay her in cash. It was done every day in the horse business by people less than honest . . . often selling horses less than sound.

The phone rang as Linda tossed a Rambo blanket over one of the horses.

The wall phone hung on the outside wall.

She picked it up. "Hello."

"Linda," the deep male voice said, "Coty Lamont was found dead in the back of his pickup truck. A knife through the heart."

She gasped. "What?"

"You're losing business." He laughed. Then his voice turned cold. "I know Sheriff Yancey questioned you."

Before he could continue she said, "Hey, I'm not stupid. I didn't say a word."

A long pause followed. "Keep it that way. Liabilities don't live long in this business. Midnight. Tomorrow."

"Yeah. Sure." She hung up the phone, surprised to find her hand shaking.

18

The pale November light spilled over her like champagne, making the deep blacks of Mrs. Murphy's stripes glisten. Her tail upright, her whiskers slightly forward, she loped across the fields to Mim's house. Alongside her and not at all happy about it wobbled Pewter—not an outdoor girl. Tee Tucker easily kept up the pace.

Mim's estate nestled not fifteen minutes from the post office if one cut across yards and fields.

"Oh, can't we walk a bit?"

"We're almost there." Murphy pressed on.

"I know we're almost there. I'm tired," complained the gray cat.

"Hold it!" Tucker commanded.

The two cats stopped, Pewter breathing hard. A rustle in the broom sage alerted them to another presence. The cats dropped to their bellies, ears forward. Tucker stood her ground.

"*Who goes there?*" Tucker demanded.

"*As fine a cat as ever walked the globe,*" came the saucy reply.

"*Ugh.*" Pewter squinted. She had never been able to stand Paddy, Mrs. Murphy's ex-husband.

Murphy stuck her head up, "*Whatever you're doing on this side of Crozet, I don't want to know.*"

"*And you shan't, my love.*" He kissed her on the cheek. "*Pewter, you look slimmer.*"

"*Liar.*"

"*What a pretty thing to say to a gentleman paying you a compliment.*"

"*What gentleman?*"

"*Pewter, be civil.*" Murphy hated playing peacemaker. She had better things to do with her time. "*Come on, you two. If we're going to get back by quitting time, we've got to move on.*"

"*Where are you going?*"

"*Mim's stable. Come along and I'll give you the skinny.*" Mrs. Murphy used an expression that she had heard Mrs. Hogendobber occasionally use when the good lady felt racy.

"*Let's trot. I am not running.*" Pewter pouted.

"*All right. All right,*" Tucker agreed to put her in a better mood. "*Remember, it's because of you that we're on this mission.*"

"*It's not because of me, it's because Coty Lamont turned up dead in the back of a pickup truck, shot in the back and with a knife through his heart. All I did was report the news of it this morning.*"

"*How is it that Harry didn't know first—or the sanctified Mrs. Hogendobber?*" Paddy smelled a heavy scent of deer lingering in the frost.

"*Cynthia told Harry second. She stopped for coffee and one of Mrs. Hogendobber's bakery concoctions. French toast today and a kind of folded-over something with powdered sugar. Next she dropped in at the post office—.*"

Tucker interjected, "*Said they'd read about it in the papers later, so she'd give them the real facts.*"

"*And then I let you talk me into coming out here. Why I will never know.*" Pewter loudly decried her sore paw pads.

"*Because Coty Lamont slipped into Mim's barn on the night or early* morning when he was killed, that's why, and no one knows it but Rodger Dodger, Pusskin, the horses, and us."

Tucker patiently explained again to Pewter. This was like teaching a puppy to hide a bone. Repetition.

Tucker knew that Pewter figured things out just fine, but in bitching and moaning she could be the center of attention. Then, too, her paw pads, unused to hard running, really were tender.

"Another human knows, all right." Mrs. Murphy spied the cupolas on the stable up ahead. "Coty's killer."

"You don't know that," Paddy said and was informed as to the events that had transpired before Coty was found, the events at Mim's stable. Stubbornly, he said, "That means Mickey Townsend, since Rodger said he snuck in and found him."

"Sure looks that way, but I've learned not to jump to conclusions, only at mice," Murphy slyly offered.

"Don't sound superior, Murphy. I hate it when you do." Pewter puffed as they entered the big open doors trimmed in dark green on white.

Addie and Chark Valiant were arguing in the tack room situated in middle of the stable.

"You've got to get serious about the money."

"Bullshit," Addie defiantly replied.

Chark's voice rose. "You'll piss it all away, Addie—"

She interrupted. "All you and Arthur think about is the money. If I burn through my inheritance, that's my tough luck."

"We should keep our funds together and invest. It's the way to make more money."

"I don't want to do that. I have never wanted to do that. You take your share and I'll take mine."

"That's crazy!" he yelled. "Don't you realize what's at stake?"

"I realize that you and Arthur Tetrick went to court two years ago to extend the term of Arthur's trusteeship." Her face was red, "It's my money. Thank God, the judge didn't extend the term!"

"You were loaded on drugs, Addie. We did the right thing to try and protect you."

"Bullshit!" She threw her hard hat on the floor.

Chark tried another approach. "What if we get another adviser?"

"Dump dear Uncle Arthur?" The word *uncle* was drenched in sarcasm.

"If it would convince you to keep our money together, yes."

A silence ensued, which Addie finally broke. "No. You and Arthur can watch over your money. I'll watch over mine."

"Goddammit, you're so stupid!"

She screamed, "I'm not going to be under your thumb for the rest of my life!"

"No, you'll just be under the thumb of whatever son of a bitch you fall in love with next—just like Mother."

The sound of a slap reverberated throughout the barn. "I could kill you. I wouldn't be surprised if *you* killed Nigel."

"You're nuts!" Chark stormed out of the tack room and out of the barn.

The animals, not moving, watched as Addie charged out of the tack room, running after her brother and bellowing at the top of her lungs, "I hate you. I really friggin' hate you!"

"Hi," Rodger called down from the hayloft. "Don't pay any attention to them, they're always fighting over money."

"Hi," called Pusskin, Rodger's adored girlfriend, sitting by his side.

"Have you heard?" Pewter loved to be first with the news, any news.

"No." Rodger climbed backward down the ladder to the hayloft. Pusskin followed.

"Coty Lamont was found murdered last night," Pewter breathlessly informed them.

"How awful." Pusskin slipped a rung, putting her hind paw on Rodger's head.

"That's why we're all here, Rodg," Mrs. Murphy said. *"Let's go into Orion's stall."*

Rodger, knowing of Paddy's reputation with the female of the species, walked between Pusskin and the handsome black cat with the white tuxedo front and white spats on his paws.

Orion stood in his stall, for he was to be clipped today, a process he loathed. The stiff whiskers on his nose and chin would be shaved off with hair clippers like the ones humans used for a buzz cut. His ears would be trimmed and a path on his poll behind his ears would be cut, a bridle path. The stall was latched.

"Orion, how are you today?" Rodger called to him from the tack trunk.

"How do you think? That damned Addie will twitch me and Chark will play barber shop." A twitch was used to keep horses standing still for such beauty treatments. A looped piece of rope at the end of a half broom handle was wrapped around his lip.

"I'll make a deal," Mrs. Murphy called out to him.

"I'm listening." Orion walked over to behold the gathering on his tack box. Tucker was seated beside it.

"I'll open this latch. I think if we cats push on the door, we can slide it back. Now, I don't care if you run out, but will you wait until we stop digging?"

The handsome horse blinked, his large brown eyes filled with curiosity. *"What's in my stall, anyway? Sure I'll promise."*

Mrs. Murphy, lean and agile, stretched to reach the bolt on the stall door. About the width of a human little finger, although longer, the metal bolt slid into a latch, a rounded piece of metal on the top, enabling a human to pull back the latch with one finger. Helped Mrs. Murphy, too. After much tugging, she pulled the fingerhold on the bolt downward, then she pushed with all her might to push the whole bolt back through its latch.

"You did it." Pewter was full of admiration.

"Now let's push." Rodger put his paws on the stall door, right below the X, which strengthened the lower door panel. Paddy put

his paws at the very base of the door. Pewter added her bulk to it, and Tucker nudged with her nose. In no time at all they rolled the door back as quietly as they could.

"*Over here.*" Rodger bounded to the spot.

"*Let's pull the shavings away from it.*" Pusskin sent shavings flying everywhere.

All the cats, plus Tucker, were sprayed with little shavings bits.

"*I can't smell anything,*" Orion added, "*and you know I have a good sense of smell.*"

"*I can't either,*" Tucker confessed. "*But, Orion, if you'll use your front hooves to crack up the hard-packed earth, we can get digging faster. We might find something. Treasure, I bet!*"

"*Treasure is sweet feed drenched in molasses.*" Orion chuckled as he tore out chunks of earth.

Mrs. Murphy mumbled. "*Too noisy—it'll bring the humans.*"

Noisy as Orion was, he dug out a deep saucer much more quickly than the combined cat and dog claws could have done. They heard footsteps outside.

"*I'm out of here.*" Orion wheeled and trotted out of his stall just as Addie, over her fury, walked back into the barn from the other end.

Once outside, Orion jumped the fence into the pasture where his buddies chewed on a spread-out round bale of hay.

Two other people came into the tack room from outside. Tucker leapt into the small crater.

"*Anything?*" Mrs. Murphy asked her trusted companion.

"*Can you smell gold?*" Pusskin innocently asked.

Pewter bit her tongue. The pretty tortoiseshell was a kitty bimbo, but she made Rodger happy in his old age.

"*I do smell something. Faint, very faint. Maybe another two feet below, maybe less.*"

"*What?*" came the chorus.

"*Well, I don't know exactly. A mammal that's been dead for a long, long time. It's so faint and dusty, like mildew after the sun hits it.*"

Before the animals could react, Addie, Charles, and Arthur Tetrick lurched into the open stall.

"What the—?" Addie opened her mouth.

"That damned Orion. He's too smart." Charles slapped his thigh. "He heard the clippers."

"How'd he get out?" Addie stared at the animals, not comprehending that they had freed the hunter. "What is this, an animal convention? Mrs. Murphy, Tucker, Pewter, Paddy, Rodger, and Pusskin even."

The animals remained silent with Tucker slinking toward the door.

Arthur inspected the hole. "Better fill this in right away. It's not good for a horse to stand in an uneven stall. Not good at all."

"But that's the funny thing." Charles removed his baseball cap and ran his fingers through his hair. "Orion isn't a digger."

Arthur snorted. "Well, he is now."

"*You would do best to dig further,*" Mrs. Murphy told Addie.

"*Yeah, Adelia, something's down there,*" Rodger added, noticing that Addie was pointedly ignoring her brother and Arthur.

"I'll get the shovel and pack this back down." Charles left the stall.

"*Keep digging!*" Tucker barked.

"That dog has a piercing bark." Arthur frowned. "I never liked little dogs."

"*I never liked fastidious men,*" Tucker snapped back, then ran out of the stall followed by the other animals.

Adelia snapped too, as she walked away from the stall, "You two are as thick as thieves. I'm going to lunch."

"Come on, Addie." Charles said, but she kept walking away.

"*Rodger and Pusskin, keep your eyes open,*" Mrs. Murphy told them as her small group left the barn. "*Anything at all. A change in routine—*"

"*We will,*" Pusskin agreed. "*But what the humans do is their own business.*"

"*Curiosity killed the cat,*" jibed the big ginger.

"*Don't say that, Rodger. I hate that expression.*" Pusskin frowned.

"*I'm sorry, my sweet.*" He rubbed the side of his face against hers.

Pewter stifled a laugh.

"Bye," they called to one another.

As Mrs. Murphy melted back into the field Paddy said, "*You are nosy.*"

"*Well . . .*" The tiger cat thought a moment. "*I didn't much care until Coty was killed and I found out he'd been in the barn the night before. I don't know—guess I am nosy.*"

"*I'm hungry.*"

"*Another ten minutes.*" Tucker babied Pewter. "*Unless you want to run.*"

"*No, not another yard!*"

"*Wish I could figure out a way to get Mom or even Mim to dig up that stall.*" Murphy thought out loud.

"*About all she knows is when to open a can of food.*" Tucker loved Harry but suffered no illusions about her mental capabilities.

"*You're right,*" Murphy sadly agreed.

"*Whatever is in that stall is going to cause a shitload of trouble,*" Paddy sagely noted. "*And Orion's got to stand on it.*"

"*If he digs it up again just out of curiosity they'll either put him in another stall to see if it's pique on his part or put a rubber mat in the stall. I doubt he'll dig, though.*" Tucker was getting hungry herself.

"*Why do you say that?*" Pewter walked more briskly since she was close to home.

"*He'll be in enough trouble for bolting his stall and digging that hole in the first place. He'll lie low for a while.*" Tucker saw Mrs. Hogendobber's house. "*Hey, I'll race you to the door.*"

"No," Pewter adamantly said, but the others took off, leaving her to grumble as she walked to the post office. "*Bunch of show-offs.*"

19

A small nicotine stain marred Arthur Tetrick's lower lip. A dedicated pipe smoker, he contentedly packed in an expensive mix as he relaxed in Mim's living room. He'd walked up to the house after Addie stalked off.

"Smartest horse. Too smart." He tapped down the tender tobacco releasing a sweet unsmoked fragrance. "You're going to have to put a combination lock on his stall door."

Mim, out of the corner of her eye, saw Chark and one of her grooms chasing Orion in the field. This was a holiday, a canceled school day for the hunter, and he was making the most of it.

"Some sherry, Arthur?"

"No, no." He waved his hand. "No libations until the sun's over the yardarm."

"Coffee or tea then? I have some wonderful teas that Little Marilyn gave me for my birthday."

"A bracing darjeeling would do me a world of good." He held the match over the bowl of his burl pipe, the bowl shining with the use of many years, the draw perfect. That same pipe today would cost well over $250, so Arthur cherished it. No true pipe smoker would stick the flame right into the bowl just as no true cigar smoker would ever put the flame to the end of the cigar.

Mim shook a tiny bell. Gretchen appeared at the doorway. Gretchen and Mim had been together so long neither could imagine life without the other no matter how unequal the terms. "Yes, Miz Big." Her shorthand for Big Marilyn.

"Some darjeeling for the gentleman and some Constant Comment for me."

"Morning, Gretchen." Arthur nodded.

"Morning, Mr. Arthur. Cream or sugar?"

"Cream, well, half-and-half if you have it."

"Oh, Miz Big, she got everything." Gretchen turned, her wiry frame almost leaving a puff of smoke, she turned so fast.

"Mim, I'm here on a mercy mission." He cleared his throat. "As you know, Adelia comes into her inheritance November fourteenth, the day after the Colonial Cup. It's a considerable fortune, as you are aware. At that time she may elect to separate her share from Charles's share, which, of course, I oppose. Adelia is a lovely, lovely girl with absolutely no head for business. She should never be allowed to get her hands on her money. The interest is sufficient to allow her to live very well indeed."

"Bonds. Are you talking bonds, Arthur?" Mim shrewdly asked.

"Well, yes and no. As it now stands the Valiant resources are so conservatively invested that they reap barely six percent per annum. I have deliberately invested conservatively so as to run no risks until they inherit. Once that happens, I would still advise them to be prudent but to diversify more than I did when they were minors. They can afford a bit of risk, you know, keep the bulk in secure investments while targeting a small portion for high-risk/high-yield investments. My fear is, Adelia will take her money and—" He held up his hands. "Shiny cars, the usual foolish pleasures . . . Mim, you and I have both seen impulsive scions run through more money than Adelia will inherit. Large as the amount is, no well is bottomless. She greatly respects you. She finds me an old bore."

"Impossible," Mim said brightly as Gretchen delivered the tea.

Mim's tea service, which had been in the family on her mother's side since George III, caught the light, holding it prisoner to the lustrous silver. No one with an eye for beauty could behold her tea service without a slight gasp of appreciation.

"Need anything else?" Gretchen smiled.

"New knees."

"I told you not to hunker down there in that garden this summer, but you didn't listen to me. You don't listen to anyone."

"I'm listening to you now, Gretchen dear."

"Yes, Miz Big, dear." Gretchen put her hands on her hips. "Mr. Arthur, you talk to her. She is the most stubborn woman God ever put on this earth. She don't listen to me. She don't listen to her husband—'course, I don't listen to mine either. She is just a whirlwind of opinion. Uh-huh." That said, Gretchen wheeled and vacated the room.

"She is one of a kind." Arthur chuckled.

"Thank God. I don't think I could stand two."

Mim used the delicate silver tongs to drop a sugar cube into her Constant Comment, making it even sweeter. "Now let me understand you fully. You want me to tell Adelia to be a bit more aggressive with her investments but not to get crazy and, of course, never, ever, on pain of death, to touch the principal. Ideally she will keep the money together with Charles's." A beat. "And you'd like to remain as an adviser, or in some capacity."

"Um . . ." He nodded in the affirmative and placed his pipe in the pipe ashtray that Mim kept in the living room as he delicately brought the thin teacup to his lips. "I say, this is marvelous tea. My compliments to Little Marilyn."

"Before I have this financial meeting with her, I want to know who you are recommending for handling the portfolio. After all, out of duty you must recommend people other than yourself. We must hope the children will be wise enough to stick with you."

"I rather like Ed Bancroft at Strongbow and McKee."

"Yes, he's very good, but he's older. They might work better with someone in his or her thirties."

Arthur paled. "Too young, too young. A young person hasn't ridden the market through a few cycles. They panic during contractions." He refused to call a recession or a depression just what it was.

"Good point." She leaned back in the silk-covered chair. "Well, you seem to be the best person for the job. There's always Arnie Skaar, should they wish a change—you know, an assertion of independence."

"Yes, Arnie's good."

"Will you be saddened if you lose your job?" she forthrightly asked.

"Oh, I never thought of it as a job, and in some ways Charles has been Adelia's guardian more than I have. Really, I'll continue to guide them as best I can no matter what happens. I was shocked, when Marylou disappeared, to discover she'd made me her executor. I thought she was so besotted with Mickey Townsend that she might have foolishly changed her will. Devastated as I was to lose Marylou, I was heartened by her caution on this matter." He drew on his pipe. "Charles and I have been able to draw together. Adelia favored Mickey, and, well—women are so unpredictable." He held up his hands as if in supplication.

"You've done your best. Being anyone's executor is a time-consuming and sad process. I was Mother's executor, and I learned more in that one year than I think I did in all the years before." Mim poured Arthur more tea. "Terrible news this morning. It's giving us all the chills."

"What?" He inhaled the delicate yet strong tea aroma.

"You haven't heard?" Mim put her cup and saucer down.

"No."

"Coty Lamont was stabbed through the heart on a dirt road off Route Twenty-Two. Dumped in the back of his pickup truck."

"Good God!" Arthur's cup slipped from his hand. He captured it with his saucer but slopped tea everywhere. "I'm so sorry, Mim."

"Scotchgard." She tinkled for Gretchen again. "Works wonders."

"Ma'am." Gretchen perceived the situation as soon as the "Ma'am" was out of her wide and generous mouth. "I'll be back."

She returned quickly with dishtowels, mopping up Arthur and dabbing the rug. "No harm done."

"I do apologize. It was such a shock."

"What shock?" Gretchen wouldn't budge.

"Oh, Gretchen, Sheriff Shaw called to tell me there's been another murder. Coty Lamont."

"That handsome good-for-nothing jockey? Why, he used to ride for you, didn't he, Mr. Arthur, back when you was in the game?"

"Yes, yes, I gave him his start. I gave a lot of men a leg up, so to speak. He left me to ride for Mickey Townsend and then moved on from there. That's the way of the world—the young and ambitious, climbing the ladder." He wiped his brow with a neatly folded linen handkerchief. "This is too much. Why didn't Adelia and Charles say something?"

"They don't know yet. Rick just called. I'd like to think I was his first call, but I doubt it. I'm going to buy one of those CBs that lets me listen to police calls."

"No, you aren't," Gretchen scolded. "You'll be running all

over the county. Bad enough that Mr. Jim does it. 'Course, being mayor he has to, I guess.''

"Something's dreadfully wrong," Mim blurted out. "Arthur, you officiate at different races. Surely, you must know something."

"No." He wiped his brow again. "Coty Lamont. It doesn't seem possible. And stabbed through the heart, you say?"

Mim nodded. "Apparently he wasn't as easy to kill as Nigel Danforth was because Rick says he was shot first. Of course, they'll do an autopsy, but he believes the shot preceded the stabbing. This grotesque symbol—the stiletto through the heart. And another playing card."

"What do you mean?" Gretchen asked, curiosity getting the better of her.

"Gretchen . . . oh, sit down and have some tea. I'll get a crick in my neck turning around to talk to you."

Gretchen quickly fetched another cup, eagerly plopped down and helped herself to some of the darjeeling.

"You see," Mim intoned, "the first man murdered had a playing card over his heart. The Queen of Clubs. Fair Haristeen found him. And Arthur, I must talk to you about Fair. Anyway, this second murder—" She paused. "The Queen of Spades."

"Mojo." Gretchen downed her tea in one big swallow.

Arthur smiled indulgently. "I don't think anyone knows voodoo in central Virginia."

"Mojo." She clamped her jaw shut.

"Well, if it isn't mojo, it still means something."

"Means something wild. You stab a man through the heart, you got to get real close. You got to look in his eyes and smell his breath. You got to hate him worse than the angel hate the Evil One. I know 'bout these things."

Arthur shuddered. "Gretchen, you are very graphic."

"When was the last time you saw Coty?" Mim asked him.

"Montpelier. I was always proud of him, you know—that I

saw his talent early and encouraged it. I emphatically did not encourage his arrogance."

Mim's tone flattened a bit. "But he was arrogant—arrogant and too clever by half."

"Ain't clever now."

"That's just it, Gretchen. Maybe he was, and like I said, he was too clever by half always playing odds with the bookies through fronts like Linda Forloines. No one could catch him at it." She smoothed over her skirt. "I suppose I'll go down and tell Charles and Adelia. Arthur, I'll wait a day or two to have that financial discussion with Adelia."

"Of course, of course. Well, I'd better be heading home. I was going to run some errands in town, then go to the office, but I think I'll go straight home and, well—ponder."

"Nothing to ponder. Somebody got a backwards passion. It's worse than hate—reverse love." Gretchen picked up the silver tray and ambled out.

20

"I resent that. I resent this whole damned line of questioning!" Mickey Townsend roared in Rick Shaw's face.

Rick, accustomed to such displays, calmly folded his hands as Cynthia Cooper, behind him, took notes. "I don't think there's any way to make this pleasant. Nigel Danforth rode for you and—"

"Rode for me for two months. How the hell did I know he was, uh—a non-person?"

"You could have checked his green card."

"Well, I didn't. He was a decent jock and I let it go, so call down the damned bloodhounds from Immigration on me. They'll harass me for hiring a skilled Brit, yet they let riffraff pour over the border and go on welfare and we pay for it!"

"Mr. Townsend, I wouldn't know about that," Rick Shaw

replied dryly. "But you are a successful trainer. You have knowledge of the steeplechase world, and two jockeys have been killed within a week of one another under similar circumstances. You knew them both. And they both rode for you at various times."

His face reddened. "Balls! Everyone in the game knew Coty Lamont. I don't like your line of questioning, Shaw, and I don't much like you."

"You're accustomed to having your own way, aren't you?"

"Most successful people are, Sheriff." Townsend folded his burly arms across his chest. "So I'm a prick. That doesn't make me a killer."

"Did you owe Nigel Danforth money?"

"Absolutely not. I pay at the end of the day's race."

"Easier when you don't have withholding taxes and Social Security to worry about, isn't it?"

"You're damned right it is, and taxes will destroy this nation. You mark my words."

"Did you owe Coty Lamont money?"

"Why would I owe Coty Lamont money?" The bushy eyebrows knitted together.

"That's what I'm asking you."

"No."

"Did you like Coty Lamont?"

"No."

"Why?"

"That's my business. He was a talented son of a bitch. That's all I'm prepared to say."

"We'll get a lot further along if you cooperate with me." He swiveled to exchange looks with Coop, who frowned. This was part of their routine before recalcitrant subjects. They could play "good cop, bad cop" but Mick was too smart for that game.

"Well, let me try another tack then. Did either Nigel Danforth or Coty Lamont owe you money?"

"No." Mick rolled his forefinger over his neat black mustache. "Yes."

"Who and how much?"

"Nigel owed me three hundred forty-seven dollars, a collection of poker debts, and Coty owed, oh, about one hundred twenty-two dollars."

"You didn't like Coty but you played poker with him?"

"Hey, there's down time in this business. I don't have to love a guy to let him sit in on a poker game."

"You're a good player?"

Mick shrugged.

Cynthia chimed in, "Everyone says you're slick as an eel."

"They say that because they don't remember which cards are out and which ones are still in the deck. If you're playing stud, that's all you gotta do." He shrugged those powerful shoulders again. "I'm not so smart."

Rick rubbed his receding hairline. It was almost as if he were searching for the hair. "Coop, can you think of anything?"

"One little thing—Mr. Townsend, do the card suits have a special significance?"

"What do you mean?"

"Well, what if—crazy, I know, but what if I had a royal flush in hearts and you had one in spades. Who would win?"

"I would. The suits in ascending order are clubs, diamonds, hearts and spades."

"But wouldn't most people declare it a draw?" Rick puzzled. "I mean most people wouldn't know the significance of the suits. At least, I don't think they would. If a situation like that occurred, wouldn't you draw off the deck, high card takes it?"

"In a situation with two royal flushes, you'd both have cardiac arrest and it wouldn't matter. The odds are impossible."

"But you know the significance of the suits," Rick pressed.

"Yes, I do."

"Isn't there another way to look at the suits, a non-poker way?" Cynthia asked.

He leaned back in his chair. "Sure."

"Can you tell me what that is?"

"You've done your homework. You tell me." He stared at her.

"All right." She smiled at him. "Clubs represent humans at their basest. Spades is a step up. Instead of clobbering one another, they work the earth. Diamonds is a higher level than that, obviously, but the highest type of human would fall into the heart category."

"Well put." Mickey smiled back at the young officer. He couldn't help himself. She was nice-looking.

"A club and a spade have been used," Rick drawled.

"So next comes a diamond. Somebody rich." Mickey folded his arms across his chest. "Won't be me. I'm not rich."

21

Totem, a Thoroughbred hotter than Hades, ditched most people who climbed on his back. The only reason he wasn't turned into Alpo was that he could run like blazes. Dr. D'Angelo had bought him on sight from Mickey Townsend at Montpelier. Linda Forloines, furious that she wasn't in on the deal and hence got no commission, plotted how to get rid of the animal.

She promised Dr. D'Angelo that she would faithfully work Totem. She'd then take a bar of soap and lather him up fifteen minutes before D'Angelo walked into the stable. This way the horse looked as though he'd been exercised. Then Linda would make up a story about how he had behaved, full of little details to cement her lies. As soon as D'Angelo left she'd hose the horse off and turn him out in the paddock.

Will, grabbing the halter with a lead chain over the nose, helped his wife walk the horse to the paddock.

"I'll get this horse out of here in two months' time," she bragged.

"How?"

"Ask Bob Drake to ride him when D'Angelo's here."

"Bob Drake can't ride this horse." Will's eyes widened.

"Exactly." She grunted as the large animal bumped into her. She hit his rib cage with her fist, hoping he'd not bump into her again.

They both breathed a sigh of relief when Totem walked into his paddock and the gate closed behind him.

"Linda, Bob could get hurt—bad."

She shrugged, "He's a big boy. He doesn't have to ride the horse."

Will pondered that. "Well, he gets planted. Then what?"

"Then I tell D'Angelo he could get sued with a horse like this. I'd better take it off his hands."

Will smiled, "The commission ought to be pretty good."

"Just remember"—she winked at him—"we're going to own our own stable—real soon. We can make money in this business. Real money."

"What if D'Angelo won't sell?"

"He will." She rubbed her hands together. "I've got him all figured out. Listen, honey, I've got to make a pick up tonight. I'll be back real late."

He frowned. "I wish you'd let me go with you."

"I'm safe. It's better if only one of us knows who the supplier is. Since I knew him first, it doesn't make sense to drag you into it. And he'd never allow it."

Will shielded his head as a gust of wind blew straw and hay bits everywhere. "It's dangerous."

"Nah."

"Two of our best customers are dead."

"Has nothing to do with us."

"God, I hope not." Will's features drained of animation.

Linda didn't want Will to know the supplier for two reasons. In a tight spot he might spill the beans, ruining everything. And he'd know the exact amount of coke being sold to her. That would never do because she didn't want him to know how much she kept back for herself. She cut it lightly once before bringing it back home. Then she and Will cut it together, using a white powdered laxative.

Will could be the brawn of the outfit. She was the brains. What he didn't know wouldn't hurt him.

Later that night, at ten-thirty, when Linda pulled out of the driveway in the truck, Will hurried outside and jumped into Dr. D'Angelo's old farm truck. He followed her, lights off, until she turned south on Route 15. He allowed a few cars to buffer the zone between himself and his wife. Then he clicked on the lights and followed her to her rendezvous.

22

Silver strands of rain poured over the windshield. Harry could barely see as she drove to work. The windshield wipers sloshed back and forth, allowing momentary glimpses of a road she luckily knew well.

Mrs. Murphy, paws on the dash, alert, helped Harry drive. Tucker wasn't quite able to rest her hind paws on the bench seat and reach for the dash.

"Big puddle up ahead," the cat warned.

Harry slowed, wondering why her tiger was so chatty.

"Mom, a stranded car dead ahead." Mrs. Murphy's claws dug into the dash.

Mickey Townsend's beautiful silver BMW rested by the side of the road, the right wheels in a drainage ditch that had swollen from a trickle to a torrent.

Harry stopped, putting on her turn signal because the old truck's flasher fuse had a tendency to blow. Of course, that wasn't as annoying as having the gear shift stick whenever she tried to put it in third gear. The passenger window looked as though Niagara were pouring over it. She couldn't see a thing.

"Damn." She pulled ahead of the beached vehicle, careful not to suffer the same fate. "Guys, stay here."

"*Don't go out in that,*" Mrs. Murphy told her. "*You'll catch your death of cold.*"

"Stop complaining, Murphy. You stay right here. I *mean* it."

She clapped her dad's old cowboy hat on her head, which channeled the water away from her face and off the back and front of the hat. She'd never found anything better for keeping the rain out of her eyes. She also wore her Barbour coat, a dark green dotted with mud, and her duck boots. They would keep her dry.

She slipped out, quickly closed the door, and prayed no one would skid around the curve as it appeared Mickey Townsend must have done. She put her hand over her eyes and peered into the driver's seat. Nothing. She walked around to the other side, just to be sure he wasn't bending over outside his car, trying to figure out how to extricate himself from this mess. He wasn't there.

She lifted herself back up into the truck, clicked off the turn signal, and rolled on down the road. By the time she walked through the back door, carrying both Mrs. Murphy and Tucker under her Barbour, Mrs. Hogendobber had sorted out one bag of mail.

"Miranda, I'm sorry I'm late. I couldn't go over twenty-five miles an hour, the visibility was so awful."

"Don't worry about it," Mrs. Hogendobber airily replied. "The water is ready for tea and I whipped up oatmeal muffins last night and another batch of glazed doughnuts. I can't bake enough doughnuts for Market. He sells out by ten o'clock."

"Oh, thanks." Harry gratefully pulled off her raincoat as

Mrs. Murphy and Tucker shook off the few drops of water that had fallen on them. Harry hung up her coat on the coat rack by the back door and poured herself a cup of tea. "I'd die without tea."

"I doubt that, but you'd sure be grouchy in the morning." Miranda helped herself to a second cup.

"Oh, I better call Rick." Harry carried the steaming cup with her to the phone.

"Now what's wrong?"

"Mickey Townsend's BMW is stranded at Harper's Curve." She punched the numbers.

"I hope he's all right. Things are so—queer just now."

Harry nodded. "Sheriff Shaw, please, it's Mary Minor Haristeen." She waited a minute. "Hi, Sheriff. Mickey Townsend's BMW has two wheels dropped in a ditch at Harper's Curve. I got out to check it and it's empty."

"Thanks, Harry. I'll send someone over once things quiet down. It's one fender bender after another on a day like this." He paused a moment. "Did you say Mickey Townsend's car?"

"Uh-huh."

His voice sounded strained. "Thanks. I'll get right on it. That curve can be evil."

The phone clicked and Harry put the receiver back in the cradle.

"Well?"

"At first he didn't seem too worried about it but now he's sending someone right over."

"You know at choir practice last night Ysabel Yadkin swore that Mickey is involved in a big gambling scam and that Nigel Danforth owed him oo-scoobs of money. I asked her what was the last steeplechase she attended and she gave me the hairy eyeball, I can tell you. 'Well, Ysabel,' I said, 'if you're going to tell tales, you ought to at least know the people you're talking about.' She fried. But then after practice she came over and declared that I was being snotty because I had horsey friends. Her Albert knows Mickey Townsend because he works on that expensive car of his.''

"Since when did Albert start working on BMWs?"

Mrs. Hogendobber drained her mug, returning to the second mailbag. "Since they offered him more money than Mercedes."

"Mrs. H., sit down, you did that first bag all by yourself. I'll do this one."

"Idle hands do the devil's work. I don't mind."

Together they tipped the bag into the mail cart just as Boom Boom Craycroft sashayed through the front door at eight o'clock sharp.

"What a morning, and the temperature is dropping. I hope this doesn't turn to ice."

"We're a little behind, Boom Boom, and it's my fault."

"I can help."

"Oh, no, don't bother," said Harry, who knew that Boom Boom's idea of help would be to sort for five minutes, then have a fit of the vapors. "Why don't you run a few errands and come on back in about half an hour?"

"I guess I could." She plucked her umbrella out of the stand where she had dropped it. "Isn't it awful about Coty Lamont?"

Before she had the complete sentence out of her mouth a soaking-wet Mickey Townsend pushed open the door and sagged against the wall.

"Mickey, are you all right?" Boom Boom reached out to him.

"Yes, by the grace of God." He began shaking; he was chilled to the bone.

"Come back here." Miranda flipped up the dividing barrier. "You need a hot drink. I'll run to the house and get some of George's clothes. They're too big for you but at least they're dry."

"Oh, Mrs. Hogendobber, a cup of coffee will put me right." His teeth chattered, belying his words.

"Now you stay right here," Miranda commanded as Harry made him a cup of instant coffee.

"Sugar and cream?" Harry opened the tiny refrigerator to reach for the cream.

"Two sugars and a dab of cream." He held out his hand for the cup, then put both hands around it, vainly trying to stop shaking.

Boom Boom joined them as Mickey dripped water all over the floor.

"*He's white as a sheet,*" Tucker noted.

"I stopped by your car." Harry threw her coat over his shoulders.

"How long ago?"

"Fifteen, twenty minutes."

"Just missed me." His teeth hit the rim of the cup. "I couldn't find a house. I headed into the cornfield there but realized I had to come back to the road because I couldn't see anything and I'd get lost. I mean, I know that territory but I couldn't see a damned thing and I was—" He gulped down a few warm mouthfuls of coffee. "God, that tastes good."

Miranda pushed open the back door, turned and shook her umbrella out the door, and then closed it because the wind was blowing the rain into the post office. A shopping bag of clothes hung on her arm. "You go right into the bathroom and towel off. There's a big towel here on top. And get into these clothes."

Mickey did as he was told, finally emerging in pants with rolled cuffs and the sleeves of George's old navy sweater rolled up, too, but he was warm.

"*Mrs. Hogendobber never throws anything out.*" Mrs. Murphy laughed. "*I guess it's a good thing.*"

He ate a glazed doughnut and continued his story. "I found the road again and knew if I could get into town you'd be in the post office early. Say, I'd better call a towing service."

"I already called Rick Shaw."

"What for?"

"I didn't know where you were or whether you were okay—things being what they are," Harry said forthrightly. "So I called him."

"Well, he's not worried about me. He treats me like the chief suspect."

"He sounded worried enough on the phone," Harry stated.

"Yeah—well." Mickey slumped a moment, then straightened his back. "I guess I'm a little worried, too."

"Everyone's worried." Boom Boom nibbled an oatmeal muffin.

"I know that road like the back of my hand. Someone swooped down behind me and ran me off the road."

"People don't pay attention to the weather—" Miranda prepared to launch into a diatribe about the bad driving habits of the younger generation, meaning anyone younger then herself.

Mickey cut her off, "No, whoever this was wanted to run me off the road—or worse."

"What?" Boom Boom stopped mid-bite.

"They nudged me from behind and then drew alongside and pushed me right off the road. If we'd been twenty yards further up the road, it would have been a steep drop, I can tell you that."

"Could you see who it was?" Harry asked.

"Hell, no, not in this rain. It was a big-ass truck, I can tell you that. I'm not even sure about the color, although I thought I caught a glimpse of black or dark blue. GMC maybe, but I don't know. It happened so fast."

"*Why don't they ask him what he was doing down that road in the first place?*" Mrs. Murphy rubbed against Tucker.

"*Too polite.*" Tucker loved it when the cat rubbed on her.

"*This is no time to be polite. And furthermore, I don't believe him.*"

"*You don't believe he was run off the road?*"

"*I believe that.*" The cat's whiskers touched and tickled Tucker's nose. "*But he's hiding something.*"

"Maybe he knows what's in Orion's stall?"

"Tucker, I don't know about that. I don't think we'll ever get the humans to dig down deep enough, and Orion can't help. He's switched to another stall, remember?"

"Yeah. So what is it about Mickey Townsend?"

"You can smell fear as well as I can."

23

Harry, Susan, Fair, Big Mim, Little Marilyn, and Boom Boom all had their noses out of joint because the rain had forced them to bag their long-planned foxhunting with Keswick Hunt Club. The only good thing about the rained-out Saturday was that Harry finally went grocery shopping.

As she wheeled her cart around the pet food aisle, always her first stop, she saw Cynthia Cooper piling bags of birdseed into her cart.

"Coop."

"Hey. Great minds run in the same direction."

"Mrs. Murphy will shred the house if I don't get her tuna. She tore the arm off the sofa last week. I still haven't put it back together."

"Because of tuna?"

"No. I left her home from Montpelier and took Tucker. Made her hateful mean."

Five years ago, hearing a story like that, Cynthia Cooper would have thought it a fabrication. However, she had grown to know Harry's cat and dog as well as other Crozet animals. The stories were true. In fact, Mrs. Murphy had pointed out a skull fragment to her on a case at Monticello. It could have been blind luck but then again—

"One of these days I'll get a cat, but I work the most terrible hours. Maybe I need a husband before the cat. That way he can take care of the cat when I'm on duty."

"Hope you have better luck than I did."

"Doesn't it make you crazy that everyone tries to get you and Fair back together—including Fair?" Cynthia laughed.

Harry rested her elbows on the push bar of the cart. "Lack of imagination. They don't believe another eligible man will come through Crozet."

"Blair Bainbridge." She was referring to the model who had bought the farm next to Harry's a few years back.

"His career takes him away for such long stretches of time. And I think Marilyn Sanburne the younger has set her cap for him."

"Quaint expression."

"I'm trying not to be rude." Harry inadvertently kicked the cart and almost fell on her face as it rolled out from under her.

"How much more shopping?" Cynthia pointed to Harry's long list.

"Forty-five minutes. Why?"

"If you buy pasta I'll make it."

"No kidding?" Harry eagerly said. Not being much of a cook, she loved being asked to dinner or having someone cook for her.

"That way we can catch up." Cynthia put her finger to her lips, the hush sign.

Harry understood right away. "Be back at the house in an hour."

As she rounded the next aisle in a hurry, she beheld Boom Boom, ear pressed to cans of baked beans.

"I'm in this aisle now." Harry had to twit her. "I mean, unless the beans are talking to you."

"You need to do something about your hostility level. I really and truly want to take you to Lifeline with me."

"I am doing something about my hostility level." Harry mimicked Boom Boom's mature and understanding voice, the one reserved for moments of social superiority. With that she pushed her cart away.

"What do you mean?" Boom Boom put her hands on her hips. "Harry, come back here."

Harry twirled around the next aisle without looking back. Boom Boom, miffed, hurried after her. "What do you mean?"

"Nothing," Harry called over her shoulder, throwing items into her cart at a fast clip.

Boom Boom, never one to miss an emotional morsel, cut the corner too close and rammed into a toilet paper display that tumbled over the floor, into her cart, and onto her head.

Harry stopped and laughed. She couldn't help it. Then she turned her cart, threw a couple rolls into it and said to the fuming Boom Boom, "Wiped out, Boom."

"Oh, shut up, Harry!"

"Ha!"

Cynthia hooted as Harry recounted the supermarket incident. She dipped a wooden fork into the boiling water to pluck out a few noodles. "Not quite ready."

Harry set the table. Mrs. Murphy reposed as the centerpiece. Tucker mournfully gazed at the checkered tablecloth.

"Here." Harry tossed the corgi a green milkbone.

"*How can you eat that stuff?*" Murphy curled her front paws under her chest.

"*I'll eat anything that doesn't eat me first.*"

"*Very funny. My grandmother told me that joke.*" The cat flicked her right ear.

"Here we go." Cynthia put the pasta on the table. "Is she going to eat with us?"

"Well—if she bothers you I'll put her on the floor, but she loves pasta with butter, so once this cools I'll fix her a plate."

"Harry, you'll spoil that cat."

"*Not enough,*" came the swift reply as Harry diced pasta for the cat and then made a small bowl for Tucker too. She put butter on her own noodles while Cynthia drenched hers in a creamy clam sauce.

"Can't I interest you in this sauce?"

"You can interest me, but I've got to lose five pounds before winter really sets in or I won't get rid of it until April. Susan and I made a vow last week not to put on winter weight."

"You aren't one pound overweight."

"You don't squeeze into my jeans."

"Harry, you're reading too many fashion magazines. The models are anorexic."

"I don't subscribe to one fashion magazine," Harry proudly proclaimed.

"Of course not. You read whatever comes into the post office."

Harry sheepishly curled her noodles onto the fork. "Well, I suppose I do."

"You're the best-read person in Crozet."

"That's not saying much." Harry laughed.

"The Reverend Jones reads a lot."

"Yes, that's true. How'd you know that?"

"Called on him yesterday in the course of my duties."

"Oh."

"I wondered how well he knew Coty Lamont, Mickey Townsend, and the rest of the steeplechase crowd, and if he knows any knife collectors."

"He knows more people than anyone except Mim and Miranda, I swear. Did he know anything about those—"

"More!" Tucker barked.

"No." Harry sternly reprimanded the greedy dog.

"Said he knew Coty Lamont from years back when he was a groom. I also asked him about Rick's bait and switch idea. Put a fake tattoo on a horse's upper lip and sell it for a lot of money. Herb said it just wouldn't work today. Rick's having a hard time giving up his pet theory since we're running into dead ends. The boss can be very stubborn."

"That's a nice way to put it." Harry scooped more pasta on her plate and used just a little of the clam sauce, which was delicious. "Did he have any ideas about what's going on?"

"No. You know Herb, he likes to rummage around in the past. He took off on a tangent, telling me about when Arthur Tetrick and Mickey Townsend were both in love with Marylou Valiant. Coty Lamont used to spy on Mickey for Arthur."

"Spy?"

"Wrong word. He'd pump the grooms at Mickey's for news about when and if he'd dated Marylou that week. She dated both of them for about six months and then finally broke it off with Arthur." She giggled. "It's hard to imagine Arthur Tetrick being romantic."

"Guess it was hard for Marylou too."

They both laughed.

Cynthia recounted what the minister had told her. "After Marylou disappeared, Herb said Arthur suffered a nervous breakdown."

"He did. They had to hospitalize him for a week or two, which made him feel even worse because he wasn't there for the Valiants. Larry Johnson admitted him."

"Mim took care of the Valiants. That's what Herb said."

"Yeah. It was pretty awful. She offered a ten-thousand-dollar reward for any information leading to Marylou's whereabouts. As soon as Arthur was released, he wanted the Valiants with him. Mim told him a woman was better able to look after their needs than a man. Arthur didn't want Mickey to see them at all and Mim disagreed with that, too. Addie was hurt enough. She needed Mickey. This provoked another huge fight between Arthur and Mickey. So Adelia was sent away to school, Charles graduated from Cornell and worked in Maryland for a while. Addie always came home to visit Mickey during her vacations. Arthur and Mickey really hate one another. Mickey didn't get a cent from Marylou. He wasn't mentioned in her will. They hadn't been together long enough, I guess. Mim did her best for the Valiants—well, for Marylou, I would say. She was a true friend."

Coop asked, "Did Mim inherit anything from Marylou?"

"A bracelet as a memento. I don't think Mim ever accepted money from Arthur for the kids' bills, except maybe tuition. Addie didn't stay at school long, of course. Hated it."

"I was brand-new to the force when all that was going on . . . the disappearance. Had nothing to do with the case. Mostly I answered the telephone and punched information into the computer until I had it out with Rick."

"I didn't know that."

"Oh, yeah. I told him he was giving me secretarial work and I was a police officer. He surprised me because he thought about it and then said, 'You're right.' We've gotten along ever since. More than that. I adore the guy. Like a brother," she hastened to add.

They ate in silence for a few moments. Mrs. Murphy reached onto Harry's plate, pulling off a long noodle. Harry pretended not to notice. Cynthia knew better than to say anything.

"Coop, what is going on?"

"Damned if I know. The autopsy report came back on Coty Lamont. Full of toot. So was Nigel. No fingerprints on the body. No sign of struggle. It's really frustrating."

Harry shook her head. "I bet a lot of those guys are on cocaine. Maybe they owed their dealer."

"Drugs are responsible for most of the crime in this country. One other little tidbit you have to promise not to tell."

"Not even Miranda?"

"No."

Harry sighed deeply. It pained her to keep a secret from Miranda or Susan. "Okay."

"There is no Nigel Danforth."

"Huh?"

"Fake name. We can't find out who he is or was. We're hoping that sooner or later someone who doesn't know he's dead will look for him, file a missing persons report." She rested her fork across the white plate. "That's a long shot though."

"Mickey Townsend doesn't know who he is?"

"No, and Rick put it to him. None too kindly either."

"Whoeee, bet Mickey doubled for Mount Vesuvius."

"He kept it in check."

"That's odd."

"We think so, too."

"*Mickey's scared,*" Mrs. Murphy interjected.

"Honey, you've had enough." Harry thought the cat was talking about food.

"*I wish just once you would listen to me,*" Murphy grumbled. "*He's scared and there's something in Mim's barn.*"

"*Something not nice,*" Tucker added.

Harry stroked the cat while Cynthia fed Tucker a bit of buttered bread. "She has the most intelligent face."

"*Oh, puleese,*" the cat drawled.

"Do you think Mickey's in on the murders?"

"I don't think anything. I'm trying to gather facts. He's got an alibi for the first murder because so many people saw him at the time of the murder. He was loading horses from the smaller barns. But then everyone's got an alibi for that murder. As for the second murder—anyone could have done it. And when we review the principals' time frame at Montpelier, most anyone could have done in Nigel Danforth. We've even reconstructed Charles Valiant's moves about the time of the murder because he and Nigel had an argument at the races. Nothing hangs together."

"Did you go through mug shots to try and find Nigel?"

"We punched into the computer. Nothing. We've sent out his dental records. Nothing. I think the guy is clean." She shrugged. "Then again . . ."

"Before the races Jim Sanburne and Larry Johnson told me to watch out because Charles and Mickey had gotten into it at the Maryland Cup last year," Harry said. "They thought there'd be trouble between the jockeys, but then they didn't know that Addie had fallen for Nigel. That's not where the trouble came from, though. Odd."

"Linda Forloines and Nigel. Yes, we've tried to piece that together. Frank Yancey interrogated Will and Linda separately. We're getting around to them. Rick's instincts are razor sharp. I wanted to drive right up Fifteen North and flush them out, but Rick said 'Wait.' He believes some other bird dog will flush their game."

"You think they're in on this? Actually, I detest Linda Forloines to such a degree that I'm not a good person to judge."

"Lots of people detest her," Cynthia said. "She's a petty crook and not above selling horses to the knackers while telling the owner she's found them a good home."

"She's so transparent that it's ludicrous—if you know horses." Harry piled more pasta on her plate.

"She's selling cocaine again. Rick thinks she'll lead us to the killer—or killers."

"You do think she's in on it." Harry's voice lowered although no one else was there.

"Linda was the one who indirectly accused Fair of doping horses."

"I'll kill the bitch!"

"No, you won't," Cynthia ordered her. "Frank Yancey saw

right through her when she planted her 'suspicion.' When Colbert Mason at National got a little worried, we sat back to see what he would do. Mim's faxing off the lawyer's letter pushed Colbert to contact Linda and tell her she had to file a formal complaint. She backed off in a hurry."

"What a worthless excuse for a human being she is."

"True, but why did she do that, Harry?"

"Because she likes to stir the pot, fish in muddy waters, use any phrase you like."

"You can do better than that." Cynthia gathered up the dishes.

"She's throwing you off the scent."

"We've been watching her. She scurried straight to some of the people she's been supplying. Less to warn them than to shut their traps. At least that's what we think. We can't keep a tail on her around the clock, though. We don't have enough people in the department. We're hoping she'll lead us to the supplier."

"Did she sell coke to Coty Lamont?"

"Yes. She also sold it to Nigel Danforth. His blood was full of it, too. Jockeys are randomly tested, and we believe they were tipped off as to when they would be tested."

Harry whistled in amazement. "Poor Addie."

"Why?"

"Jeez, Cynthia, she was about to get mixed up with a user."

"My instincts tell me she's back on it again."

"I hate to think that."

"You can help me." Cynthia leaned forward. "The stiletto used in these murders is called a silver shadow. They retail for anywhere from ninety to one hundred ten dollars. I've checked every dealer from Washington to Richmond to Charlotte, North Carolina. They don't keep records of who buys knives. It's not like guns. Apparently a stiletto is not a big seller because it's not as useful as a Bowie knife. Only six have been sold in the various shops I called. Anyway I'm still checking on this, but it's slipping down on my things-to-do list because we're being overwhelmed after the second murder. The pressure from the press isn't help-ing. Rick's ready to trade in the squad car for a tank and roll over those press buzzards." She paused. "If you should see or hear anything about knives—tell me."

"Sure."

"One other thing." Harry's expression was quizzical as Cynthia continued. "If this is about drugs, the person commit-ting these crimes might not be rational."

"Do you think murder can be rational?"

"Absolutely. All I'm saying is, keep your cards close to your chest." She winced. "I wish I hadn't said that."

"*Me, too,*" the cat chimed in.

24

The foxes stayed in their burrows, the field mice curled up in their nests, and the blue jays, those big-mouthed thieves, didn't venture out. The rains abated finally, but temperatures plummeted, leaving the earth encased in solid ice.

Fortunately, since it was Sunday, there wasn't much traffic. While this cut down on the car accidents, it also made most people feel marooned in their own homes.

Mrs. Murphy hunted in the hayloft while Tucker slept in the heated tack room. Simon, the opossum, was fast asleep on his old horse blanket, which Harry had donated for his welfare. The owl also slept overhead in the cupola.

The tiger knew where the blacksnake slept, so she avoided her. By now the snake was five years old and a formidable presence even when hibernating.

Hunched on top of a hay bale, an aromatic mixture of orchard grass and alfalfa, Murphy listened to the mice twittering in the corner. They'd hollowed out a hay bale in the back corner of the loft and into it dragged threads, pieces of paper, even pencil stubs until the abode was properly decorated and toasty. Mrs. Murphy knew that periodically a mouse would emerge and scurry across the hayloft, down the side of a stall, then slide out between the stall bars. The object was usually the feed room or the tack room. They'd eaten a hole in Harry's faded hunter-green barn jacket. Mrs. Hogendobber patched it for her because Harry couldn't imagine barn chores without that jacket.

Harry fed Tomahawk, Gin Fizz, and Poptart half rations, which caused no end of complaining down below. If the horses couldn't be turned out for proper exercise, Harry cut back on the food. She feared colic like the plague. A horse intestine could get blocked or worse, twisted, and the animal would paw at its belly with its hind hooves, roll on the ground in its torment, and sometimes die rapidly. Usually colic could be effectively treated if detected early.

The three horses—two geldings and one mare—sassy in their robust health, couldn't imagine colic, so they bitched and moaned, clanged their feed buckets against the walls, and called to one another about what a horrible person Harry was to cheat on food.

Mrs. Murphy had half a mind to tell them to shut up and count themselves lucky when one of the mice sped from the nest. The cat leapt up and out into the air, a perfect trajectory for pouncing, but the canny mouse, seeing the shadow and now smelling the cat, zigzagged and made it to the side of the stall.

Mrs. Murphy couldn't go down the stall side, but she walked on the beam over it, dropping down into Poptart's stall just as the mouse cruised through the stall bars. Mrs. Murphy rocked back on her haunches, shot up to the stall bars, grabbed the top with her paws, then slipped back into the stall because her claws couldn't hold on to the iron.

"Dammit!" she cursed loudly.

"You'll never get those mice, Murphy." Poptart calmly chewed on her hay. "They wait for you to appear and then run like mad. She's eating grain in the feed room right now, laughing at you."

"Well, how good of you to tell me," Murphy spat. "I don't see you doing anything to keep the barn free of vermin. In fact, Poptart, I don't see you doing much of anything except feeding your face."

Placidly rising above the abuse, the huge creature stretched her neck down until she touched Murphy's nose. "Hey, shortchange, you're trapped in my stall, so you'd better watch your tongue."

"Oh, yeah."

With that the cat leapt onto the horse's broad gray back. Poptart, startled, swung her body alongside the stall bars. With one fluid motion Mrs. Murphy launched herself through the stall bars, landing on the tack trunk outside.

Poptart blinked through the stall bars as Mrs. Murphy crowed, "You might be bigger but I'm smarter!"

Having a good sense of humor, the horse chuckled, then returned to her orchard grass/alfalfa mix, which tasted delicious.

The cat trotted into the feed room. Sure enough, she could hear the mouse behind the feed bin. Harry lined her feed bins with tin because mice could eat their way through just about anything. However, grains spilled over and the mice had eaten a tiny hole in the wall. They'd grab some grains, then run into the hole to enjoy their booty.

Mrs. Murphy sat by the hole.

A tiny nose peeped out, the black whiskers barely visible. "I know you're there and I'm not coming out. Go home and eat tuna."

Murphy batted at the hole and the little nose withdrew. "I'm a cat. I kill mice. That's my job."

"Kill moles. They're more dangerous, you know. If one of these horses steps into a mole hole? Crack."

"Clever, aren't you?"

"No, just practical," came the squeak.

"We're all part of the food chain."

"Bunk." To prove the point the mouse threw out a piece of crimped oat.

"I will get you in good time," Mrs. Murphy warned. "You fellows can eat a quart of grain a week. That costs my mother money, and she's pretty bad off."

"No, she's not. She has you and she has that silly dog."

"Don't try to flatter me. I am your enemy and you know it."

"Enemies are relative."

Mrs. Murphy pondered this. "You're a philosophical little fellow, aren't you?"

"I don't believe in enemies. I believe there are situations when we compete over resources. If there aren't enough to go around, we fight. If there are, fine. Right now there're enough to go around, and I don't eat that much and neither does my family. So don't eat me . . . or mine."

The tiger licked the side of her paw and rubbed it over her ears. "I'll think about what you said, but my job is to keep this barn and this house clean."

"You already cleaned out the glove compartment of the truck. You've done your job." The mouse referred to Murphy's ferocious destruction of a field mouse family who took up residence in the glove compartment. They chewed through the wires leading into the fuse box, rendering the truck deader than a doornail. Once Murphy dispatched the invaders, Harry got her truck repaired, though it cost her $137.82.

"Like I said, I'll think about it."

"Murphy," Harry called. "Let's go, pussycat."

Murphy padded out of the feed room. Tucker, sleepy-eyed, waddled behind Harry. Fit as she was, Tucker still waddled, or at least that's how she appeared to Mrs. Murphy.

"Whatcha been doing?"

"Trying to catch mice. You should have heard the sneak holed up there in the feed room where I finally trapped him with my blinding speed."

"What did he say?"

"One argument after another about how I should leave him and his family alone. He said enemies were relative. Now that's a good one."

As Harry rolled open the barn door, a blast of frigid air caused the animals to fluff out their fur. Tucker, wide-awake now, dashed to the house through the screen door entrance and into the kitchen through the animal door. Mrs. Murphy jogged alongside Harry, who was sliding toward the back porch.

"I can handle snow but I hate this ice!" Harry cursed as her feet splayed in different directions. She hit the hard ice.

"Come on, Mom." Mrs. Murphy brushed alongside her.

Tucker, feeling guilty, emerged from the house. Her claws, not as sharp as Murphy's, offered no purchase on the ice so she stayed put unless called.

"Crawl on your hands and knees," Tucker advised.

Harry scrambled up only to go down again. She did crawl on her hands and knees to the back door. "How did I get to the barn in the first place?"

"You moved a lot slower, and the sun is making the ice slicker, I think," Mrs. Murphy said.

Finally Harry, with Mrs. Murphy's encouragement, struggled onto the screened-in back porch. She removed her duck boots and opened the door to the kitchen, happy to feel the warmth. Mrs. Murphy kept thinking about the mouse saying enemies were relative. Then another thought struck her. She stopped eating and called down to Tucker, "Ever notice how much bigger we are than mice, moles, and birds? Our game?"

"No, I never thought about it. Why?"

"We are. Occasionally I'll bring down a rabbit, but my game is smaller than I am."

"And faster."

"Oh, no, they're not!" Mrs. Murphy yelled back at Tucker. "No one is faster than I am. They have a head start on me, and half the time I still bring them down. Anyway, they have eyes on the sides of their heads. They can see us coming, Tucker."

"Yeah, yeah." Tucker, pleased that she had twitted feline vanity, rested her head on her paws, her liquid brown eyes staring up at angry green ones.

"I'm not going to continue this discussion. I'll keep my revelation to myself." Haughtily she turned her back on the dog and walked the length of the kitchen counter. She stopped before the painted ceramic cookie jar in the shape of a laughing pig.

"Don't be so touchy." Tucker followed along on the floor.

"I don't see why I should continue a discussion with an animal who has no respect for my skills." She was feeling a little testy since she couldn't nail the barn mouse.

"I'm sorry. You are amazingly fast. I'm out of sorts because of the ice."

Eagerly the cat shared her thoughts, "Well, what I've been thinking is how small jockeys are. Like prey."

25

Tricky November. The mercury climbed to 55°F. The ice melted. The earth, soggy from the rain, slowly began to absorb the water. One confused milk butterfly was sighted flying around Miranda's back door.

Harry and Mrs. Hogendobber sorted through the usual Monday morning eruption of mail. Pewter visited but grew weary of Mrs. Murphy and Tucker describing their dramas on the ice. She fell asleep on the ledge dividing the upper from the lower post boxes. Lying on her side, some of her flabby gray belly hung over.

"Now you are coming, aren't you?" Mrs. Hogendobber asked about her church's songfest. "It's November nineteenth. You write down the date."

"I will."

Mrs. Murphy stuck her nose in Mrs. H.'s mailbag. "Mrs. Murphy, get out of there."

"*Don't be an old poop face.*"

Mrs. Hogendobber reached down into the bag, her bangle bracelets jangling, and grabbed a striped kitty tail.

"*Hey, I don't grab your tail!*" The cat whirled around.

"Now I told you to get out. I don't even like cats, Murphy. For you I make an exception." Mrs. Hogendobber told half the truth. When Harry took over her husband's job, bringing her animals to work, Mrs. Hogendobber had been censorious. During her period of mourning she would find herself at the post office, not sure how she'd arrived at that destination. She'd helped George for the nearly four decades that he was postmaster. An unpaid assistant, for the Crozet post office, small and out of the way, did not merit more workers. Of course, the volume of mail had increased dramatically over the years. When Harry took over as postmistress, as they preferred to call the position, her youth allowed her to work a bit harder than George could at the end of his career, but even she couldn't keep up with the workload. Entreaties for an assistant fell on deaf federal ears. No surprise there. Out of the 459,025 postal employees, less than 10 percent worked in rural areas. They tended to be ignored, a situation that also had its good side, for rural workers enjoyed much more freedom than urban postal employees, trapped in a standard forty-hour week with some power-hungry supervisor nagging them.

Mrs. Hogendobber began coming once or twice a week to pitch in. At first, Harry had welcomed her company but asked her not to work because she couldn't pay her. But Miranda knew the ins and outs of the routine, the people at the central post office in Charlottesville on Seminole Trail, even the people in Washington, not to mention everyone in Crozet. She proved invaluable. Since George, prudent with money, had left her with enough to be comfortable, and she was making more with her baking, she didn't need the money. More than anything, she needed to be useful.

Over time she and Harry grew close. And over time, despite her reservations, Mrs. Hogendobber grew to love the two furry friends at Harry's side. She'd even learned to love the fat gray cat presently knocked out on the ledge. Not that she wanted anyone to know.

Murphy, having pressed her luck, backed out of the bag, danced sideways to the counter, and leapt on it. She collapsed on her side and rolled over, showing lots of tummy.

"Murphy, you're full of yourself this morning." Harry patted her stomach.

"I'm bored. Pewter's sacked out. Tucker's snoring under the table. It's a beautiful day."

Harry kissed her on the cheek. A light knock at the back door put a stop to the kissing. Mrs. Murphy could take but so many human kisses.

Miranda opened the door. "Adelia, come right in."

Addie, still wearing her chaps, stepped inside.

"Breeze all your babies?" Harry asked as Tucker lifted her head, then dropped it back down again.

"Oh, yeah." Addie sniffed as the vanilla odor from hot sticky buns reached her nostrils.

"Your mail's on the table," Miranda said as she carried two handfuls of mail to the big bottom boxes used by the small businesses in town.

"Thanks."

"Ready for the Colonial Cup?" Harry referred to the famous steeplechase in Camden, South Carolina, which had also been started by Marion duPont Scott.

"Well, Ransom Mine is coming along. You remember, he came in second at Montpelier. Royal Danzig, dunno, off these last couple of days, and Bazooka—I think I need a pilot's license to ride him. Mickey Townsend sent over two horses right after Nigel was killed." She paused a moment. "He said he wanted me to work them. They're really going great. Mickey's always backed me, you know. Chark's crabby about it, but he knows it's extra money so he shut up."

"What are you all talking about, 'breezing' a horse?" Miranda paused, oblivious to Pewter who was rolling over in her sleep.

"*Watch out!*" Mrs. Murphy called.

Too late. Pewter tumbled into one of the large business mailboxes.

"Pewter." Mrs. Hogendobber leaned over the befuddled cat. "Are you all right?" She couldn't help it. She burst out laughing.

"*Fine.*" Pewter picked herself up and marched right out of the box, over to the table where she tore out a hunk of pastry with her claws before Harry could stop her.

"Actually, I think you all have more work with these critters than I do with the horses," Addie observed. "Breezing—uh, I limber up the horse a little, jog a little, and then I do an exercise gallop around the track. Chark gives me the distance. You work a horse for conditioning and for wind. I guess that's the easiest way to describe it."

"Aren't you ever afraid up there?" Miranda asked.

"Right now I'm more afraid down here."

"Why? Has someone threatened you?" Mrs. Hogendobber walked back to Addie.

"No." Addie sat down on the chair by the sticky buns. "Everything's a mess. Arthur bombards me with daily lectures about how to handle my inheritance when I turn twenty-one. Mim's giving me the same lecture but with a lot more class. My brother shrugs and says if I blow it it's my own fault and he's not keeping me, but then I never asked him to. That's on a good day. On a bad day he yells at me. Everybody's acting like I'm going to go hog-wild."

"*Pewter's the one who goes hog-wild,*" Murphy snickered.

"*Shut up,*" Pewter replied, sitting on the other chair at the

table. She thought the humans, engrossed in conversation, wouldn't notice her filching another piece of bun.

They did. Addie stretched over and lightly smacked the outreached paw. "You have no manners."

"I'm hungry," Pewter pleaded.

Mrs. Hogendobber reached into her voluminous skirt pockets and pulled out a few tiny, tiny fish, Haute Feline treats. She lured Pewter away from the table. Mrs. Murphy leapt off the counter and hurried over, too.

"I never thought I'd live to see the day." Harry laughed.

"If I don't do this, there won't be anything left for us." Miranda laughed, too. She turned her attention back to Addie. "One of the terrible things about wealth is the way people treat you."

"Well. Uh, well, I'm not wealthy yet." Addie rubbed her finger on the table making designs only she could see. "Actually, I came by, Harry, to see if you'd lend me a hundred dollars. I'll pay you right after Camden—speaking of money." She smiled sheepishly.

Harry, not an ungenerous soul, hesitated. First, that was a chunk of change to her. Second, what was going on? "Why won't Chark lend you the money?"

"He's mad at me. He's being a butthole." Her voice rose.

"So, what did you do with the money you won at Montpelier?" Harry juggled a load of mail on the way to the post boxes.

"Uh—"

"I'm not lending you a cent until I know why you're short. The *real* reason."

"And what's that supposed to mean?" Addie flushed.

"Means your deceased boyfriend had a coke habit. How do I know you don't have one?"

This stunned Miranda, who stopped what she was doing, as did the cats and dog. All eyes focused on Addie, whose face transformed from a flush to beet red.

"He was trying to stop. Until Linda got hold of him. I hope

she gets a stiletto through her heart. Except she doesn't have one."

"What about you?" Harry pressed.

"I'm off all substances. Anyway, I had the example of Mother."

"Now, now, your mother was a wonderful woman. She was a social drinker, I grant you." Miranda defended Marylou.

"She was a drunk, Mrs. Hogendobber," Addie's voice became wistful. "She'd get real happy at parties and real sad at home alone. She leaned on Mim a lot, but a best friend isn't a lover, and Mother needed that. She'd be morose at home . . . and out would come the bottle.

"Well . . ." Miranda was obviously reluctant to give up her image of Marylou Valiant. "At least she always behaved like a lady."

Harry crossed her arms over her chest. "You still haven't answered my question. Why do you need a hundred dollars?"

"Because I owe Mickey Townsend from a poker game the night before the Montpelier Races," she blurted out.

"He won't wait?" Miranda was curious.

"Mickey's a good guy. I adore him. I wish Mother had married him. But when it comes to poker, I mean, this is *serious*." She rubbed her thumb and forefinger together.

"Come on, he won't let you work off a hundred dollars with the horses he brought over?" Harry waited for the other shoe to drop.

"I haven't asked."

"Addie, I don't believe a word of this!" Harry figured they were long past the point of subtlety. Mickey was a bum excuse.

"I really do owe Mickey a hundred dollars. I just want to get it out of the way. And I don't want Arthur to find out."

"Mickey won't tell him." Mrs. Hogendobber stated the obvious, which had no effect on the young woman.

Out of the blue, Harry fired a question. "And how much did Nigel really owe Mickey?"

Without thinking it through, Addie answered, "About two thousand. He'd have made good on it, you see, because he took a kilo from Linda and Will—"

"A kilo!" Harry exclaimed.

"Yes, he thought he could sell it off after cutting it and make a lot of money." Addie realized she'd let the cat out of the bag. "Don't tell Rick Shaw or Deputy Cooper!"

"This could have some bearing on the case," Mrs. Hogendobber replied sensibly.

"Then why hasn't anyone mentioned the kilo? Where the hell is it? Whoever killed him probably carted it away and is further enriching himself." Harry threw her hands in the air, disgusted that Addie would hold back something so vital.

"I have it." Her voice was small.

"*You what?*" The humans and animals said in unison.

"My God, Adelia, you're crazy. People have killed for less than a kilo of cocaine, and you know that Linda and Will will be on your tail *soon.*" Harry was emphatic.

"They already are." She put her head in her hands. "I put it in my big safe deposit box at Crozet National Bank when Nigel asked me to help him out. No one else knows. The sheriff from Orange County and Rick combed through his truck and his quarters. Nothing. Clean. Linda knows the cops haven't found the coke. She wants it back."

"I'll bet she does!" Harry exploded.

"She says she'll blackmail me if I don't return it. She says nobody will believe that I'm not in on the drug sale, and if I accuse her, it's her word against mine. She says that if I give her back the coke, that will be the end of it."

"So why *do* you need the hundred dollars?" Miranda picked up the refrain.

"For gas for the dually and for pocket change. I'll drive the coke up tonight. I haven't any spare money because I've been paying off money I owe Linda"— she paused, thinking—"over a horse deal."

"How much? Really, how much?" Tucker and Harry both asked.

"Uh . . ." A long pause followed. "As of today, one thousand and fifteen dollars."

"Good God, Addie." Harry sank into the chair that Pewter had vacated when she was offered the Haute Feline. She knew instinctively that Addie owed Linda Forloines on her own drug tab. Addie was lying to her.

"Pretty stupid, huh?" She hung her auburn head.

"Box of rocks." Harry made a fist and tapped her skull.

Miranda's imposing figure overshadowed the two seated young women. "This is foolishness and will lead to more pain. 'As a dog returneth to his vomit, so a fool returneth to his folly,' Proverbs twenty-six eleven."

"I *resent that*," Tucker barked.

"Gross," Addie said.

"I am not giving you one hundred dollars. And we're calling Rick Shaw right this minute."

"No! He'll tell Arthur, and Arthur'll tell Chark. They'll get the damn trusteeship extended. I'll never get my money!"

"Your mother's will is your mother's will. It can't be broken," Miranda told her.

"Maybe not, but they sure can drag it out. It's my money."

"But you've got to give the sheriff this information. You've got to get out before you get in too deep—you've already aided and abetted a felon."

"Coty Lamont was on cocaine too, wasn't he?" Mrs. Hogendobber inquired.

Addie nodded.

"For all we know, Addie, you deliver that kilo and you'll wind up with a knife through your heart." Harry sighed.

"I can't tell Rick," Addie wailed.

Miranda lifted the receiver from the phone as Addie bolted for the door. Tucker tripped her and Harry pounced on her.

"Let me go."

"Dammit, Addie, you're gonna get killed. You give Linda and Will that kilo and you'll be in business with Linda for the rest of your life. She'll bring you horses. She'll want special favors. If you're lucky, she'll take the kilo and blow town. If she stays . . ."

"If you're not lucky, cement shoes," Pewter matter-of-factly stated.

26

Rick Shaw, being an officer of the law for all his adult life, never expected people to tell him the truth right off the bat. The truth, like diamonds, had to be won by hand, by pick, by dynamite.

His anger when he heard the dismal story at the post office was not so much provoked by Addie's withholding information, although he wasn't happy about that, as by the way she had foolishly placed herself in jeopardy. He also made a mental note that Mickey Townsend had drastically downplayed the amounts of money Nigel and Coty owed him. He had never mentioned Addie's debt at all.

As soon as he dismissed Addie, after taking her back to his office for a full disclosure, he and Cynthia Cooper hopped into the squad car. He'd taken the precaution of calling the president of the bank, advising him not to let Addie into her safe deposit box. It could be opened only in Rick's presence.

"Did you call Culpeper?" Cynthia asked in shorthand, meaning the sheriff of Culpeper County.

"Uh-huh."

They drove in silence. When they reached Dr. D'Angelo's place, Romulus Farms, Sheriff Totie Biswanger was waiting for them.

"Gone," was all he said.

"Both of them?" Cynthia asked.

"Ey-ah," came the affirmative. He pointed to their cottage on Dr. D'Angelo's farm.

"Neat as a hairpin. Nothing moved. Clothes in the closet. Food in the refrigerator."

"Kind of funny, ain't it?" Totie folded his arms over his barrel chest and stared at his shoes.

27

"They dropped the whole damn thing!" Fair's radiant face underscored the happy news.

Harry had encountered him at Mim's, where she'd gone to deliver an express package. Mim and Chark Valiant, also on hand, were nearly as excited as Harry was at Fair's news.

They were all gathered at the barn, where Mrs. Murphy and Tucker nosed around. Rodger Dodger and Pusskin were nowhere to be found.

"Well, let me have a look at Royal Danzig," Fair said. "Didn't mean to talk so much."

"Oh, he can wait another minute. Once we get down to business, we'll forget to ask the details." Mim invited them into the tack room.

"Where's Addie?" Fair asked.

Mim, who knew, said nothing for Chark was in the dark about his sister's unholy mess. Another request of Rick Shaw's.

"She called from Charlottesville," Chark answered. "Said she was tied up and didn't know when she'd be back."

"Oh, okay." Fair grabbed a cup of coffee. He'd been up since four o'clock that morning because of an emergency at a hunter barn. "As near as I can make out, or as much as Colbert Mason wants to tell me, he contacted my accuser, Linda Forloines. She claimed he entirely misunderstood what she had said. She was furious he'd even think that and she had no intention of bringing charges against me. So that's that." He sat in the comfy old leather chair and immediately regretted it because he knew he wouldn't want to get up.

"Typical," was Mim's reply.

"She's not worth talking about," Chark added.

They all knew Linda's modus operandi. She'd act as though she had inside information, she'd hint, intimate, change the inflection of her voice to convey the full weight of her words. This way she could say that people misunderstood her, implying there must be a problem with you if you could even think such a thing.

"Well, let me take a look at Royal Danzig." Fair forced himself out of the chair.

They walked down the beautiful center aisle and Chark pulled the flashy guy out of his stall. As Fair ran his hands over the horse's legs, Rodger Dodger, fresh from patrolling the paddocks, sauntered into the barn, his beloved Pusskin by his side.

"*Royal, what's the buzz?*" the old ginger cat asked.

"*Kinda tender on my left leg. I think I put a foot wrong when I was turned out in the paddock.*"

"*Hope it's nothing serious,*" Rodger politely replied.

"*Me, too, I want to go to Camden.*"

"*Rodger, how you been?*" Mrs. Murphy called out when she heard Rodger's voice. She and Tucker had been in the tack room. It smelled so good and was toasty warm.

"Murphy. Hi, Tucker," Rodger said as Pusskin murmured her greetings.

Mrs. Murphy sat down, curling her tail around her. "*I've got a proposition for you, Rodger.*"

"*What proposition?*" Tucker's ears pointed up. "*Why didn't you tell me?*"

" *'Cause I've been cooking it.*" Mrs. Murphy turned back to Rodger. "*There's a chance your barn mice know what's in Orion's stall.*"

"*Why not ask the horses?*" Tucker asked.

"*I did.*" Rodger flicked his tail for a minute. "*They didn't remember anything, not even Orion, and he's the oldest, being twelve. 'Course, it could be that whatever is in there was buried in summertime years back. The foxhunters are always turned out in the far pastures in summer, so only the mice and I would have been here. I don't remember anything, but summers I go up and rest in the big house because of the air conditioning.*"

"*If you made a deal with the mice, maybe they'd talk to us.*" Mrs. Murphy kept to her agenda.

"*What kind of deal?*"

"*Not to catch them.*"

"*I can't do that. Mim will be furious if I don't deliver mice to the tack room. She asks Chark every day if Pusskin and I have done our duty.*"

"*She's real fussy,*" Pusskin added.

"*I thought of that.*" Mrs. Murphy wanted to bat Pusskin. She tried to make her meow sound pleasant. "*What I propose is that you catch field mice and deliver them to the tack room. The humans don't know the difference.*"

Rodger rubbed his whiskers with his forepaw. He wrinkled his brow. A wise old fellow, he wanted to consider the ramifications of such a bargain. "*It will work for a time, Murphy, but as the grain goes down and the barn mice population doesn't decrease, the humans will figure out something's wrong. I don't want Pusskin or me to get the boot.*"

"*Mim would never do that,*" Tucker rightly surmised.

"*I'd like to think that.*" Rodger knew other cats who were out of work or worse because they got lazy. "*But even if she let us stay, she* might bring in another cat, and I don't want to be bothered with that. This is my barn."

"What if we asked the barn mice not to show themselves?" Mrs. Murphy tried to figure out a solution. "At least so the humans wouldn't see them. You know how they get about mice."

"Seeing is bad enough. It's the grain I'm worried about," Rodger said sensibly.

"Can't they get by on what the horses throw on the ground? You know, horses are the sloppiest eaters," Pusskin chimed in. Not a bad idea for a slow kitty, Mrs. Murphy admitted.

"Less food. More safety," Rodger purred. "It's a trade-off. Worth a try, I suppose, but Murphy, why do you care what's in Orion's stall?"

"Don't say curiosity," Tucker warned.

Mrs. Murphy breathed in the crisp air. Her head felt quite as clear as the air around her. "I think the murders aren't over, and I think whatever's in Orion's stall might be part of the answer."

"If humans kill one another, that's their business," Pusskin, not a major fan of the human race, hissed.

"But what if this puts Mim in danger? Think about that." Mrs. Murphy reached out with a paw to Pusskin as though she were going to cuff her. "Something has happened in her barn. Something that goes back a few years at least. Mickey Townsend pulled a gun on Coty Lamont in the middle of the night. Coty was in Orion's stall, digging. Mickey makes him cover it back up, then takes him away. Coty's truck wasn't here. He'd walked in from somewhere and Mickey snuck up on him. Pretty peculiar. The next day Coty Lamont is dead in the back of the pickup, a knife through the heart and another playing card on it, the Queen of Spades. That's what Cynthia Cooper told my mom when they had supper night before last." She took a breath.

Pusskin blurted out, "That means Mickey's the killer."

"Maybe yes and maybe no. Addie has a kilo of cocaine in her safe deposit box that she says belonged to Nigel Danforth."

"Oh, no!" Rodger and Pusskin exclaimed together.

"She told Rick Shaw. Now she's in deep doo-doo." Tucker felt the same urgency that her best friend did. "And I don't think she would have told him, but Mom and Mrs. Hogendobber forced her to do it. I reckon we haven't heard the end of it because Addie was supposed to deliver the kilo to Linda Forloines, and what's Linda going to do when it doesn't show up?"

"So Addie might be in danger?" Rodger liked Addie.

"Anybody might be in danger, especially if I'm right about there being a secret in Orion's stall. What if, by pure accident, Mim stumbles on the truth? You can't expose your owner to that kind of danger. I know you aren't house cats, but Mim is fair and she takes care of you. And"—Mrs. Murphy lowered her voice—"what would have happened if she hadn't rescued you all from the SPCA? There are too many kittens, and no matter how good a job the SPCA does—well, you know."

The animals remained silent for some time after that grim reminder.

Finally Rodger spoke, firmly. "It's a debt of honor. We'll do our best for Mim. Pusskin?"

"Whatever you say, darling."

He filled his red chest, licked the side of Pusskin's pretty face, then said, "Let's parlay with the mice."

The mice were partying in the walls of the tack room. Mim had insulated the tack room so there was plenty of space between the two walls, filled with warm insulation, easy for mice to get in and out of because they burrowed from the stall next door. By this time they had created many entrances and exits, driving Rodger Dodger to distraction because even if he and Pusskin divided to cover holes, they'd still miss the mice.

The raucous squeaking stopped when the mice heard and smelled the approaching cats.

"Must be an army of them," the head mouse, a saucy female, warned.

Rodger put his pink nose at the entrance to one of the holes. "Loulou, it's Rodger and Pusskin. Mrs. Murphy and Tucker, the corgi from over by Yellow Mountain, are with us."

"The post office animals," Loulou replied, her high-pitched voice clear and piercing.

"How do they know that?" Mrs. Murphy wondered.

"We know everything. Besides, we have cousins at Market Shiflett's store. Pewter's too fat to run anyone down."

Murphy giggled. So did Tucker.

"Loulou, I've come with an offer you should consider."

A moment of silence was followed by a wary Loulou. "We're all ears."

"Do you know what's buried in Orion's stall?"

"As the oldest mouse, I do," Loulou swiftly replied. "But I'm not telling you."

Rodger kept his temper in check, but Pusskin complained, "She's a real smartass."

Mrs. Murphy whispered for her to shut up.

"Loulou, I don't expect something for nothing. Pusskin and I agree not to catch any barn mice for a year"—that last part was Rodger's own flourish—"if you agree not to let the humans see you. Otherwise they'll think Pusskin and I are lazing about and we'll get in hot water, and Mim might try to bring in another cat. You can understand our position, can you not?"

"Yes."

"Well, a year of freedom for the information—and try not to breed too much, will you?"

"It's an open shot to the feed room. The humans will see us." Loulou was playing for time as the excited chatter in the background proved.

"There's plenty of grain under the horses' feed buckets. Just don't show your faces in the barn during the day, and if you hear a human coming at night, duck for cover. Otherwise, we'll all be in a real bad situation."

"I'll get back to you," Loulou replied.

The three cats and the dog patiently waited. Harry walked by on her way to the john. "What are you all doing?"

"High-level negotiations," Mrs. Murphy informed her.

"Sometimes you're so cute." Harry smiled and continued on her way.

"Whew." Tucker sighed. "She could have screwed up the whole deal."

"Yeah, the last thing we want any of them to see is this entrance here with all of us sitting around like bumps on a log." Rodger shifted his weight from one haunch to the other.

They heard a chorus of tinny voices. "Aye." Then one lone "Nay."

"Rodger Dodger!" Loulou said peeking her little head out of the entrance. She was a feisty mouse and a confident one.

"Yes."

"We are almost unanimous. We agree to your terms, a free year, but I have a personal favor to ask."

"What?"

"Can you talk to Lucy Fur and Elocution, the Reverend Jones's two cats? My youngest sister's family lives behind the tapestry of the Ascension. Lucy Fur and Elocution hassle them constantly. I'm not asking for a moratorium, just a little less hassle, you know?"

"I don't know those cats," Rodger honestly replied.

"I do," Mrs. Murphy quickly said. "I'll talk to them. You have my word."

"You must have mice at your barn," Loulou pushed.

"I do, but you all are browns and they are grays. I doubt any of your family is out my way."

A pause followed. "You're probably right, but you will talk to these barn cats?"

After a long pause Murphy agreed, "Yes. Now, will you tell us what is in Orion's stall, and whether you remember any of the people involved."

Loulou coughed, clearing her throat. "I was very young. Mother was still alive but I remember it as if it were yesterday. Five years ago last July. Hotter than Tophet. Coty Lamont and a fellow called Sargent dug a deep hole in the corner of the stall. Had to be two in the morning, and about four when they finished. The earth was soft there, so they made good work of it. We could smell how nervous they were. You know, that sharp, ugly odor." She caught another big breath. "They left, then came back with a heavy canvas tarp and a man holding either end. I couldn't see what was in it but I could smell blood."

"Damn," Mrs. Murphy whispered.

Loulou listened to a squeak then said, "Mom and I and the older mice, no longer living, of course, watched from the hayloft. When they lifted the tarp to lower it in, I guess they were tired because they dropped it, and one end unraveled a little. Lots of brassy hair spilled out. Mother got a good look at the face because she ran along the top of the stall beam."

All the animals held their breath as Loulou continued. "It was Marylou Valiant."

28

Livid, Addie Valiant opened her safe deposit box at Crozet National in the presence of five onlookers. Rick Shaw and bank president, Dennis Washington, stared at the brown-paper-wrapped package. By opening the box in the evening they had avoided the regular ebb and flow of banking traffic, diminishing the chances of someone getting wind of Addie's escapade.

"I don't know why everyone has to be here." Addie pouted. Arthur stood next to Dennis. Chark, arms folded across his chest, leaned against a wall of small stainless steel safe deposit boxes.

Cynthia Cooper held the small brass key. She wouldn't give it back to Addie. "Arthur is your guardian until midnight November fourteenth. And I would think you'd be glad your brother is here."

"I'm not glad."

Rick had waited until the last minute to pull in Charles and Arthur, fearing that the earlier he informed them, the likelier they were to leak the news. That could be dangerous.

Addie's young face wrinkled in rage. "I'll hear about my poor judgment for the rest of my life." She wheeled on Arthur. "And I bet you find a way to extend your trusteeship with help *again* from my *loving* brother!"

"You're under duress," Arthur said in a measured voice. "This was an extremely foolish thing to do. As to your money, the wishes of your mother will be followed to the letter."

"I don't believe that. You think I'm stupid about money."

Arthur opened his mouth, then shut it. Addie, fiery like her mother, wouldn't hear anything he said.

"Sis, I ought to wring your neck for this stunt," Chark said through clenched teeth as Cynthia Cooper reached into the deep safe deposit box and lifted out the wrapped kilo.

"It wasn't what you think. Nigel bought this to pay off his debt to Mickey."

"This goes far beyond a debt to Mickey Townsend," Rick replied. "This represents a lot of money on the street."

"He used you!" Chark yelled.

"He didn't use me."

"Let the dead sleep in peace." Arthur held up his hands to stop the argument. "Whatever his intentions were we'll never know."

Rick motioned for Cynthia to lock up the box.

"I have something to tell you all." Rick's eyes narrowed. "And Addie, if you're holding anything back, out with it." She glared at him as he continued. "There is no Nigel Danforth."

"What do you mean?" Alarm flashed on her face while confusion registered on Chark's and Arthur's visages.

"I mean, there is no record of such a person in England. And there is no green card registered to anyone by that name in this country. Our only hope is his dental records, which we have sent out by computer to every police station we can reach, here and in England. A real long shot. His fingerprints are not on file in either the U.S. or England."

Addie sank like a stone. "I don't understand."

Chark caught his sister and gently lowered her in a chair. "He lied even more than I thought," he said.

She put her head in her hands and sobbed. "But I loved him. Why would he lie to me?"

Arthur placed his hand on her shoulder. "Sheriff, might he perhaps be from some British colony—or French colony?"

"Coop thought of that. Can't find a thing. We don't know who this man was, where he came from, or his exact age. All we know is that he gave a kilo of cocaine to Addie to keep for him. Saying he bought it from Linda Forloines—"

"Well, get them!" Addie wailed.

"We tried to arrest them yesterday. They're gone." Rick, embarrassed, saw the dismay on their faces.

"Is my sister"—Chark could hardly get the words out—"under arrest?"

"No. Not yet anyway," Rick said.

"Now see here, Shaw." Arthur stood up straight. "She's been a foolish girl, but many a woman's been led astray by a man. She is no drug dealer. She isn't even a user anymore."

Shaking, tears down her cheeks, Addie choked, "Well—uh, sometimes."

"Then your brother and I will put you in a clinic." Arthur's tone brooked no contradiction.

"What about Camden? Anyway, I only use a little to celebrate. Really. I'm not an addict or anything. Test my blood."

"We'll settle this between us." Arthur took control. "Sheriff, does Adelia have permission to ride in Camden?"

"Yes, but"—he focused on Addie—"don't try anything stupid—like running away."

"Do you think Will and Linda will show up there?" Chark asked.

"I don't know," Rick replied.

"They're out of the country by now." Addie wiped her red eyes. "Linda always said she was going for one last big hit."

"Why didn't she do that a long time ago?" Arthur's voice was hard.

"Because she was using too. She said she'd cleaned up, though. Now it's strictly business. She wanted a haul. And out of here." Addie dropped her head in her hands again.

"There's lots of this around the steeplechase world, isn't there?" Cynthia jotted notes in her book.

Addie shrugged. "Goes in cycles. I don't think there's any more drug abuse on the backstretch than there is in big corporations."

"In that case, America's in trouble," Chark said.

"We'll deal with America tomorrow." Arthur smiled tightly. "Right now my first priority is getting this young lady straightened out. Sheriff, is there any more that you need from us tonight?"

"No," Rick said. "You're free to go."

Later, when Rick and Cynthia were about to get into the squad car, she asked him, "Do you think she's telling the truth? That she really didn't know about Nigel?"

"What's your gut tell you?"

Cynthia leaned against the door of the car. The night, crystalline and cold, was beautiful. "She didn't know."

"What else?" He offered her a cigarette which she took.

Cynthia bent her head for a light and took a drag. She looked up, noticing how perfectly brilliant the stars were. "Rick, this thing is a long way from being over."

He nodded in agreement, and they finished their cigarettes in silence.

29

The big purple van with the glittering gold lettering—DALMALLY FARM on both sides and HORSES on the rear—was parked next to an earthen ramp. The loading ramps, heavy and unwieldy, could injure your back so Mim had had an earthen ramp built. The horses walked directly onto the van without hearing that thump-thump of metal underneath them. Of course, once they were at the races, the loathed ramp did have to be pulled out from the side of the van, but still, any easing of physical labor helped.

Harry loved to inspect Mim's vans. Mim also had an aluminum gooseneck trailer for hunting. Although purple was the racing color of her mother's family, for hunting Mim used red and gold on her three-horse slant-load Trailet. Harry coveted this trailer as well as the Dodge dually with the Cummins turbo-diesel engine that pulled it. That was red, too.

She'd stopped by the stable after work to see if Little Marilyn was around. She didn't want to seem as though she was checking up on her peer, but she was. Little Mim had finally sent out the invitations for the wild-game dinner, but she hadn't reported who had RSVPed and who hadn't. As it was, Susan Tucker had had to pick up the invitations from the printer in Charlottesville.

Just as Harry climbed back into her truck, Big Mim cruised into the parking lot in her Bentley Turbo R. Mim never stinted on machines of any sort. It was an irrational thing with Mim: she couldn't resist cars, trucks, or tractors. Fortunately, she could afford them. She probably ran the best-equipped farm in Albemarle County. She even had a rolling irrigation system, a series of pipes connected to huge wheels that ran off a generator.

"Harry."

"Hi. I was trying to find Little Marilyn but no one's around."

"She's in Washington today." Mim opened the heavy door and slid out. "Worried about the dinner?"

"A little."

"Me too. Well, don't worry overmuch. I'll check the messages on the service and tell you who's accepted. I'll resort to the telephone tree, too, if necessary." She mentioned the system wherein designated callers were each responsible for calling ten people.

"I can do that."

"No, she's my daughter, and as usual, she's falling down on the job." Mim fingered her Hermes scarf. "Marilyn hasn't been right since her divorce was final last year. I don't know what to do."

Harry, forthright, said, "She isn't going to learn much if you do it for her."

"Do you want the game dinner to fall apart? My God, the hunt club would have our hides. I'd rather do it and get after her later."

Harry knew that was true. Their foxhunting club, the Jefferson—which chased foxes, rather than truly hunting them—was filled with prickly personalities, big egos, and tough riders as well as those of calmer temperament. Foxhunting by its nature attracts passionate people, which is all very well until the time comes for them to cooperate with one another. Little Marilyn would stir a hornets' nest if the game dinner didn't raise the anticipated revenue.

"I wish I could help you, but Marilyn has never much cared for me."

"Now, Harry, she's not demonstrative. She likes you well enough."

Harry decided not to refute Mim. Instead, her attention turned toward Tucker and Mrs. Murphy chattering loudly about who had been in Orion's stall.

"Mrs. Murphy and Tucker appear to be hungry," Mim said.

"Mim, I wish *you'd listen.*" Mrs. Murphy mournfully hung out the driver's window.

"Yeah, well, let me know if there's anything I can do to help," Harry said.

"You're part of the telephone tree." Mim started for the stable, then turned. "Harry, what are you doing next weekend?"

"Nothing special."

"How would you like to come to Camden this weekend to see the Colonial Cup? It would mean a lot to Adelia and Charles, I'm sure."

"*Don't go.*" A bolt of fear shot through Mrs. Murphy and she didn't know why.

"If Miranda will take care of my babies, I'd love to go."

"I thought Miranda might like to attend as well. Her sister lives in Greenville. Perhaps she could drive over."

"Let me see what I can do about the kids here, but I'd love to go."

"It's Adelia's twenty-first birthday. I thought we could celebrate down there and put her troubles behind us."

"Good idea."

30

Gray clouds hung so low Harry felt she could reach up and grab one. Although the temperature stayed in the mid-forties, the light wind, raw, made her shiver.

She dashed out of the bank on her lunch hour just as Boom Boom dashed in.

"Harry."

"Boom Boom."

"I'm sorry I lost my temper in the supermarket."

"Uh, well, an avalanche of toilet paper will do that to you." Harry continued down the steps.

Boom Boom placed a restraining, manicured hand on her shoulder. "Miranda says you can have the next hour off."

"Huh?"

"I was just in the post office and I asked her if I could borrow you for an hour."

"What?"

"To go to Lifeline with me."

"No."

"Harry, even if you hate it, it's an experience you can laugh about later."

Harry wanted to bat Miranda as well as throttle Boom Boom, a vision in magenta cashmere and wool today. "No. I can't do something like that."

"You need to reach out to other people. Release your fears. We're all knotted up with fear."

Harry breathed deeply, removing Boom Boom's hand from her shoulder. "I'm afraid to die. I'm afraid I won't be able to pay my bills. I'm afraid of sickness, and I guess if I'm brutally honest, I'm afraid to grow old."

"Lifeline can not only banish those fears but teach you how to transform them to life-enhancing experiences."

"Good God." Harry shook her head.

Mickey Townsend walked up behind her, a deposit envelope in his gloved hand. "Harry, Boom Boom. Harry, are you all right?"

"No! Boom Boom keeps pressuring me to go to Lifeline with her. I don't want to go."

"You'd be surprised at the number of people who do go." Boom Boom fluttered her eyelashes. Harry assumed this was for Mickey.

"I've never been to Lifeline, but—" He paused. "When Marylou disappeared I went to Larry Johnson. He prescribed anti-depressants, which made me feel like a bulldozer ran over me, except I could function. I hated that feeling so I went into therapy."

"You?"

"See!" Boom Boom triumphantly bragged.

"Shut up, Boom. Lifeline isn't therapy."

"Did it help? I'm sure it did." Boom Boom smiled expansively.

Mickey lowered his already low voice. "I found out I'm a real son of a bitch, and you know what else I found out?" He leaned toward Boom Boom, whispering, "I like it that way."

Harry laughed as Boom Boom, rising above the situation, intoned, "You could benefit from Lifeline."

"I could benefit from single malt scotch, too." He tipped his hat. "Ladies."

Harry, still laughing, bade her improvement-mad tormentor good-bye.

"You know what, Harry?" Boom Boom shouted to her back. "This is about process, not just individual people. Process. The means, not the ends. There are positive processes and negative processes. Like for Mickey Townsend. Ever since the whole town turned on him for courting Marylou—*negative* process."

Harry stopped and turned around. "What did you say?"

"Process!" Boom Boom shouted.

Harry held up her hands for quiet. "I hear you. I think I'm missing something."

"A lot."

"Go back to Marylou."

"Not unless you come with me to Lifeline."

"Look. I've got to pack now, I'm going to Camden for the weekend. I haven't got time to go with you to Lifeline. Talk to me about process right now. I promise I'll go when I return."

"Set a time frame."

"Huh?"

"You could come back and say you'll go with me next year."

"In a week."

Boom Boom, thrilled, stepped closer, looming over Harry from her much greater height. "Nothing happens in isolation. All emotions are connected like links in a chain. Marylou Valiant couldn't cope without her husband. She began to drink too much. Squander money. That set off Arthur, who loved her. He chased off that greedy movie star and what happens? She falls in love with Mickey Townsend."

"So?"

"Process. No one directly confronts and releases their emotions. Arthur becomes embittered. He wins over Chark. Mickey wins over Addie. The men fight over Marylou through her children."

Harry, silent for a long time, said, "This is Act Two."

"Yes—until everyone involved stops hanging on to hardened, dead patterns. But people's egos get hung up in their anger and their pain. So they pass it along."

"What goes around comes around," Harry said, thinking out loud.

"Not exactly. This is about breaking patterns."

"I understand. I think." She rubbed her temples. "Didn't mean to be, uh, reductive."

"You will go with me?"

"I said I would."

"Shake on it."

Harry extended her hand. She ran back to the post office, pushed the door open. "Miranda, how could you?"

Miranda, glasses down on her neck, said to Herb Jones, "Ignore her."

Harry strode up to the counter, Murphy, Pewter, and Tucker watching her every move. "You told Boom Boom you'd relieve me for an hour so I could go to Lifeline. How could you?"

"I did no such thing. I told her if you wanted to go you could. It's a slow day."

"Damn. I should have known." Harry propped her elbow on the smooth, worn counter. "Well, I am going." She held up her hand for stop. "Not today. Next week."

"Harry, I'm proud of you." The reverend beamed.

"Why?"

"You're showing the first signs of forgiveness."

"I am?"

"You are." He slapped her on the back, reaching over the counter. "You girls enjoy the races."

As he left, Harry repeated to Miranda her entire conversation with Boom Boom Craycroft.

"She wasn't talking about the murders—she was just talking." Miranda pushed her glasses up to the bridge of her nose.

"Yeah, but it made me wonder if Nigel and Coty's murders aren't part of a process—something started before drugs . . . or during drugs. Fixing races. Betting. That was everyone's first thought, remember?"

"Yes. It proved unfounded."

"Well, Mrs. H., they weren't just killed because someone didn't like them. They were links in a chain."

"*She surprises me.*" Pewter lay down crossing her paws in front of her. "*Humans can reason.*"

31

Since no one claimed Nigel Danforth's body, he was buried in a potter's grave at the expense of the taxpayers of Ablemarle County.

His belongings were in his tack trunk back in the over-crowded locker room at the station.

Cynthia Cooper called Mickey Townsend to pick them up. The department had tagged and photographed each item.

He followed her back to the locker room.

"I was going to turn this over to Adelia since he had no next of kin. But the more I thought about it, the more I decided against it. It could upset her too much, and the big race is this weekend. You were his employer. You'll have to stand in for next of kin."

"May I open it?"

"Sure."

He knelt down, lifting the brass hasp on the small wooden trunk. A riding helmet rested on top of folded lightweight racing breeches. He placed it on the ground with the breeches beside it. Two old heavy wool sweaters and a short winter down jacket were next. Assorted bats and whips rested on the bottom along with a shaving kit.

"Feel that." Mickey handed her a whip, pointed to the leather square at the end.

"It's heavy. What's in there?"

"A quarter. It's illegal but nothing says he can't use it during workouts. A crack with that smarts, I promise."

"Not much to show for a life, is it?" she said.

"He had some beautiful handmade clothes from London. Turnbull & Asser shirts. That kind of thing. He made money somewhere."

"Yeah. I remember when we went through the cottage. Still, not much other than a few good clothes. The only reason we kept the tack trunk so long is he was sitting on it. We dusted it inside and out."

Mickey slid his hands into the pockets of the down jacket. He checked the inside pocket. Empty.

It wasn't until he got home and hung the jacket on a tack hook, wondering to whom he should give the clothing—maybe some poor, lean kid struggling to make it in the steeplechasing world—that he noticed a folded-over zipper where the collar met the yoke of the down jacket. Nigel had worn the jacket so much that the collar squinched down, covering the zipper. The tack hook straightened out the collar. A hood would be inside, another aid against foul weather.

Out of curiosity, Mickey unzipped it, unfurling the hood. A dull clink drew his eyes to the soft loam of the barn aisle.

He bent over, picking up a St. Christopher's medal. He started to shake so hard he steadied himself against the stall.

Beautifully wrought, the gold medal was the size of a half-dollar. Over the detailed relief of St. Christopher carrying the Christ child was layer after layer of exquisite blue enamel. The engraving in perfect small script on the gold non-enameled back read: *He's my stand-in. Love, Charley.*

Mickey burst into tears, clutching the medal to his chest. "St. Christopher, you failed her."

That medal had hung around Marylou Valiant's neck on a twisted thick gold chain.

Once he regained control of himself, Mickey stood up. He started for the phone in the tack room to call Deputy Cooper. His instinct told him it would have been easy to miss the hood in the collar. If he hadn't hung up the coat, he would have missed it himself.

He sat down behind the old school desk and picked up the receiver.

He thought to himself, *What if they did see it and photograph it? Maybe they're trying to bait me. I'm a suspect.* He put the receiver back in the cradle. *No, no they missed it.* He held the beautiful medal in both palms. *Marylou, this medal will lead me to your killer, and I swear by all that's holy I'll take him out. If Nigel killed you, then may he fry in Hell for eternity.*

He stood up abruptly and slipped the St. Christopher's medal in his pocket.

32

"She's got Susan to take care of us and the horses," Tucker moaned. "She's packing her bags. What are we going to do?"

"I can hide under the seat of the Ford and then jump into the racing van." Mrs. Murphy lay on her side. She'd worried about this so much she was tired.

"But I can't fit under the seat," Tucker wailed. "And you need me. Mother needs me, she just doesn't know it."

"I'm thinking."

Tucker dropped her head between her white paws so that her face was in front of Mrs. Murphy's. "There will be more murders! Everyone will die!"

"Don't get carried away. Anyway, be quiet for a minute. I'm still thinking." Five long minutes passed. "I have an idea."

"What?" Tucker jumped up.

Mrs. Murphy also sat up. She didn't like to have Tucker hanging over her. *"Go into her bedroom and beg, plead, cry. Make her take you."*

"What about you?" Tucker's soft brown eyes filled with worry.

"She won't take me. We both know that. I can travel as well as you, but Mother has it in her head that cats don't like to travel."

"It's because you—"

"I only did that once!" Mrs. Murphy flared. *"I wish you'd forget it."*

"Mother doesn't. I'm trying to think like she does," Tucker hedged.

"The day we think like a human we're in trouble. We outthink them, that's the key. She won't take me. If she'll take you, one of us will be there at least. She needs a keeper, you know. If she blunders into something she could make a real mess. I'm a lot more worried about Mim, actually."

"Mim?" Tucker's tongue flicked out for a minute, a pink exclamation point.

"Marylou Valiant is buried in her barn. Coty Lamont and someone called Sargent put the body there five years ago. Right? Well, Mim may be safe and sound but the fact remains that a murdered woman, a dear friend of hers, is buried on her property. What if she finds out?"

Tucker, knowing her friend well, picked up her train of thought. *"It's a small circle, these 'chaser people. Mim's important in that world."*

"One thing is for sure."

"What?"

"The murderer carries a deck of cards."

"So does half of America." Murphy brushed against Tucker's chest, tickling the dog's sensitive nose with her tail.

"Here's what really bothers me. Once a murder is committed, the last thing a murderer would want to do is dig up the corpse. It's the corpse that incriminates them."

"Maybe they forgot to take off her jewelry or there was money buried with her."

"Possible, if the murderer or murderers were rattled. Yes, it's possible but Coty had enough time to collect his wits. He would have stripped her of anything

valuable. I'd bet on that. Then, too, we don't know for sure if Coty or the other guy killed her."

"Don't forget Mickey Townsend."

"I haven't." Murphy paced, her tail flicking with each step. "Mickey must know where Marylou is, though. Otherwise, why did he stop Coty from digging that night?" She paced some more. "But it doesn't feel right, Tucker. Mickey was in love with Marylou."

"Maybe at the last minute she thought Arthur was the better choice. Maybe she told him and he lost it and killed her—lover's passion," Tucker said soberly.

"I don't know, but you've got to go to Camden, Tucker. Mickey will be there. They'll all be there—and that's what scares me."

"I'll do my best."

"Go into that bedroom and put on a show."

Tucker trotted into Harry's bedroom. She'd placed her duffle bag on the floor. Her clothes lay on the bed and she was folding them.

Tucker crawled into the duffle bag. "Mom, you've got to take me."

"Tucker—" Harry smiled. "Get out of there."

Mrs. Murphy bounded on the bed. "Take her, Harry."

"Murphy—" Harry shooed her off a blouse. The cat sat on another one. "Now this is too much."

"Tucker needs to go with you."

"Yes, it's very important," the dog whined.

"Throw back your head and howl. That's impressive," the cat ordered.

Tucker threw back her pretty head, emitting a spine-tingling howl. "I wanna go!"

Harry knelt down and hugged the little dog. "Ah, Tucker, it's only for the weekend."

Tucker repeated her dramatic recitation. "I wanna go! Don't leave me here!"

"Oh, now, come on." Harry comforted the dog.

"Oo-oo-oo!"

"That's good." Mrs. Murphy moved to another blouse. If she

couldn't go she could at least deposit as much cat hair as possible on Harry's clothes.

"Well—" Harry weakened.

"*Oh, please, I'm the best little dog in the world. I won't make you walk me to go to the bathroom. I won't even eat. I'll be real cheap—*"

"That's pushing it, Tucker," Mrs. Murphy grumbled.

"*She's eating it up.*"

"Oh, Tucker, I feel so guilty about leaving you here."

"*Oo-oo-oo!*"

Harry picked up the phone by the bed and punched in Mim's number. "Hello, Mim. I have the unhappiest dog in front of me, curled up in my duffle bag. May I bring Tucker?" She listened to the affirmative reply. "Thank you. Thank you, too, for Tucker." Then she called Sally Dohner, who agreed to fill in for her at the post office.

"*Way to go!*" Mrs. Murphy congratulated her friend.

"*Oh, boy!*" Tucker jumped out of the duffle bag and ran around in small circles until she made herself dizzy and fell down.

"Now how did you know you were going?" Harry laughed at the dog. "Sometimes I think you two understand English." She petted Mrs. Murphy, who nestled down in a sweater. "I'm sorry, Murphy, but you know how you are on a long trip. You take care of Susan—she's going to spend the weekend here. She said she'd love a break from being a wife and mother." Harry sat on the bed. "Bet she brings the whole family with her anyway. Well, you know everyone."

"*Yes. I'll be a good kitty. Just tell her I want lots of cooked chicken.*"

"She even promised to fry pork chops for you."

"*Ooh, I love pork chops.*" Mrs. Murphy purred, then called out to Tucker: "*Tucker, you've got to remember everything you see, smell, or hear.*"

"*Got ya.*"

33

Camden, South Carolina, settled in 1758 and called Pine Tree Hill at that time, sits in a thermal belt, making it perfect for horsemen. While the air freezes, the sand does not, so in wintertime Thoroughbred breeders, trainers, chasers, hunters, and show horse people flock to the good footing and warmer temperatures. While not as balmy as Florida, Camden isn't as crowded either, nor as expensive.

Mrs. Marion duPont Scott had wintered in Camden, falling in love with the town. The relaxed people, blessed with that languid humor peculiar to South Carolina, so delighted her that she decided to use her personal wealth to create the Colonial Cup, a Deep South counterpoint to great and grand Montpelier. She developed a steeplechase course that allowed spectators in the grandstand to see most of the jumps, a novelty.

Over the years the races grew. The crowds poured in. The parties created many a wild scandal. The pockets of the citizens of Camden bulged.

The only bad thing that could be said about this most charming of upcountry towns in South Carolina is that it was the site of a Revolutionary War disaster on April 16, 1780, when General Horatio Gates, with 3,600 men, lost to Lord Cornwallis's 2,000 British troops. After that the British decided to enjoy thoroughly the comforts of Camden and the attentions of the female population, famed for their exquisite manners as well as their good looks.

Harry, thrilled to be a guest at the Colonial Cup, walked around Camden with her mouth hanging open. She and Miranda had decided to tour the town before heading over to the track. The races wouldn't commence until the following day, and they were like schoolgirls at recess. Harry dutifully asked Mim, then Charles, then Adelia, and even Fair if they needed her assistance. As soon as everyone said "No," she shot out of the stable, Tucker at her heels.

"I could get used to this." Harry smiled as she regarded a sweeping porch that wrapped around a stately white frame house. Baskets of flowers hung from the ceiling of the porch, for the temperature remained around 65°F.

"How I remember Mamaw sitting on her swing, passing and repassing, discussing at length the reason why she lined her walkway with hydrangeas and why her roses won prizes. Oh, I wish Didee were coming." Miranda used the childhood name for her sister. "That husband of hers is too much work."

"What husband isn't?"

"My George was an angel."

Harry fought back the urge to reply that he was now. Instead she said, "He had no choice."

Mrs. Hogendobber stopped. The crepe on the bottom of her

sensible walking shoes screeched, which made Tucker bark. That made the West Highland white on the wraparound porch bark. "Do I detect sarcasm?"

"Hush, Tucker."

"*I'm on duty here,*" Tucker stoutly barked right back. "*If that white moppet wants to run his mouth and insult us, I am not remaining silent.*"

"Will you shut up!"

"My husband listened better than your dog."

"Let's move on before every dog in the neighborhood feels compelled to reply. Tucker, I don't know why I brought you. You've been a real pain in the patoutee. You sniffed everything where we slept. You rushed up and down the barn aisles. You ran out in the paddocks. You dashed into every parked van. Are you on canine amphetamines?"

"*I'm searching for information. You're too dumb to know that. I'm not rushing around like a chicken with its head cut off. I have a plan.*"

"Apparently, Tucker isn't too pleased with you either," Mrs. Hogendobber noted.

"She'll settle down. Let's go on up the road. The second oldest polo field in the United States is there."

They walked down a sandy path; the railroad track lay to their right. Within moments the expanse of manicured green greeted them, a small white stable to one side. On the other side of the field were lovely houses, discreetly tucked behind large boxwoods and other bushes.

A flotilla of corgis poured across the field, shooting out of the opened gate of one of the houses. Tee Tucker stopped, her ears straight up, her eyes alert, her non-tail steady. She had not seen so many of her own kind since she was a puppy.

"*Who are you?*" they shouted as they reached midfield.

"*Tee Tucker from Crozet, Virginia. I'm here for the Colonial Cup.*"

Before the words were out of Tucker's lips the corgis swarmed around her, sniffing and commenting. Finally the head dog, a large red-colored fellow, declared, "*This is a mighty fine repre-*"

sentative of our breed. *Welcome to the great state of South Carolina. Might I invite you to our home for a refreshing drink or to meet my mistress, a lovely lady who would enjoy showing you Camden hospitality?"*

"Thank you, but I've got to stay close to Mom. On duty, you know."

"Why, yes, I understand completely. My name is Galahad, by the way, and these are my numerous offspring. Some were blessed with intelligence and others with looks." He laughed and they all talked at once, disagreeing with him.

"Have you ever seen so many corgis?" Mrs. Hogendobber watched all those tailless behinds wiggling in greeting.

"Can't say that I have," Harry said, laughing.

"Galahad," Tucker asked politely, *"have there been any murders at the Colonial Cup?"*

"Why, no, not in my recollection, although I think there were many who considered it, humans being what they are. Given their tendency to rely on copious libations for sociability—I'd say it was remarkable that they haven't dispatched one another into the afterlife."

"Oh, Daddy." One of the girls faced Tucker. *"He does go on. Why do you ask a thing like that?"*

"Well, there've been two steeplechase jockeys murdered since Montpelier. I was curious. You know, maybe it's not so unusual."

"Plenty unusual. Steeplechasing doesn't attract the riffraff that flat racing does," Galahad grumbled.

"These days, how can you tell riffraff from quality, Daddy?" the petite corgi asked, knowing full well what the answer would be.

"Bon sang ne sait mentir," came the growled reply.

"What's that?" Tucker's eyebrows quivered.

"Good blood doesn't lie."

"Ah, blood tells," Tucker said. She laughed to herself because that old saw drove Mrs. Murphy wild. Being an alley cat, she would spit whenever Tucker went off on a tangent about pure-bred dogs. *"Well, I am charmed to have met you all. As you can see, the humans are moving off. By the way, I'm staying at Hampstead Farm. If anything should pop into your heads, some stray thought about the racing folks, the 'chasers, I'd appreciate your getting word to me."*

"*You some kind of detective?*" the pretty little one asked.

"*Yes. Exactly.*" Tucker dashed to catch up with Harry and Miranda, hearing the oohs and aahs behind her. She neglected to tell them she worked with a partner, a cat. They'd never meet Mrs. Murphy, so what the heck?

34

Dr. Stephen D'Angelo's farm truck had been discovered in an abandoned barn near Meechum's River in western Albemarle County.

Rick Shaw and his department thoroughly searched the area, turning up nothing, not even a scrap of clothing.

"Think they ditched the truck and stole another?"

"We'd know. I put out a call to the local dealers and to other county departments. Nada. For the first day they were in their truck, the Nissan. After they got rid of D'Angelo's truck."

"By now they know we're on their trail. They've swapped off the Nissan," Coop said.

"That's more like it. No telling, though."

"Sooner or later someone was bound to find this truck."

She sighed. "Well, they've got two days' head start." Cynthia put on her gloves.

"They got it. They could have driven to any airport out of state by now or picked up the train. Or just kept driving. I expect those two have more fake IDs than a Libyan terrorist. They've got seventy-one dollars in cash." He squinted as a tiny sunburst of light reflected off the outside mirror. "Linda withdrew the money at one o'clock on the day they disappeared."

"Let's get this thing dusted for prints."

"Coop, you're methodical. I like that in a woman." He smiled. "Got your bags packed?"

"I always keep a bag packed, why?"

"We're going to Camden."

"No kidding."

"As spectators. If I notify the sheriff down there, it's one more department to fool with. They don't know what we do and I'm not inclined to tell them. It's enough that I have to handle Frank Yancey day in and day out."

"He's getting a lot of pressure from the newspaper." Her mind returned to Linda and Will. "The Forloines have a booming business. And there's someone higher up on the food chain."

"Right. You might want to wear your shoulder holster."

"Good idea."

35

Nerves tight before a race were stretched even tighter today. Fair Haristeen noticed the glum silence between the Valiants when he checked over Mim's horses early that morning.

Brother and sister worked side by side without speaking.

Arthur Tetrick stopped by on his way to the racecourse. He, too, noticed the frosty air between the siblings.

Addie, on sight of her guardian, practically spat at him. "Get out of my face, Arthur."

His eyebrows rose in a V; he inclined his head in a nod of greeting or acquiescence and left.

"Jesus, Addie, you're a bitch today." Charles whirled on her as Arthur shut the door to his car and drove out the sandy lane.

She looked into her brother's face, quite similar in bone structure to her own. "You, of course, are a prince among men!"

"What's that supposed to mean?"

"That you and Arthur are ganging up on me again. That I know he called on Judge Parker the day I spilled the beans about Nigel's stash. God, I was stupid. You'll both use it against me in court."

"This isn't the day to worry about stuff like that."

"You *knew* he went to see Parker, didn't you?"

"Uh"—Chark glanced outside, the sun filtered through the tall pines—"he mentioned it."

"Why didn't you tell me?"

"You'd had enough stress for one day."

"Liar."

"I'm not lying."

"You're withholding. It amounts to the same thing."

"Look who's talking. You lied to me about drugs. You withheld the truth about Nigel. A kilo is a lot of coke, Addie!"

"It wasn't for me!" she shouted.

"Then what were you doing with Nigel?"

"Dating him. Just because he was really into it doesn't mean I was, too."

"Come on, I'm not stupid."

She pointed her finger at him. "So what if I took a line or two. I'm okay. I stopped. This isn't about coke. It's about my money. You want my share."

"No, I don't." He pushed her finger away. "But I don't want to see you ruin everything Dad worked for. You have no sense of—" He struggled.

She filled in the word for him. "Responsibility?"

"Right." His eyes blazed. "We have to nurture that money. It seems like a lot but it can go faster than you think. You can't be cautious and we both know it."

"No risk, no gain."

"Addie." He tried to remain patient. "The only thing you know how to do is spend money. You don't know how to make it."

"Horses."

"Never."

"Then what are you doing as a trainer?" She was so frustrated tears welled up in her eyes.

"I get paid for training. I'm not running my own horses. Jesus, Addie, the board and vet bills alone will eat you alive. 'Chasing is for rich people."

"We *are* rich."

"Not if you try to be a major player overnight. We have to keep that money in solid stocks and bonds. If I can double the money in ten years, then we can think about owning a big string of our own."

"What's life for, Charles?" She used his proper name. "To hoard money? To read balance statements and call our stockbroker daily? Do we buy a sensible little farm or do we rent for ten years? Maybe I think life is an adventure—you take chances, you make mistakes. Hey, Chark, maybe you even lose money but you live."

"Live. You'll wind up with some bloodsucker who married you for your fortune. Then there'll be two of you squandering our inheritance."

"Not our inheritance. My inheritance. You take yours and I'll take mine. It's simple."

"I'm not going to let you ruin yourself."

"Well, brother, there's not a damn thing you can do about it." She stopped, blinked hard, then said in a low voice, "You could have killed Nigel. I don't put it past you." She drew close to his face. "I'll do one thing for you though. You're so worried about me? Well, this is my advice to you. Dump dear old Uncle Arthur. He's a dinosaur. And a very well-off dinosaur, thanks to Mom's will. He got his ten percent as executor. And after you dump the old fart, do something crazy, Chark. Something not useful. Buy a Porshe 911 or go to New York and party every night for a month. For once live your life. Just let go." She turned and walked outside.

He yelled after her, "I didn't kill Nigel Danforth!"

She cocked her head and turned back to face him. "Chark, for all I know you'll kill me, then you can have the whole ball of wax."

"I can't believe you said that." His face was white as a sheet.

"Well, I did. I've got races to run." She left him standing there.

36

The making of a good steeplechaser, like the making of a good human being, is an arduous melding of discipline, talent, luck, and heart. The best bloodlines in the world won't produce a winner, although they might fortify your chances.

Thoroughbreds a trifle too slow for the flat track find their way to the steeplechasing barns of the East Coast. Needing far more stamina than their flat-racing brethren, the 'chasers dazzle the equine world. Many a successful steeplechase athlete has retired to foxhunting, the envy of all who have beheld the creature soaring over fences, coops, ditches, and stone walls.

They gathered at the Springdale track for the $100,000 purse of the Colonial Cup, the last race in the season. After this race the points would be tallied, and the best trainer, horse, and jockey would emerge for the season.

Harry and Mrs. Hogendobber figured the most useful thing they could do was to keep Mim occupied despite her nervousness. They knew better than to disturb the Valiants before a race. Keeping Mim clear of them seemed a good policy.

Tucker, on a leash, complained, but Harry refused to release her. "You don't know where you are and you might get lost."

"Dogs don't get lost. People do."

"She's yappy this morning." Miranda, wearing her favorite plaid wraparound skirt and a white blouse with a red cable knit sweater, seemed the essence of fall.

"The crowd excites her."

"I'm on a recon mission. I need to chat up any animal who will talk to me."

Heedless of Tucker's tasks, Harry pulled her along to the paddock. After being dragged a few feet Tucker decided to give in and heel properly. If she couldn't have her way, she might as well make the best of it.

The lovely live oaks sheltered the paddock. The officials busied themselves in the final hour before the first race.

Colbert Mason spied Mrs. Hogendobber and waved to her. Miranda waved back.

Arthur bustled out of the small officials' office, his Worth and Worth trilby set at a rakish angle. Most of the other men wore hats, too: porkpies, cowboy hats, lads' caps in every imaginable fabric, and one distinguished navy blue homburg. The manufacturers of grosgrain ribbon would survive despite the dressing down of America. Horsemen had style.

The one blond uncovered head among the group belonged to Fair, who had ridden over in the van. He walked over to join his ex-wife and Miranda.

"May I get you ladies a drink or a sandwich?"

"No, but I'd like to sit a spell. This commotion is tiring." Miranda dumped herself on a park bench.

"Imagine how the horses feel." Fair sat next to her.

"Fair, make her let me go," Tucker implored.

He reached down and scratched those big ears. "You're so low to the ground, girl, I bet all these shoes and legs are bewildering."

"*No, they're not.*"

"Ignore her. She's whined and whimpered since the moment we arrived." Harry sternly raised her forefinger to the dog.

"You know, when we were married, I always wanted to bring you here, but somehow I never got the time."

"I'm here now."

"Do you like it?"

"It's wonderful. Miranda and I toured the town. I had no idea it was so lovely."

"People here know how to garden." Miranda's passion, apart from the choir and baking, was gardening. "I'm tempted to ask for cuttings."

"Bet they'd give them to you." Fair smiled. He put his arm around Harry's shoulders.

"Where's Mim?" she said. "We started out with her—"

"We drove over with her and Jim. That's not the same as starting out." Miranda chuckled. "That Mim, no sooner had we parked than she rocketed out of her car."

"Don't worry. Arthur headed her off before she could get to Addie and Chark. And Jim stuck right with her. He's the only one of us capable of dissuading Mim from her plans."

"She doesn't mean to lean on those youngsters." Mrs. Hogendobber stretched her legs out in front of her, wiggling her toes. She'd walked more in the last twenty-four hours than in the preceding month. "Oh, that feels good."

"Nerves," Harry succinctly said.

"There are plenty of owners worse than Mim. We practically had to tranquilize Marylou Valiant in the old days." He laughed.

"If I'd been dating Mickey Townsend I'd have to be tranquilized too." Harry giggled.

"I thought you liked Mickey." Miranda finally released her purse from her death grip and set it on the ground next to her.

"I do like Mickey. He's full of energy. He's got plenty of that burly masculine charm that Marylou could never resist. But he loses money at the races and doesn't pay his staff until he wins it back."

Fair crossed his arms over his chest. "If he'd married Marylou, he wouldn't have had those worries. Racing isn't for folks who need a weekly paycheck. Plus you need nerves of steel. He has them. I worry more about his temper than the money. He comes up with it somehow."

"It's the somehow I'm worried about," Harry said under her breath.

"Why?"

"Fair, two jockeys are under the ground and—" She looked up then blurted out, "What the hell—?"

Miranda, Fair, and Tucker turned their heads left in the direction of Harry's amazed look. "Gracious!" Miranda exclaimed.

"Bet you didn't recognize me in street clothes," Cynthia Cooper joked.

Fair, a gentleman, stood up and offered Cynthia Cooper his seat as she and Rick Shaw approached.

"Well, do I look the part?" Rick wore a plaid lad's cap, a tweed jacket, and baggy pants.

"Do you think you're incognito?" Harry smiled at him.

"You look splendid." Miranda praised the sheriff, a man with whom she might have disagreements but for whom her affection never dimmed.

Harry lowered her voice. "You know the Virginia gang will recognize you."

Cynthia replied, "Sure, we know that. We've never seen a steeplechase, and the boss here had an impulse, so . . . voilà!"

Harry, not believing a word of it, simply smiled. Rick and Cynthia were aware none of the three believed them; probably Tucker didn't either, but they'd go along with the story.

Loud voices at the paddock grabbed their attention.

"You're behind this—" Chark's voice rose.

He shut up when Mickey's fist jammed into his mouth.

Within seconds the two men were knocking the stuffing out of each other.

Fair, Cynthia, and Rick rushed over. Tucker lunged to help but Harry held on to the leash.

"I'll kill you, you dumb son of a bitch," Mickey cursed, then landed a right to the breadbasket. "You're too stupid to know who's on your side and who isn't."

"With you as a friend I don't need enemies." Chark gasped, then caught Mickey on the side of the head with a glancing blow. He reeled back, going down on one knee. The St. Christopher's medal fell out of his pocket, face down on the grass.

Rick and Cynthia deftly stepped between the two men. Rick grabbed Mickey as Cynthia pulled Chark's left arm up behind his back and put a hammer lock around his throat.

"Easy, Chark. Let's end this before it gets a whole lot worse." Cynthia's regulation size .357 Magnum flashed as her blazer opened up. Chark couldn't see it, but as she pressed against him he could feel it. He immediately stopped struggling.

Mickey, however, didn't. Fair stepped in and he and Rick took Mickey down together.

"Goddammit, man." Fair shook his head. "Things are bad enough."

Mickey tried to shake them off. "Bad ain't the word. Let me go." He saw the medal and reached over to pick it up. Fair held him. Rick picked up the medal and handed it to Mickey.

Chark noticed but the object didn't fully register at that moment.

Two uniformed police officers arrived at the scene and brusquely told Cynthia, Rick, and Fair to step back. Then the skinny one noticed her gun.

"You got a license to carry that, ma'am?"

"Deputy Cynthia Cooper, Albemarle County Sheriff's department. I'd shake your hand but I'm occupied. Until you all can talk sense into Mickey Townsend there, I'll remain occupied. We can be formally introduced later."

"Want some help with the perp?" the cop asked Cynthia using the shorthand for perpetrator.

"I'll take care of him. Thanks."

"Coop, I'm okay. I lost my temper." Chark sighed. "Why go out of my way to piss on a skunk?"

"Can't comment on that. Come on, I'll walk you back to the weigh-in. Okay?"

"Yeah. On the way you can tell me what you're doing here."

"A first-class chickenshit!" Mickey, oblivious to the crowd around him, spat out the words as Chark walked away.

Fair whispered, "Mickey, shut up."

"Huh?" Fair's words filtered through the hammer pounding in Mickey's brain.

"Two jockeys who owed you money are dead. No one believes you were playing Old Maid. Chill out," Fair warned.

Mickey shut up.

Rick turned to the two uniformed cops. "This man lives in my county. Nothing to worry about." The two cops nodded and watched Rick and Fair walk away, Mickey between them, the crowd bubbling about what they'd just witnessed.

"You're bullshitting me," Mickey said under his breath to Rick. "You don't know one end of a horse from the other."

"Mickey, you are your own worst enemy." Fair shook his head.

"It's obvious, isn't it?" Mickey spoke to the vet he used and trusted. "Rick Shaw's here to spy on me. Everyone thinks I killed Nigel and Coty. Dammit! Why the hell would I kill my own jockey?"

"You tell me," Rick said.

"I didn't! That's the long and short of it." Mickey's handsome face sagged, and he suddenly appeared old.

"Lying takes so much energy. Just tell the truth," Rick said nonchalantly. "You knew Nigel didn't have a green card. Let's start there."

"Ah, man, give me a break." Mickey squared his shoulders, looking his forty-five years again. "I don't give a shit if the guy had a polka-dot card. He knew how to ride a horse. And don't give me this crap about protecting American workers or protecting abused immigrants. I didn't abuse anyone, and if an American worker can do the job as well as the limey, hey, he's hired. Screw the government."

He was so incorrigible, Rick and Fair had to laugh.

"Mickey, if you'd just give it to me straight I wouldn't have to see you as a prime suspect."

Mickey looked up at Fair imploringly. "Suspect for what?"

"Just talk to the man," Fair said in an even tone.

Mickey gazed over the tops of their heads, over the tops of the trees, all the way up to a robin's-egg-blue sky. "All right."

37

With a half hour to the first race, Mickey Townsend asked if he might give directions to his jockey, obviously new to the job.

Fair had returned to the paddocks.

Cynthia and Rick walked along with Mickey, Cynthia flipping open her notebook as they headed back to his horses.

"I will tell you everything, but I've got to see the races."

"That's fine," Rick said. "You're not under arrest—yet. You've got enough time to start talking before the first race."

Mickey exhaled deeply, shut his eyes, and then opened them. "Nigel Danforth owed me two thousand dollars, give or take, on a gambling debt—not horses, poker. Coty Lamont owed me over seven thousand from last season. I owe Harvey Throgmorton five and a half grand. His wife had her first child, he's had a bad-luck year with the horses, and he needs the money. I want to pay him off. I didn't kill Nigel and I didn't kill Coty Lamont." He took another deep breath, involuntarily clasping and unclasping his hands. "I got a little crazy. I thought about beating them up, and Coty really pissed me off. He promised to pay me, and—that was on the night he was killed or early that morning. I'd heard one lie too many. I don't know . . . when he didn't show up at my barn at ten that night as agreed, I roared on over to his house. To make a long story short, I threatened him, pulled a gun, told him he'd better pay me by morning or he would be history." He walked over to the cooler and plucked a soft drink out for himself. "Want some?"

"No, thanks."

"All this talking makes me thirsty." Mickey popped the top and drank. "I left. What he didn't figure on was that I'd wait for him. I waited at the end of the driveway behind a big bush, had my lights off. When he drove out of there about half an hour later, I tailed him. Guess I've seen too many cop shows. Anyway, I followed him to Mim Sanburne's stable. He didn't drive in, though, which was the weird thing. He left his truck behind the old Amoco station about half a mile from her main gate. But here's what really made me wonder—he covered his license plate with a rag or something. Josh at the Amoco is always fixing cars, I mean the lot is always full of stuff, but Coty covered up that license plate.

"He didn't hear me because I stayed way far behind, far enough to muffle my motor, and then I cut it. About twenty minutes later I ran out of patience, so I walked into Mim's myself. Had my gun. I found him in the stable. He had her hunter in the crossties. I walked over to the stall, scared the shit out of him. He'd been digging in the corner of the stall. I asked him what the hell was he doing and he said getting my money. I asked him what was down there and he said pirate's treasure, real smartass, you know. I was so mad, I said, 'Cover the hole back up, you're jerking me around—if there was anything of value down there you'd have claimed it by now.' Coty always thought people were stupid, that he could stay one step ahead. He was about to tell me something but then he shut up and we both got scared for a minute because we heard a noise. Turned out it was nothing but mice in the hayloft. You know, when it's real quiet at night you hear things like their feet, those little claws. Damnedest thing.

"Well, he filled the hole back in. He hadn't gotten very deep anyway. Put the horse back in the stall. I walked him out to my car by the road, then drove him back to his truck and told him he had until five o'clock before I took his truck as collateral.

"That was the last I saw of Coty Lamont." Pale, he finished his soda, then said as an afterthought, "Doesn't look too good for me, does it?"

"No," Rick said.

"If you're telling the truth, you'll be all right," Cynthia added.

"Do you know about the coke?" Rick listened as the call to the first race was announced.

"Uh—" Mickey stalled.

"Were they users?" Rick asked.

"Yes."

"Are you?"

"I wouldn't have lasted this long in the business if I were hooked on that stuff."

"Do you know who sells it?"

"Sheriff, it's not hard to get."

"That's not what I'm asking."

"Linda Forloines."

"Thank you, Mickey. After the races you'd best go back to Albemarle County and not leave without checking in with me. Go on, the first race is about to start."

Mickey rose, his knees cracking. He walked to the course, his hands deep in his pockets, his fingers wrapped around Marylou's medallion. He was tempted to tell Cynthia and Rick, sorely tempted, but he'd keep the St. Christopher's medal a secret for a little bit longer.

Cynthia flipped her notebook shut. "You believe him?"

"You know better than to ask me something like that."

"Yeah, but I always do, don't I?"

╔══════════╗
║ **38** ║
╚══════════╝

The light breeze made Arthur Tetrick's sky-blue official's ribbon flap. His brisk walk assisted the flapping.

Chark and Addie sat behind the weigh-in station. As they had no horse in the first race they watched everyone else.

"Are you all right?" Arthur asked, noticing Chark's swollen lip.

"I'm embarrassed." Chark ignored the dribble from his bleeding lip.

"What happened?"

"Mickey Townsend acted like Mickey Townsend." Chark spoke ruefully. "I walked out of the official's tent and bumped into him. By mistake. I wasn't looking where I was going. I've got Ransom Mine on my mind, you know. He made some crack about how I excel at the bump and run. He's still pissed off about the Maryland Hunt Cup last year. 'Course, I'm a little tense . . .''

"That's the understatement of the year." Addie spoke out of the side of her mouth.

He held up his hands in supplication. "I saw red. No excuses. I was wrong. I made a spectacle of myself."

"No harm done. I'll head off Mim if I can." Arthur checked his watch. "Hmm. I take that back. I'll try to find Harry and Miranda. Maybe they can keep Mim occupied so you don't have to go over the whole story again. Or get chewed out."

Chark winced as Addie dabbed at his lip with a handkerchief. She couldn't stand the dripping blood anymore. "I'm so ashamed."

"If I had half a chance I'd like to thrash him myself."

Addie peered up at Arthur. "I still like Mickey. You two will never cut him a break."

Arthur snapped, "Mickey Townsend cares for nobody but Mickey Townsend. For reasons I will never fathom he casts a spell over the female of the species."

"Yeah, sure." Addie threw down the hankie. "Arthur, I know you went to see Judge Parker."

Arthur's face clouded. "Just a formality."

"No, it wasn't. You were filing papers to extend your trusteeship."

"I did no such thing." He glared at her. "You inherit your fortune at midnight on your birthday . . . tomorrow night. The paperwork will be done on Monday. That's why I went to see Judge Parker."

"You think I'm not competent. Because of the drugs."

Arthur lowered his voice. "This is neither the time nor the place! But Adelia, I have come to the mournful conclusion that I can do nothing to help you. You may not believe me, but I will be relieved to no longer be your trustee or the executor of your mother's will. I wash my hands of you." He drew in a gulp of sweet air. "I only hope your mother will forgive me if she's looking down upon us."

"What rot." Addie left them. She needed to push everything and everybody out of her mind to concentrate on the horses and the course. Each time she saw Arthur or talked to her brother, she felt she was being pulled back into a white-hot rage. This was the first race without Nigel, and that hit her harder than she thought it would.

Arthur followed her with his eyes, then sadly said, "Well, I've upset her. I didn't mean to but . . ."

"She started it."

"So she did, Charles, but I'm old enough to know better."

"You're right about Mickey though. He twisted Mom around his little finger and Addie thought he could do no wrong. Know what else I don't get?" Chark stood up, found he was a trifle shaky, and started to sit back down.

"Here, Chark, you're hurt." Arthur put his hand under Chark's arm to steady him.

"I'm shook up, not hurt. I can't believe I lost control like that."

"You're too hard on yourself." Arthur discreetly glanced at his wristwatch, then sat next to Chark for a moment. "Now, what is it that you don't understand? You lost your train of thought."

"If Mom was so in love with Mickey, why did she refuse to marry him?"

"Ah—" Arthur tipped back his head. "I'd like to think because she knew it wouldn't work in the long run."

"Addie says it was because I didn't like Mickey. Makes me feel guilty as hell."

"Oh, now—"

"You know how she was. She'd do anything for Addie. I used to beg her to marry you. Funny, isn't it?"

"Not to me," Arthur said sadly.

"I used to scream at her that Mickey was a gold digger.

When I think of the stuff I said to my mother," he hung his head, covering his eyes, "I feel so terrible."

Arthur put his arm around Chark. "There, there. You're overwrought. You were young. She forgave you. Mothers always do, you know."

Chark shook his head. "I know, but—"

"Let's talk about something pleasant. I picked up Adelia's birthday cake. It's three tiers high since I figured everyone will wind up back at Mim's place anyway. It's got a jockey's cap on it, Mim's colors, with two crossed whips. Chocolate inside, vanilla icing on the outside. Her favorite."

"That's great, Arthur—just great."

"Big birthday, twenty-one." His own twenty-first had receded into memory, a kind of warm blur. "I've got to go. I'll do my best to find Harry or Mim before I take up my post."

"Thanks."

"Don't mention it." Arthur walked away, the sandy soil crunching underfoot.

39

Addie found Mickey under a huge sweet gum tree on the back side of the course. His stopwatch in his hand, he furtively checked between it and the announcer's stand.

"You mad at me, too?" he said.

"Nah." She drew alongside him.

" 'Bout five more minutes," he said.

"You might win this race."

"Oh, I might win every race." He smiled weakly. "Just depends who the gods smile on that day, right?"

"I think it depends upon the brilliance of the jockey and the heart of the horse."

"That helps." He shifted his weight from one foot to the other. "Do you know why Nigel and Linda beat each other up at the Montpelier Races? He never would tell me, and I think it might be why he's dead."

"Nigel bought a kilo of cocaine from Linda. Or at least I thought he bought it. He was going to sell it to pay off debts, yours being one, and then buy a little place and start training horses himself. He said he knew he couldn't be a jockey forever."

"Yeah, well, you don't just go from being a jockey to being a trainer." Mickey folded his arms across his chest. "Think he was hooked?"

"No."

"Did you tell the sheriff?"

"Finally I did. I mean, I'm in a lot of trouble because I stashed the kilo in my safe deposit box."

"Addie—"

"Yeah, well, I told them that, too. They've impounded it."

Mickey chewed the inside of his lip. "What else did you tell them?"

"Not any more than I had to. Look, just because you're a riverboat gambler doesn't mean you killed anybody. It wasn't enough money to kill someone over."

"What do you think?"

"No way." She grinned.

"Tell you one thing, pretty girl." He felt protective toward Addie, who reminded him a lot of Marylou. "We need a soothsayer to help us."

"Soothsayer won the Eclipse Award. Hell, if we had a soothsayer life would be perfect."

He laughed. "You're too young to remember that horse."

Her face darkened a moment. "There's one thing I did lie about, though."

"Huh?" His senses sharpened.

"Nigel never paid for the cocaine. He said he'd pay as soon as he sold it. He only paid for about a fourth of it. I told Sheriff

Shaw that Nigel paid for it." She helplessly held up her hands. "I don't know why I lied."

"Addie!" He blanched.

"I don't want Linda coming after me." Her face flushed. "If Linda thinks I set her up, hey . . ." She didn't need to finish the thought.

Mickey rolled his shoulders forward and back, something he did to relax his muscles. "She's in so much shit. Hell, they know she sells it. She's a suspect with or without your help."

"Selling ain't killing. You coming to my birthday party?" She fell in with his step.

"No."

"I'll talk to Chark."

"Don't. Let well enough alone, Adelia. I'd be a wet blanket."

"Oh, please come. You'd make me happy." She sighed. "Be a lot happier if Nigel were still here."

He patted her on the back. "Believe it or not, honey, I know how you feel. There isn't a day that goes by that I don't miss your mother." He waited, cleared his throat. "Addie, you aren't the only person withholding information from the sheriff." He reached into his pocket, placing the beautiful St. Christopher's medal into Adelia's hand.

She stared, blinked, then the tears gushed over her cheeks. She brought the medal to her lips, kissing it. "Oh, no. Oh, no." Although she knew her mother must be dead, the medal brought home the full force of the loss; not a vestige of hope remained.

"Where did you get this?" she whispered.

Mickey, crying too, said, "From Nigel Danforth's down jacket." He explained the whole sequence of events to her. "This will lead us to her murderer. My gut tells me it wasn't Nigel. But how did he get this medal?"

"Mickey, let me have it."

"After we flush out the rat."

"No. Let me have it now. I want to wear it just like Mom did."

"Addie, it's too dangerous."

"Please. You can stick close to me. I want Mom's medal, and I want everyone to see it."

40

Despite being on a leash, Tucker wiggled with excitement. The smells alone thrilled her: aromas of baked ham, smoked turkey, roast beef, and fried chicken mingled with the tang of hot dogs, hamburgers, and mustard. Three-bean salad, seven-layer salad, simple cole slaw, and rich German potato salad emitted a fragrance not as tantalizing as the meats, but food was food and Tucker wasn't picky. The brownies, angel food cakes, pound cakes with honey drizzled on top, and pumpkin pies smelled enticing, too. The sour mash whiskey, bracing single malt scotches, sherries, port, gin, and vodkas turned her head away because these odors stung her nostrils and her eyes.

For Tucker, the Colonial Cup was a kaleidoscope of smells and of more people than she could possibly greet. Tucker knew her social obligations. She was to rush out and sniff each human nearing her mother. If she knew them, she would wag her non-existent tail. If she didn't, she'd bark her head off, the cheapest and most effective alarm system yet devised. But with thousands of people swarming about, she couldn't bark at everyone. Instead she practiced her steely gaze technique. If someone approached Harry, she braced herself, never removing her eyes from the person's face. Once she felt sure the person was not going to lunge for Harry or Mrs. Hogendobber, she relaxed.

Although bred for herding, corgis are also mindful of their special human and will defend that person to the best of their ability. In Tee Tucker's opinion the best dog for human defense was and ever would be a chow chow. Fanatically devoted to their masters, chows first growled a warning and then, if the warning was ignored, the dog would nail the potential attacker, whether it was another canine, a human, or whatever. Tucker wasn't that ferocious but she was devoted to Harry. Sometimes she wished Harry had another dog. Mrs. Murphy could be so superior some-times, and she hated it when the cat looked down at her from a table or a countertop. She loved Murphy, but she couldn't play rough with her or the cat would shred her sensitive nose.

"Mother, these tailgates tempt me. If I have to walk by you, you should beg food for me."

The day had warmed up, and the time between races was more exhausting than the races themselves. Miranda, parched from the dust and the sun, pulled Harry toward a drink stand.

Harry longingly viewed the bar set out on the back of a station wagon, but since she didn't know the jolly people cele-brating the sunshine, the horses, the day, and one another, she moved on, to the stand.

"I thought Fair wasn't going to work this race," Miranda said.

"You know how that goes." Harry bought a Coke, glanced down at her panting pooch, and asked for an empty paper cup.

She walked over to the water fountain, filled it up, and Tucker happily slurped.

"Guess being married to a vet is like being married to a doctor."

"I'm not married to him."

"Oh, will you stop."

"Yes, it's like being married to a doctor, and Fair is so conscientious. He works on animals whether the people pay or not. I mean, they always tell him they're going to pay, but they don't. If an animal is in trouble, he's there."

"Isn't that why you loved him?"

"Yes." Harry finished her Coke.

"Mmm." Miranda watched the three jockeys, their silks brilliant, standing in the paddock.

Harry followed her gaze, particularly noticing one wiry fellow, hand on hip, crop in hand. "Funny, isn't it? Those behemoth football players get paid a fortune and we worship them for their strength, but these guys have more courage. Women, too. Pure guts, gristle, and brains out there."

"Well, I've never understood how—" Miranda stopped. "Harry, is it rude to talk to jockeys before they ride? I would guess it is."

"They aren't up next. I recognize the silks."

Miranda charged over to the three men. One looked much younger than the others—about sixteen. "Excuse me," she said.

Tucker bounded forward, surprising Harry, who was pulled off balance.

"Ma'am." The eldest of the three, a man in his middle forties, removed his cap.

"Did you know Nigel Danforth?" Miranda demanded.

"I did." The teenager spoke up.

"This may sound like an odd question, but, did you like him?"

"Didn't really know him." The older man spoke up quickly. The youngest one, in flame-orange silks with two black hoop bands on each sleeve, said, "He acted like he was better than the rest of us."

Harry smiled. That English accent set off people every time.

As if reading her thoughts, the middle jockey, twenty-five or so, added, "It wasn't his accent, which sounded phony to me. He used to strut about, cock of the walk. And brag."

"That he was a better rider?" Harry joined in.

"No," the younger one said. "That he was going to marry Addie Valiant. Addie deserves better than that."

"Yes, she does," Harry agreed.

Now the oldest jockey, in deep green silks with pale blue circles on them, decided to talk. "Don't get me wrong. None of us hated him enough to kill him, and he wasn't a dirty rider, so you have to give the man credit for that, but there was something about him, something shifty. You'd ask him a question, any question, and he'd dance around it like he needed time to think of an answer."

"What did Addie see in him?" the youngest one asked, eyebrows quizzical. His longing tone betrayed a crush on Addie.

Miranda, in her "Dear Abby" voice, replied, "She wasn't thinking clearly. She would have come to her senses."

"Why do you want to know about Nigel Danforth?" the older man asked.

Harry jumped in. "Guess we were as curious as you all were—we couldn't figure out what she saw in him either."

They exchanged a few more words, then Harry, Miranda, and Tucker hastened to the small paddock where jockeys mounted their horses before they were led out onto the track.

Addie, riding for a client other than Mim in this race, walked around led by Chark. Her mother's medal gleamed on her neck. She had the top button of her silks undone. Chark, taut before the race and upset over Mickey Townsend as well as his argument with his sister, didn't notice.

Colbert Mason, the Sanburnes, Fair Haristeen, Arthur Tet-

rick, Mickey Townsend, Rick Shaw, and Cynthia Cooper, plus
hundreds of others, observed the horses. Within a few minutes
they'd be called toward the starting cord.

Miranda's mouth fell open. "It can't be," she half-
whispered.

"What?" Harry leaned toward her.

"Look at Adelia's neck."

Harry peered, the light bouncing off the royal blue enamel.
"Some kind of medal. I don't remember it. Must be an early
birthday present."

"No early present. I'd know that medal anywhere. It was
Marylou's. She never took it off her neck after Charley died. Not
even for fancy balls. She'd drape her rubies and diamonds over
it."

Harry focused on the medal. "Uh—yes, now that you mention it. I recall Marylou wearing that."

Mim, across the paddock, also stared at the medal. She
grabbed Jim's arm.

Mim, Miranda, and Jim converged on Rick Shaw, pulling
him away from the rail and possible eavesdroppers.

Once he persuaded them to talk in sequence, he listened
intently as did Deputy Cooper.

"You don't know if it's the exact medal. Someone could
have given her a replica," Rick said.

"Flip it over." Mim's lips were white from emotion.

"Even if it carries the same message, it could be a replica."
Rick pursued his line of thought.

"It was made by Cartier expressly for Marylou." Mim
wrung her hands.

"I appreciate this. I really do. After the races we can ask
Adelia to remove the medal so you all can have a closer look, and
she can tell us where she got it." Rick hoped the medal was
meaningful, but he needed to keep Marylou's old friends calm.
He wanted to approach this evidence quietly and sensibly.

"The minute the Colonial Cup is run." Mim was pleading, unusual for her.

"I promise," Rick said firmly.

The trumpet called contestants from the paddocks to the track.

Harry, Mrs. Hogendobber, the Sanburnes, and Tucker raced to the stands. The horses lined up, the cord sprang loose, and they shot off. Addie hung in the pack, easily clearing the fences, but on the second lap the horse was bumped over a fence and lost a stride or two. She couldn't make it up by the finish line, and they were out of the money.

As the humans hollered and exchanged money among themselves, Tucker, happy to see another dog come up into the stands, a jaunty Jack Russell, called out, "Hello."

"Hi," the Jack Russell answered. "I hope we sit near one another. I've had about all the humans I can stand. My name is The Terminator."

"Mine is Tucker."

Fortunately, the owner, a nervous-looking, thin, middle-aged woman, took a seat in front of Tucker. "This is good luck. Are you with anyone in the races?"

"Mim Sanburne," Tucker replied.

"She might win the cup this year," the Russell said sagely. "My human, ZeeZee Thompson—she's a trainer, you know—thinks Mim has a good chance. In fact, my human has been in the top five trainers in winnings for the last ten years."

"Oh." Tucker sounded impressed.

"ZeeZee used to ride in England, but she took a bad fall, ruptured her spleen and damaged her liver plus she broke some ribs. So as soon as she recovered, she learned how to train."

"She must have known Nigel Danforth in England."

The Terminator paused, lowering her voice. "Nigel Danforth is no more a Brit than you or I, my friend. My mother's afraid to talk about him 'cause of the murders, you see. She doesn't want to be next."

"Is she in danger?" Tucker surged forward on her leash. Harry

paid no attention, so Tucker moved next to the smooth-coated Jack Russell.

"I hope not, but you see, she is the only person who knows where Nigel came from, and if the killer figures that out, she might be in trouble."

"The killer's only taking out jockeys." Tucker comforted the other dog.

"I don't know, but whoever is doing this knows 'chasing inside and out."

"How did your mother know Nigel Danforth?"

"Montana. One summer—I guess it must have been six years ago, when I was a puppy—we went out to Bozeman. He was a ranch hand, but he was good with a horse. Mom told him the money back East was better than punching cows. He had a full mustache and beard then. Men look real different to humans when they shave them off. They smell the same, of course."

"What was his real name? Do you remember that?"

"Sargent Wilcox." Tucker's eyes widened as the little dog continued. "I sure hope my mother is safe. Wilcox only worked for Mom for a little bit. He was too wild for her."

Tucker hoped so, too, because she was beginning to get the picture, not the whole picture but the very beginning, and it was terrifying.

41

The Colonial Cup, for which they had waited, was about to be run.

Mim joined her husband, Harry, Mrs. Hogendobber, and Fair in the box in the grandstand. She'd run up from the paddock where she'd smiled at Addie and wished her well, all the while keeping her eyes on the St. Christopher's medal. When Chark gave his sister a leg up, Mim returned to the grandstand for fear her own nerves would make the Valiants agitated. Her beige suede outfit topped with her ubiquitous Hermes scarf showed not a wrinkle, crease, or stain despite her dashing about. She sat down, jaw tight. Little Marilyn would have gladly tightened the scarf around her mother's neck. She hated it when Mim tensed up like this, so she sat with ZeeZee Thompson down the aisle.

No one spoke. Not even Tucker, who sat motionless in Harry's lap.

Addie, shimmering in purple silks, circled on Bazooka, then came into the starting area. The yellow rope stretched across the track. The horses lined up, prancing sideways and snorting. Then twang—the rope snapped back—and off they shot.

Bazooka gunned out front. Chark, down near the starting area, ran back toward the grandstand for a better view and in the process ran into Mickey Townsend again. He said he was sorry and kept going, leaving Mickey to dust himself off. The horse Mickey trained, a client's from West Virginia, was in the middle of the pack.

"She's on too fast a pace," Mim murmured through the tension-narrowed slit that was her mouth.

"Don't fret, honey. Addie knows what she's doing."

Arthur Tetrick, up in the race director's box for this one, stood, mouth hanging open. He peeked over Colbert Mason's shoulder at the big digital timer. "She'll never make it."

"A scorcher," Colbert laconically replied.

Bazooka's stride lengthened with every reach of his black hooves. Addie appeared motionless on top of him, moving only as they landed after each successful jump.

Try as it might, no horse could get near her. The race, so perfect, seemed like a dream to Addie's cheering section. The crowd screamed as much in disbelief as in excitement.

At the next to last fence, Bazooka vaulted over, another perfect landing, and four strides after the fence Addie and the saddle slipped off and under Bazooka. She hit the ground with a thud.

If she'd fallen off at a jump she would have been thrown clear. But the saddle dropped to the left side and slightly underneath Bazooka. His left hind hoof grazed her head. She rolled into a ball.

One fractious horse, seeing Addie on the ground, exploded. The rider fought hard but the animal plunged right over the fallen jockey.

Bazooka crossed the finish line first just as the ambulance reached an unconscious Addie on the track.

42

Chark, with Mickey Townsend not far behind, tore down the grass track. Arthur Tetrick blasted out of the booth and ran down the concrete grandstand steps faster then anyone thought possible.

Huge Jim Sanburne was immediately behind them. Fair was already on the track on the other side of the finish line. An outrider led Bazooka over to him.

Rick Shaw grabbed Cynthia Cooper's arm as they ran out from the tailgate section.

"I should have seen it coming. Damn me!" He cursed. "You stay here. You know what to do. I'll ride in the ambulance."

"I'll finish up at Hampstead Farm."

"Right." He flashed his badge at a shocked track official and sprinted out to the ambulance, where Addie's unconscious form was being carefully slid into the back. Chark, tears in his eyes, hopped in with her.

Arthur reached the ambulance the same time Rick did. "Sheriff." Rick opened his badge for the ambulance attendants. "Arthur, go back to the booth and get me a video of this race. Now!"

"Yes, of course." Arthur turned and ran back to the grandstand, passing the two slow-moving Camden police.

"Jim, get her saddle. See that no one touches it but you. Hurry before some do-gooder gets there first," Rick commanded.

Jim, without comment, lurched toward the next to last jump.

"Mickey, go find Deputy Cooper. She'll be in the paddock . . . help her. You know these people. They'll talk to you."

"You got it." Mickey peeled off toward the paddock, jumping the track rail in his hurry.

"Chark, I'm coming with you." He hoisted himself into the back of the ambulance.

The driver's assistant closed the heavy door behind them. With its flashers turned on, the vehicle rolled along the side of the track. The driver, savvy about horses, would save his siren until they reached the highway.

"Who saddled the horse?" Rick waved to the gesticulating policemen.

"I did." Chark held his sister's hand.

"Where do you keep your tack?"

"At the stalls."

"Hampstead Farm?"

"No, no—the stalls at the track. We pick up the saddle pad number, we draw for position first, then we saddle up."

"Wouldn't be hard for someone to mess with the saddle or the—" Rick stopped to think of the term.

"Girth," Chark said.

"Girth, yes."

"Yes, but I saddled Bazooka. I'd have seen it." He squeezed

his sister's hand, the tears coming down his face. He reached over and touched the St. Christopher's medal, turning it over. "What in God's name . . ." he whispered.

"What is it?"

"This is Mother's. We haven't seen it since the day she disappeared." He stared, uncomprehending, at Rick.

The emergency rescue worker held Adelia's head firmly between her hands. If Addie's neck were broken, one bump could make a bad situation very much worse.

Rick, on his knees, bent over. He read aloud the inscription: *He's my stand-in. Love, Charley*

"Dad gave that to Mom the year they were married."

"And you haven't seen this since your Mother disappeared?"

"No."

Rick sat back on his haunches as the ambulance sped to the hospital.

"Sheriff."

"Huh?" Rick's mind was miles away.

"Whoever had this killed my mother."

Rick reached over and put his hand on Chark's shoulder. He said nothing, but he was praying hard, praying that Adelia would live, praying she wouldn't be paralyzed, and praying he could persuade Camden's police to provide twenty-four-hour protection until she could be moved to Albemarle County.

"Charles, you understand that my job forces me to ask unseemly questions."

"I do, sir."

"Could your sister have killed your mother?"

"Never." Chark's voice was level even as the tears kept flowing.

"Adelia comes into her majority tomorrow. Did you want her dead?"

"No," Chark whispered, shaking his head.

"What about Arthur Tetrick? Would he gain by your sister's death?"

Chark regained his voice, "No. His term as executor expires tomorrow at midnight. Even if"—he choked—"she doesn't make it, he has nothing to gain."

"Do you have any idea who would do this?"

"I can only think of one person. Linda Forloines. Because of the cocaine."

"We thought she might show up. Disguised. It's a bit far-fetched, but"—he squeezed Chark's shoulder—"we were worried."

"She could have paid someone to do this."

"Yes. Deputy Cooper is working over the officials and jockeys pretty hard right about now."

"Sheriff, I had a stupid fight with Addie. If anything should happen—" he covered his eyes, "I couldn't live. I couldn't."

"She's going to be okay." Rick lied, for he couldn't know. "You'll have plenty of time to mend your fences."

Rick looked imploringly at the rescue-squad woman, who looked down at Addie.

43

A small incident occurred during the questioning of track personnel, owners, trainers, and jockeys.

When Jim Sanburne brought Addie's light, small racing saddle to Deputy Cooper, Mickey Townsend reached for it and Arthur Tetrick slammed him across the chest with a forearm.

They slapped each other around until the men in the paddock quickly separated them.

"He's trying to smear the prints," Arthur protested.

"No, I wasn't!" Mickey shouted from the other side of the paddock.

After they quieted down, Cynthia resumed her questioning. Harry and Miranda helped by organizing people in a line and by quickly drawing up a checklist of who was in the paddock area.

Fair turned Bazooka over to a groom after checking the animal thoroughly for injury. As a precaution he drew blood to see if Bazooka could have been doped. An amphetamine used on a horse as high octane as Bazooka was a prescription for murder. He conferred with a reputable local equine vet, an acquaintance, Dr. Mary Holloway. She took the vial, jumped into her truck, and headed for the lab.

Fair reached the paddock and joined Coop. "What can I do?"

"Got a pair of rubber gloves?"

"Right here." He pulled the see-through gloves from his chest pocket.

"Inspect the saddle, will you? But be careful—remember, it has to be fingerprinted. Jim Sanburne, Chark and Addie will have prints on the saddle. We're looking for—well, you know."

"I'll be careful." Fair picked up the saddle, lifted the small suede flap. The leathers, beltlike with buckles, were solid on both sides. Then he inspected the girth, torn in two. "That's how they did it." He flipped over the girth and could see on the underside the razor cut, which ran its width. As the outside of the girth was not cut, someone could tighten the girth and not realize it was cut underneath.

"Would someone need to know a lot about horses or racing to do that?" Cooper asked.

"It would help. But with a little direction anyone could do it."

Troubled, Coop pressed her lips together. "Next."

A slight young man stepped forward. "Randy Groah. I ride for Michael Stirling here in Camden."

"Where were you before the last race?"

As Cynthia questioned, Harry wrote down everyone's statistics, name, address, phone number, etc. . . .

Tucker, having easily slipped her collar, followed The Terminator. They checked the changing room, hospitality tents, and the on-site stables. They turned up nothing except for doughnut crumbs, which they ate, certain the food had nothing to do with the case.

A long, low whistle stopped the Jack Russell. "*That's my mom.*"

"*I'll follow you over.*" Tucker trotted alongside her feisty new friend.

"Terminator, let's go." ZeeZee clapped her hands.

"*I'll walk along for a bit.*" Tucker fell in beside The Terminator.

They reached the stables, where ZeeZee's Explorer was parked in front.

"Come on, Term." She scooped up the little guy and put him on the passenger seat.

"*Good luck,*" the Jack Russell called out.

"*You, too.*" Tucker scampered back to the paddock while ZeeZee peeled out of there.

Three and a half hours later Harry, Miranda, Fair, and Cynthia Cooper finished questioning jockeys and track officials. The Sanburnes left for the hospital as soon as Cynthia dismissed them. Mim had told Coop about the St. Christopher's medal, and Miranda confirmed it.

Coop stopped by the jockeys' changing tent to check over Addie's gear bag. She unzipped it. "I will slice and dice this son of a bitch!"

On top of Addie's clothes rested a Queen of Diamonds.

44

When Harry finally walked into her kitchen at 2:30 A.M. and saw Susan, all the horrors of the day, which now seemed years ago, began to spill out. Susan had heard about Addie's accident on the radio and had waited at the farm to talk to her friend.

The two dear friends sat down at the kitchen table. Harry told her that Chark was under suspicion but hadn't been arrested.

"*So you see, Sargent Wilcox is Nigel and it was Sargent who, along with Coty Lamont, buried Marylou Valiant.*" Tucker lay down nose to nose with Mrs. Murphy, flat out on her stomach.

"*And you say this Jack Russell met Nigel in Bozeman, Montana?*" Mrs. Murphy gently swished her tail back and forth like a slender reed in slowly moving water. "*Not that I would put much faith in anything a Jack Russell says, but still——*"

"*This was a reputable Russell, not one of those yappers.*"

"Oh, you'll stick up for any dog."

"No, I won't. You've never heard me say anything good about a Chihuahua, have you?"

The cat allowed as to how that was a fact. She flicked her pink tongue over her black lips. "Apart from ZeeZee Thompson, no one there knows that Nigel Danforth is Sargent Wilcox."

"No," Tucker said, "but that's not all. Mrs. Hogendobber and Mim—Jim, too—were upset about a St. Christopher's medal Addie wore after the first race."

"Why?"

"It was her mother's. No one has seen it since Marylou disappeared."

"Maybe that's why Coty Lamont was digging"—she paused—"except he didn't reach the body. Oh, this is giving me a headache!"

"Whoever had the St. Christopher's medal has had it for the last five years. And you know what else?" Tucker panted. "Someone put the Queen of Diamonds in Addie's gear bag."

Mrs. Murphy put her paws over her eyes, "Tucker, this is terrible."

45

"Son of a bitch!" Rick Shaw exploded.

"You couldn't have known." Cynthia offered him a cigarette. He snatched one out of the pack.

"He's playing with us." He lit his cigarette and clenched so hard on the weed that he bit it in half, sending the burning tip falling into his crotch. He batted out the fire.

Cynthia, too, smacked at the glowing tip. "Sorry."

He paused a minute, then glanced down at her hand in his crotch. "Ah—I'm sure there's something I could say to cover this situation, but I can't think of it right now." He dropped the stub in the ashtray.

Cynthia lit him another cigarette. "Don't bite, just inhale."

It was five in the morning and they circled the growing city of Charlotte with ease—too early for traffic. Rick and Cynthia had stayed to assist the Camden police since the crimes in their respective jurisdictions were most likely linked. The Camden police had insisted on booking Charles Valiant on suspicion of attempted murder. Rick finally let them, figuring twenty-four hours in Camden's jail would be twenty-four hours in which they would know Chark's whereabouts. Arthur would free him on bail early Monday morning.

"The Queen of Diamonds! Son of a bitch!"

"Boss, you've been saying that for the last hour and a half. There's one bloody queen left and—"

"Bloody queen is right. I know this guy will strike again, I know it. If only I could figure out the significance of the cards." He slammed the dash.

"Your blood pressure's going to go through the roof."

"Shut up and drive!" He glowered out the window and then turned to her. "I'm sorry."

"It's a bitch. I never saw it coming, either," she said sympathetically.

"If we only knew what they had in common."

"Jockeys."

"Not enough." He shook his head.

"They all knew one another."

"Yes." He began to breathe a bit more regularly.

"They're all young people."

"Yes."

"They owed money to Mickey Townsend. They all used cocaine."

"Yes." He rubbed his eyes with the back of his hands. "Oh, Coop, it's staring me right in the face and I can't see it."

46

It was a subdued group that gathered at Miranda's on Sunday night: Harry, Rick Shaw, and Cynthia Cooper, plus Pewter, Mrs. Murphy, and Tucker.

The big news from Camden was that Addie had suffered a severe concussion. The doctors, afraid that her brain would swell, insisted on keeping her in the hospital for two more days. She'd also broken her collarbone. Given what could have happened, the consensus was that she was a lucky woman. And a rich one. She had attained her majority.

The Camden police, in a burst of efficiency, arrested Mickey Townsend on suspicion of the murders of Nigel Danforth and Coty Lamont. A pack of cards found tucked in his car's side pocket was missing the queens of clubs, spades, and diamonds. A stiletto rested under the seat of his silver BMW.

He protested his innocence. He'd be sent up to Ablemarle County as soon as the paperwork was completed between Rick's department and Camden's. Rick didn't protest the Camden police holding Mickey. Secretly, he felt Mickey'd be safer in custody.

Harry told Rick she didn't think Mickey was the killer. The gambling debts, though sizable, weren't large enough to kill over, and Mickey wasn't that stupid.

Rick, hands interlocking over his stomach, listened. "You don't buy Charles Valiant as the murderer?"

All said, "No."

Cynthia added, "Bazooka wasn't doped. The blood tests came back negative. Fair was on the ball to pull blood."

"Rick, what haven't you told us?" Miranda addressed him in familiar fashion as she offered him one of her famous scones.

Delicately he bit off a piece and chewed before answering. "I know that Mickey Townsend followed Coty Lamont to Mim's stable on the night of Coty's death. He admits to pulling a gun on Coty and marching him out of there. He swears he didn't kill him."

"Why was he in Mim's stable?" Miranda picked up her knitting needles then dropped them in the basket.

"That I don't know. Coty was digging in a stall in the back. Said he would pay Mickey when he unearthed the treasure, well, I don't think those were his exact words. He told me that at Camden yesterday. Lord, it seems like a week ago." He wiped his forehead. "Guess we'd better visit the stable."

At the mention of Mim's stable, Mrs. Murphy sprang to her feet. *"Go crazy! Run around! Bark! Steal a scone! We've got to let them know they need to go over there right now!"*

Mrs. Murphy ran toward the wall, banked off it then jumped clean over Mrs. Hogendobber's laden tea trolley, narrowly missing the steaming tea pot.

"I say—" Miranda's mouth fell agape.

"Go to the stable! Go to the stable now!" Tucker barked.

Pewter, lacking in the speed department, hurried to the center of the living room, rolled over, displayed her gargantuan tummy, and said, *"Pay attention to us! Right now, you stupid mammals!"*

Tucker ran in faster circles and Mrs. Murphy ran with her. Pewter jumped up, considered jumping over the tea trolley, realized she couldn't and instead leapt on the armchair and patted Harry's cheek.

"Harry, these animals are tetched," Miranda finally sputtered.

"No, we're not. We know what's in Orion's stall. We've known for days, but we haven't been able to tell you. You're on track now. GO TO THE STABLE!" Mrs. Murphy lifted her exquisite head to heaven and yowled.

Harry stood up and walked over to the cat who eluded her grasp. "Calm down, Murph."

"Maybe she's got rabies." Miranda drew back.

"You say that any time an animal gets excited. She's cutting a shine. Aren't you, Murphy?"

"No, I am not."

"Me neither. Listen to us," Pewter pleaded.

"Murphy, I'm exhausted. Can I stop now?" Tucker continued circling the humans.

"Sure."

The dog conveniently dropped by the tea trolley where some crumbs had fallen on the rug.

Rick clapped his hands on his knees. "Well, I'm going over to Mim's to see if she'll let us dig up that stall. Which stall was it?"

Cynthia checked her notes. "Orion's."

"Hallelujah!" Mrs. Murphy declared.

47

The cold crept into the stable. At first nobody noticed, but as Harry, Miranda, and the two animals stood watching Rick Shaw's team dig into Orion's stall, the chill crept into their bones.

When the sheriff's crew arrived, they surveyed the fourteen-foot-square stall and didn't know where to start, so Tucker began digging at the spot. The humans followed suit because Cynthia Cooper remarked that dogs, thanks to their keen noses, could smell things humans could not.

Mrs. Murphy grew tired of sitting on the center aisle floor, so she climbed into the hayloft where, with Rodger Dodger, Pusskin, and the mice, she gazed down as the humans labored. Spadeful after spadeful of crush-or-run and then clay was carefully piled to the side.

Mim, her shearling jacket pulled tightly around her, joined the humans. "Anything?"

"No," Harry answered.

"You don't think this is some kind of nutty tale on Mickey's part—a wild-goose chase?" she asked.

Rick, arms folded across his chest, replied, "I've got to try everything, Mrs. Sanburne. Don't worry, we'll put everything back just as we found it."

A car pulled up outside, the door slammed, and a haggard Arthur Tetrick strode into the stable. "Mim?" he called out. "Are you out here?"

"Here."

Arthur shouted as he walked up. "I've gotten Chark released! He'll fly home tomorrow. An ambulance will bring up Adelia on Thursday if the doctors agree." He noticed the digging. "What's going on?"

"We don't know exactly," Mim answered.

Harry shivered.

"Why don't you go back to the tack room," Miranda suggested. "You don't have enough meat on your bones to ward off the cold. Not like I do."

"No. I'll walk around a bit." Harry jiggled her legs and walked up and down the aisle. Tucker walked with her.

"You racking up brownie points, Tucker?" the tiger hollered.

"Oh, shut up. You can be so green-eyed sometimes."

That made Rodger Dodger and Pusskin laugh because Mrs. Murphy had beautiful green eyes.

One of the officers hit something hard. "Huh?"

Rick and Cynthia drew closer. "Be careful."

The other two officers carefully pushed their spades into the earth. "Yeah." Another light click was heard.

They worked faster now, each shovelful getting closer until a rib cage appeared.

"Oh, my God!" Mim exclaimed.

"What is it?" Arthur pushed his way to the edge, saw the rib cage and a now partially exposed arm as the men feverishly dug.

Arthur hit the ground with a thud.

"*Wuss.*" Mrs. Murphy turned her nose up.

48

Charles Valiant appeared far older than his twenty-five years. Dark circles under his eyes marred his handsome appearance. He'd eaten nothing since Addie's fall. Neither Fair nor any of his friends could get him to eat. Boom Boom took a turn with him as did everyone. She spoke passionately of Lifeline, leaving him some literature, but he was far too depressed to respond.

Fair sat with him in the living room of the little cottage on Mim's estate. Harry boiled water for a cup of instant soup. Mrs. Murphy and Tucker quietly lay on the rug.

"Chark, you've got to eat something," Harry pleaded.

"I can't," he whispered.

A knock on the door propelled Fair out of a comfortable old chair. He opened the door. "Arthur."

A subdued Arthur came inside, quickly shutting the door behind him. He forced a smile. "Well, we know one thing."

"What?" Fair's blond stubble made him look like a Viking. "It can't get any worse."

Harry said nothing for she thought it could indeed get worse, and if the killer weren't apprehended soon, it would.

"Charles, Adelia will be fully recovered before you know it. She'll be home before the week is out. Please eat something so she doesn't worry about *you*," Arthur reasoned.

"He's right," Fair said.

"Well, I stopped by to see how you're doing." Arthur held out his hand. "I nearly forgot. Congratulations on coming into your inheritance. I know you'll use it wisely."

"Oh," Chark's voice sounded weak, "I'd forgotten all about it."

"This troublesome time will pass. All will be well, Charles. And as for Adelia"—he folded his hands together—"perhaps she is right. She needs to go her own way and be her own person. I truly believe things will work out for the best."

"Thanks, Arthur." Chark shook his hand.

"Well, I'd better be on my way."

"I'll walk you to your car." Harry opened the front door, asking as they walked, "Do they know yet who it was in Orion's stall? I mean conclusively?"

Arthur shook his head. "No, but I think we all know." A strangled cry gurgled in his throat. "To see her like that when I thought never to see her again . . ." He collected himself. "I will advise Mim on an excellent criminal lawyer, of course."

"Why?" Harry innocently asked.

"The body was found on her property. I should think she'll be a suspect and possibly even arrested."

Harry's voice rose. "Has everyone lost their minds? Marylou Valiant was one of her *best* friends."

"Most murders are committed among people who are family or friends." He held up his hands. "Not that I, for one minute, think that Mim Sanburne murdered her. But right now, Mim is in a vulnerable position. Go inside before you catch your death."

Harry walked back into Chark's cottage, closing the door tightly behind her, and thought about the phrase "catch your death"—as though death were a baseball hurtling through the azure sky.

49

Mrs. Murphy left the stable at six-thirty in the morning, cutting across the hay fields . . . she needed time to herself to think. She brushed by some rattleweed, causing the odd metallic sound that always startled city people upon first hearing it. The light frost, cool on her pads, would melt by ten in the morning, lingering only in areas of heavy shade or along the creek bottom.

A deep, swift creek divided Harry's farm from Blair Bainbridge's land, property that had once belonged to the family of the Reverend Herbert Jones. Murphy hoped Blair would return soon, because she liked him. As a model he was one of that growing number of Americans who made a lot of money at his job but preferred to live somewhere lovely instead of in a big city. He was often on the road, though.

She stopped at the creek, watching the water bubble and

spray over the slick rocks. Mrs. Murphy, never overfond of water, liked it even less when the mercury was below 60°F. She bent over the deep bank, for there were quiet pools, and if she stayed still she could see the small fish that congregated there. She'd watched Paddy, her ex, catch a small-mouth bass once, a performance that must have heated up her ardor for him although now she couldn't understand what she had ever seen in that faithless tom. Still, he was handsome and likable.

A flip of a tail alerted her to the school of fish below. She sighed, then trotted to where Jones's Creek, as it was known, flowed into Swift Run and thence into Meechum's River.

The scent of fallen and still dropping leaves presaged winter. They crunched underfoot, which made hunting field mice a task. She followed the twists and turns of Jones's Creek, admiring the sycamores, their bark distinctive by the contrasts of gray peeling away to beige. She startled ravens picking grain out of a cornfield. They hollered at her, lifted up over her head, circled, and returned after she passed.

Another ten minutes and she reached the connection where the creek poured into Swift Run. A big willow, upturned in last week's rains and wind, had crashed off the far bank into the river. A lone blue heron, a silent sentinel, was poised about fifty yards downstream from the willow.

As Mrs. Murphy was on the opposite shore, the heron, enormous, worried not at all about the small predator. Then again, the bird was so big that if Mrs. Murphy had swum Swift Run and catapulted onto her back, the heron could have soared into the air, taking the cat with her.

She looked up from her fishing, giving Mrs. Murphy a fierce stare. The heron's methods depended on stillness followed with lightning-fast reflexes as she grabbed a fish—or anything else that caught her fancy—with her long beak.

The tiger cat sat and watched the great bird. An odd ripple of current under the willow's trunk drew her gaze away from the heron. The water would strike the obstacle and whirl around it, the obstacle would roll a bit, then the water would break free on its way downstream.

She walked along the bank to get a better look, reveling in her good eyes, so much better than human or dog eyes. She focused and another little gusher of water lifted up the obstacle. An arm broke through the surface and then sank again. Another hard rain and the corpse would be free from the branches of the willow.

Mrs. Murphy, fur fluffed out, watched. The next surge of water pushed the body up a bit farther, and she saw what was left of Linda Forloines's face. The eyes and nose were gone, courtesy of hungry fish and crawdads. The face was bleached even whiter and bloated, but it was Linda Forloines without a doubt. Mrs. Murphy remembered her from when she had worked at Mim's stable.

She trotted back to her original spot and called out to the heron, "I'm sorry to disturb your hunting. Is this your territory?"

"Of course it's my territory," came the curt reply.

"Do you know there's a dead human back at the willow?"

"Yes."

"Do you know how long it's been there?"

The heron cocked her head, her light violet-crested plume swept back over her head. "Not quite a week. There's another body one mile from here as I fly, more miles on the ground. That one is stuck in a truck." She snapped her long powerful beak. "I wish they'd have the decency to bury their dead."

"The murderer was in a hurry," the cat called over the creek.

"Ah." She stretched her graceful neck to the sky then recoiled it. "They exhibit a strange penchant for killing one another, don't they?"

"A genetic flaw, I suppose." Mrs. Murphy also thought human violence most unanimal-like. After all, she and her kind only killed other species, and then for food, although she had a difficult time resisting dispatching the occasional mouse for sport.

The heron spread her wings, exposing each feather to the

warming sun. *"Oh, that feels good. You know, if I felt like it, I could fly right over there and pick you up by your tail."*

"You'd have to catch me first," Mrs. Murphy countered.

"You'd be surprised at how fast I can fly."

"You'd be surprised at how fast I can zig and zag." Mrs. Murphy's toes tingled. She unsheathed her claws. *"Tell you what. I'll get a head start and you see if you can catch me. Don't pick me up, though, because I haven't hurt you—why hurt me? Just a game, okay?"*

"All right." The heron flapped her wings while still standing.

Mrs. Murphy took off like a shot. She raced along the edge of Jones's Creek back toward the cornfields as the heron lifted off to her cruising altitude. She ducked into the cornfields, which infuriated the crows, who soared up like pepper dashed into the sky. They saw the heron approaching and complained at the top of their considerable lungs.

The heron swooped low over the corn calling, *"No fair."*

"You never said I couldn't seek cover."

The crows dive-bombed back into the corn, forgetting for a moment about Mrs. Murphy, who leapt forward, nearly swatting one iridescent black tail.

"HEY!" The crow clamped its yellow beak together, then zoomed out of there, the others following.

The heron circled, landing at the edge of the cornfield, eyes glittering. Mrs. Murphy walked to the end of the corn row. She was maybe ten feet from the huge creature.

"You could run out and attack me before I could get airborne," the heron taunted the cat.

"Maybe I could, but why would I want to pull feathers from a bird as elegant as yourself?" Mrs. Murphy flattered her. She knew that gleam in the eye, and she didn't trust the heron even though she wasn't on the bird's customary menu.

The compliment pleased the heron. She preened. *"Why, thank you."* She stepped toward Mrs. Murphy, who didn't back into the corn row. *"You know that dead woman back there at the willow?"*

"I know who it was. No one I care about, but there's been a rash of murders among the humans."

"Um. My mother used to tell me that she could give me a fish or she could teach me how to fish. Naturally, I was lazy and wanted her to give me the fish. She didn't. She swallowed it right in front of me. It made me so mad." The big beak opened, revealing a bright pink tongue. "But I got the message, and she taught me how to fish. If you don't know how to fish you look at everyone as a free meal or you become bait yourself. I expect that dead thing back there couldn't fish."

"Partly true. She liked fishing in troubled waters." The cat intently watched the heron. Those huge pronged feet looked out of place in the cornfield.

"Ah. Well, I enjoyed talking to you, pussycat. I'm going back to my nest."

"I enjoyed you too."

With that the heron rose in the sky, circling once. Mrs. Murphy walked out of the cornfield, then made a beeline back to the old barn as the heron made a wider circle and cawed out to her below. Even though she felt the heron wouldn't attack, the sound of that caw pushed her into a run. She flew, belly flat to the land, the whole way home.

"Why, Mrs. Murphy, you look as though you've seen a ghost," Harry said as Murphy careened into the barn, her eyes as big as billiard balls.

"No, just Linda Forloines."

Tucker tilted her head. "Not in the best of health, I presume." Then she laughed at her own joke.

"She was useless in life. At least she's useful in death."

"How?"

"Fish food."

50

"Do you know what you're doing?" Miranda paced, her leather-soled shoes sliding along the worn shiny floorboards of the post office.

The old railroad clock on the wall read 7:20. Darkness had enveloped the small building. The shades were drawn and only a glimmer of light from the back room spilled out under the back window. The front door, kept unlocked, every now and then opened and closed as Crozet residents, on the way home from work or to a party, dashed in and picked up their mail if they had been unable to get there during the day.

As a federal facility, a post office, no less, the front part of the building where the boxes were had to be kept open to the public. The back was locked, and the crenelated door was pulled down to the counter much like a garage door, and locked from behind.

"I'll be at your choir show a tad late," Harry said.

"You shouldn't be here alone. Not with a killer on the loose."

"*She's right,*" Mrs. Murphy, Tucker and Pewter echoed.

Pewter, seeing the light, had sauntered in from next door. "*Market's open until eleven, but still someone could sneak in here and he'd never know. He's too busy watching television.*"

"Harry, come on. You can do this tomorrow."

"I can't. I've got this one little hunch."

"If you're not at our choirfest by intermission, I am calling Rick Shaw. Do you hear me?"

"Yes."

With reluctance, Mrs. Hogendobber closed the door, and Harry locked it behind her.

Working with the mail meant she saw every catalog under the sun. She knew of three hunting catalogs, five gun catalogs, which also featured knives, and one commando catalog for those who envisioned themselves soldiers of fortune. If the police hadn't traced the knives that the killer used, it might very well be because they had confined themselves to local stores.

She started calling. Since all the catalog companies had twenty-four-hour 800 numbers, she knew she'd get someone on the end of the line.

An hour later she had found Case XX Bowie knives for over $200, replicas of sabers, double-edged swords, saracens, and even stilettos, but not the kind she wanted. She'd spoken to college kids moonlighting, crusty old men who wanted to discuss the relative merits of government-issue bayonets, and even one aggressive man who asked her for a long-distance date.

The two cats nestled into the mail cart, since there wasn't anything they could do to help. Tucker fell asleep.

Having exhausted her supply of catalogs, Harry had hit a dead end. She couldn't think what to do next. She'd even called a uniform supply company on the outside chance someone there might be a cutlery enthusiast, as she put it.

"Call L.L. Bean. They know everything," Mrs. Murphy called out from the bottom of the mail cart.

Harry made herself a cup of tea. She checked the clock. "If I don't get over to the Church of the Holy Light in about twenty minutes Mrs. H. will fry me for breakfast."

"I told you, call L.L. Bean."

Harry sat down, sipped her tea. She felt more awake now. She kept an L.L. Bean catalog, her own, stacked next to the sugar bowl.

"Tucker, has she got it yet?"

"No." The dog lifted her head. *"Forget it."*

"Sometimes people drive me around the bend!" the sleek cat complained, leaping out of the mail bin.

"Why bother?" Pewter stretched out in the bottom. *"She won't listen about Linda's body. She won't listen now either."*

Mrs. Murphy jumped onto the table, rubbed Harry's shoulder then stuck out her claws and pulled the L.L. Bean catalog toward Harry.

"Murph—" Harry reached out and put her hand on the catalogue, fearful the cat would shred it. "Hmm." She flipped open the pages, filled with merchandise photographed as accurately as possible.

She gulped down a hot swallow, jumped up, and dialed the 800 number.

"Could I talk to your supervisor, please?"

"Certainly." The woman's voice on the other end was friendly.

Harry waited a few moments and then heard, "Hello, L.L. Bean, how may I help you?"

"Ma'am, pardon me for disturbing you. This has nothing to do with L.L. Bean, but do you know of any mail-order company that specializes in knives?"

"Let me think a minute," the voice said, that of a middle-aged woman. "Joe, what's the name of that company in Tennessee specializing in hunting knives?" A faint voice could be heard in the background. "Smoky Mountain Knife Works in Sieverville, Tennessee."

"Thank you." Harry scribbled down the information, "You've been great. May I make one suggestion about your duck boots? I mean, I always call them duck boots."

"Sure. We want to hear from our customers."

"You know the Bean Boot you all started making in 1912? Well, I love the boot. I've had mine resoled twice."

"I'm glad to hear that."

"But women's sizes don't carry a twelve-inch upper. Ours only go to nine inches, and I work on a farm. I would sure like to have a twelve-inch upper."

"What's your shoe size?"

"Seven B."

"You wear a seven and a half in this—you know, a little bigger for heavy socks."

"Yes, thank you for reminding me."

"Tell you what, can you call me back tomorrow and I'll see what we can do? The sales force is twenty-four hours, but I'll have to wait until regular hours tomorrow to see if I can accommodate your request. What's your name?"

"Mary Minor Haristeen."

"Okay then, Miss Haristeen, you call me tomorrow afternoon and ask for Glenda Carpenter."

"Thank you, I will."

Harry pressed the disconnect button and got the phone number for the Sieverville company. Hurriedly she punched in the phone number.

A man answered, "Smoky Mountain."

"Sir, hello, this is Mary Minor Haristeen from the Crozet post office in central Virginia. I am trying to trace back orders for folks here. A resident says he had the knives sent to my post office, and I swear they must have gone to the main post office in Charlottesville instead. It's no mistake on your part, by the way— just one of those things."

"Gee—that could be a lot of orders."

"Maybe I can help you. It would either be repeat orders or a bulk order for that beautiful stiletto, uh, I forget the name, but the handle is wrapped in wire and it's about a foot long."

The voice filled with pride. "You mean the Gil Hibben Silver Shadow. That's some piece of hardware, sister."

"Yes, yes, it is." Harry tried not to shudder since she knew the use to which it had been put.

"Let me pull it up on the computer here." He hummed. "Yeah, I got one order to Charlottesville. Three knives. Ordered for Albemarle Cutlery. Nice store, huh?"

"Yes. By the way, is there a person's name on that?" Harry didn't tell him there was no Albemarle Cutlery. The name had to be a front.

"No. Just the store and a credit card. I can't read off the number, of course."

"No, no, I understand, but at least I know where the shipment has gone."

"Went out two months ago. Hasn't been returned. I hope everything is okay."

"It will be. You're a lifesaver."

She bid her good-byes and then called down to the central post office on Seminole Road.

"Carl?" She recognized the voice that answered.

"Harry, what's doing, girl?"

"It only gets worse. Between now and December twenty-fifth we might as well forget sleep. Will you do me a favor?"

"Sure."

"Do you have a large post office box registered to Albemarle Cutlery?"

"Hold on." He put the phone down.

Harry heard his footsteps as he walked away, then silence. Finally the footsteps returned. "Albemarle Cutlery. C. de Bergerac."

"Damn!"

"What?"

"Sorry, Carl, it's not you. That's a phony name. Cyrano de Bergerac was a famous swordsman in the seventeenth century. The subject of a famous romance."

"Steve Martin. I know," Carl confidently replied.

"Yes, well, that's one way to remember." Harry laughed and wondered what Rostand, the playwright, would make of Steve Martin as his hero. "Listen, would you fax me his signature from the receipt?"

"Yeah, sure. You up to something?"

"Well—yes."

"Okay, I'll keep my mouth shut. I'll pull the record and fax it right over. Good enough?"

"More than good enough. Thanks."

"*Mother, calm down,*" Mrs. Murphy told her. "*The fax will come through in a minute.*"

Harry froze when she heard the whirr and wheeze of the fax. Her hands trembled as she pulled the paper out. Mrs. Murphy hopped on her shoulder.

"It can't be!" Harry's hands shook harder when she saw the left-leaning, bold script.

"*Well, who is it?*" Pewter called from the mail bin.

"*I don't know,*" Murphy called back. "*I don't see the handwriting of people like Mother does. I mean, I know Mom's, Fair's, Mim's, and Mrs. Hogendobber's, but I don't know this one.*"

Tucker scrambled to her feet. "*Mother, call Rick Shaw. Please!*"

But Harry, dazed by what she now knew, wasn't thinking straight. Shaken, she folded the paper, slipping it into the back pocket of her jeans.

"Come on, gang, we've got to get to church before Mrs. Hogendobber pitches a hissy."

"Don't worry about Mrs. Hogendobber," Pewter sagely advised. "Call the sheriff."

"Everyone will be at the choirfest, so she can see him there," Tucker added.

"That's what I'm afraid of." Mrs. Murphy fluffed out her fur and jumped off Harry's shoulder.

"What do you mean?" Pewter asked as she crawled out of the mail bin. She was too lazy to jump.

"Everybody will be there—including the killer."

51

The heater, slow in working, sent off a faint aroma in Harry's blue truck. She gripped the steering wheel so tightly her knuckles were white. Puffs of breath lazed out into the air as she sped along, a big puff from her, a medium puff from Tucker, and two small puffs from Mrs. Murphy and Pewter.

"I'm proud of Mom," Tucker said. "She figured this one out all by herself. I couldn't tell her about Nigel being Sargent, although we still don't know all that we need to know about him."

"Humans occasionally use their deductive powers." Mrs. Murphy wedged close to Harry's leg, Pewter next to her, as they huddled down to get warm.

"But if she figured out about the knife place, don't you think Rick Shaw and Cynthia have figured that out as well?" Pewter asked.

"Maybe, but only Mom knows the signatures."

"*Maybe he's afraid of exposing her to risk. Whoever this is is ruthless. Let's not forget that this started years ago,*" Mrs. Murphy prudently noted.

The parking lot of the Church of the Holy Light, jammed from stem to stern, testified to the popularity of the evening's entertainment. The choirfest, one of the church's biggest fundraisers, drew music lovers from all over the county. They might not be willing to accept the Church's strict message, but they loved the singing.

Harry scanned the lot for a place to park but had to settle for a spot along the side of the road. She noticed that the squad car was near the front door. Mim's Bentley Turbo R, Susan and Ned's Conestoga—as they called their station wagon—were there, Herbie's big Buick Roadmaster; in fact, it looked as though everyone was at the choirfest but her.

She forgot to tell the animals to stay in the truck. They hopped out when she opened the door, following her into the church just as the choir made its measured entrance to enthusiastic applause. Intermission was over and the folks could expect a rousing second half.

Harry noticed her little family as did some of the other people who turned to greet her. Tucker quietly sat down next to Fair. Mrs. Murphy and Pewter, not exactly sacrilegious but not overwhelmed either, decided to check out the gathering before picking their spot.

"You kitties come back here," Harry hissed, staying at the back of the church.

"*Don't look at her,*" Mrs. Murphy directed her fat gray sidekick.

"Mrs. Murphy! Pewter!" Harry hissed, then stopped because the choirmaster had lifted his baton, and all eyes were on him. The organist pressed the pedals and the first lovely notes of "Swing Low, Sweet Chariot" swelled over the group.

Tucker, realizing Harry wouldn't chase after her, decided to follow the cats, who generally led her into temptation.

Chark Valiant sat in the front row with the Sanburnes and Arthur Tetrick. Rick and Cynthia stood off to the side. Harry, not finding a seat, leaned against the wall, hoping to catch Rick's or Cynthia's eye unobtrusively.

Mrs. Hogendobber stepped forward for her solo. Her rich contralto voice coated the room like dark honey.

"Mrs. H.?" Mrs. Murphy was so astonished to hear the good woman that she walked right in front of everyone and sat in front of Miranda, her pretty little head tilted upward to watch her friend, the lady who formerly didn't like cats.

Miranda saw Mrs. Murphy, now joined by Pewter and Tucker. The two kitties and the dog, enraptured, were immobile. A few titters rippled throughout the audience, but then the humans were oddly affected by the animals listening to Miranda singing one of the most beautiful spirituals, a harmonic record of a harsher time made endurable by the healing power of music.

Herb, also in the front row, a courtesy seat from the church, marveled at the scene.

When Miranda finished, a moment's hush of deep appreciation was followed by thunderous applause.

"You were wonderful," Mrs. Murphy called out, then trotted down the center aisle to check over each face in her passing.

"What are we looking for?" Pewter asked.

"Someone guilty as sin."

"Ooh-la," she trilled.

"And in church, too," Tucker giggled.

"Will you get back here!" Harry whispered.

"Ignore her. No matter how red in the face she gets, just ignore her."

"You're going to get it," Pewter warned.

"She has to catch me first, and remember, she left me to go to Montpelier and then Camden. I just pray"—she remembered she was in a church—"we can get her out of here before the fur flies."

The next song, a Bach chorale, held everyone's attention. Mrs. Murphy jumped onto a low table along the back wall near Harry but far enough away so she could jump off if Harry came after her. Pewter followed. Tucker lagged behind.

"Count the exits."

"Double front doors, two on either side of the nave. There's a back stair off the balcony but that probably connects with the doors off the nave."

"And I'm willing to bet there's another back door." She swept her whiskers forward. "Tucker, get up here."

"Tucker, there are four exits. The one behind, two on the side, and one behind the proscenium, I think. If something goes wrong, if he gets scared or anything, we can run faster than he can. You go back to the nave exit, we'll stay by this one. If anything happens, stay with Mom and we'll go out our door and catch up with you. We'll be out the door before the humans know what hit them."

"Well, let's hope nothing happens." Pewter, not the most athletic girl, wanted to stay put.

Rick edged his way toward Harry, careful not to make noise. Cynthia moved to the front door.

Harry reached in her back pocket and pulled out the fax. "Come outside with me for a minute."

The sheriff and his deputy tiptoed out with Harry. Keenly, Miranda observed them as she sang. A few other people noticed out of the corners of their eyes.

"Harry, you've been meddling again," Rick said in a low voice as they closed the doors behind them.

"I couldn't help it. I figured if we could trace the knives we'd have a first down, goal to go."

Cynthia studied the fax sheet with a little pocket flashlight.

Rick held it steady in his hands, as Harry told him whose handwriting it was. "I'm not surprised," he said.

"*Was* the body Marylou Valiant's?" Harry asked.

"Yes." Cynthia answered. "Dr. Yarbrough brought the dental records right over a half hour ago. It is Marylou."

"Did you have any idea?" Harry asked Rick.

"Yes, but I thought this was about money. It's not." He rubbed his nose, the tip of which was cold. "The cards and knife in Mickey Townsend's car—right over the top. That brought me back to the real motive: jealousy." He shook his head. "When you get down to it, motives are simple. Crimes may be complicated, but motives are always simple."

"What do we do now?" Harry shuffled her feet.

"*We* don't do anything," Rick said as more applause broke out inside. "We wait."

"He's got good alibis," Coop commented.

"But if you broke down each murder, minute by minute, wouldn't you find the loophole?"

"Harry, it's not that easy. We've pinpointed the time of the murders as close as we can, but that still gives him a healthy thirty-minute comfort zone. A good lawyer can chip away at that very easily, you know, try to get the jury to believe the coroner's report is fuzzy. Things like the temperature inside the barn versus the temperature outside would affect the corpse, as would the victim's health while alive. They'll erode the time frame of each murder as well as planting doubt in the jury's mind as to how he could have escaped notice at Montpelier. Then they'll indulge in character assassination for each prosecution witness. Right now it's a cinch he'll get off with a good lawyer. Case is totally circumstantial." Rick hated the way the system worked, especially if a defendant had money.

"Yes, but what about Marylou's murder?" Harry's lips trembled she was so angry. "Can't we pin him down there?"

"Maybe if Coty were alive," Coop said. "He obviously knew where Marylou was buried."

"Rick, you *can't* let that son of a bitch go free."

"If I arrest him before I've built my case, he *will* go free, scot free, Harry." Rick's jaw clenched. He folded the fax. "This is a big help and I thank you for it. I promise you, I will do everything I can to close in."

More applause from inside roused Harry. "I guess I'd better go back in and make sure Murphy hasn't caused another commotion."

"A musical cat." Cynthia smiled, patting Harry on the back. "I know this is upsetting, but we just can't go out and arrest people. We'll keep working until we can make it stick. It's the price we pay for being a democracy."

"Yeah." Harry exhaled from her nose, then opened the door a crack and squeezed through.

The two cats remained on the table.

The last song, a great big burst from Handel's *Messiah*, raised the rafters. The audience cheered and clapped for an encore. The choir sang another lovely spiritual and then took a final bow, separating in the middle and filing out both sides of the stage.

The audience stirred. Harry walked over to the table, ready to scoop up Mrs. Murphy and Pewter when Mim, Jim, Charles, and Arthur came over, Fair immediately behind them.

Harry, overcome with emotion at the sight of the murderer, blurted out, "How could you? How could you kill all those people? How could you kill someone you loved?"

Arthur's face froze. He started to laugh but a horrible flash of recognition gleamed in Mim's eyes and in Chark's. Lightning fast he grabbed Harry, pulled a .38 from under his coat, and put it to her head. "Get out of the way."

Fair ducked low to tackle him. Arthur fired, grazing his leg. Fair's leg collapsed under him as people screamed and ran.

Mrs. Hogendobber, not yet off the stage, ran out the side door and hopped into her Ford Falcon. She started the motor.

Rick and Cynthia, hearing the shot, rushed back in through the double doors just as Arthur dragged Harry out.

"You come one step closer and she's dead."

"What's another one, Arthur? You're going to kill me anyway." Harry thought how curious it was to die with everyone looking on. She felt the cold circle of the barrel against her head, saw the contorted anguish on the faces of her friends, the snarling rage of her dog.

No one noticed the two cats streaking by. Tucker stayed with Harry.

"Don't rile him, Mother. The minute he shifts his eyes I'll nail him," the sturdy little dog growled.

"Arthur Tetrick!" Mim shrieked. "You'll rot in hell for this. You killed Marylou Valiant, didn't you?"

Arthur fired over her head just for the joy of seeing Mim frightened. Except she wasn't. People around her hit the ground but she shook her fist at him. "You'll never get away with it."

Chark, the time for talk past, lunged for Arthur. A crack rang out and the young man slumped to the ground, grabbing his shoulder.

Arthur ran outside now, propelling Harry, the cold air clarifying his senses, but then Arthur was always coolly assessing the odds in his life. His car was parked near the front. He pushed Harry into the driver's side, keeping the gun on her at all times, making her slide over to the passenger seat.

"Can you get a shot off?" Rick, on one knee, asked Cynthia, also on one knee, pistol out.

"No. Not without jeopardizing Harry."

Fair limped out, trailing blood. Herbie Jones ran after him, struggling to hold him back. "He'll kill her, Fair!"

"He'll kill her for sure if we don't stop him."

"Fair. Stay where you are!" Rick commanded.

Tucker had reached the car where Harry was and grabbed Arthur's ankle as he started to get in. Arthur shook the dog off, not noticing that Mrs. Murphy and Pewter had leapt into the backseat. He quickly turned the gun back on Harry, who had her hand on the passenger door handle.

"Keep down in the backseat," Mrs. Murphy told Pewter. "Once he gets in the driver's seat and reaches for the ignition, we've got him."

Pewter, too excited to reply, crouched, her fur standing on end, her fangs exposed.

To Arthur's shock, Mrs. Hogendobber roared through the parking lot, stopping the Falcon directly in front of him.

"I'll kill that meddling biddy!" he screamed, losing his temper for the first time.

He opened the driver's window and took aim, firing through her passenger window. Mrs. Hogendobber opened her door and rolled out, lying flat on the ground. Arthur could no longer see her.

"Run for it, Miranda, he's going to ram the car!" Herb shouted as he rushed forward, crouching to help Miranda. She scrambled to her feet, her choir robes dragging in the stone parking lot.

Just as Arthur cut on his ignition he heard two hideous yowls behind him.

"*Die, human!*" Mrs. Murphy and Pewter leapt from the backseat into the front, attacking his hands.

Murphy tore deeply into his gun hand before he registered what had happened.

Seizing the opportunity, Harry grabbed his right hand, smashing his wrist on the steering wheel. He tried to reach over the steering wheel for her with his left hand but Pewter sank her fangs to their full depth into the fleshy part of his palm. He screamed.

Harry smashed his wrist again as hard as she could against the steering wheel. He dropped the gun. She reached down to grab it. He kicked at her but she retrieved it.

Now Arthur Tetrick felt the cold barrel of a gun against his right temple.

Rick Shaw, his .357 Magnum pressed against Arthur's left temple, said, "You are under arrest for the murders of Nigel Danforth, Coty Lamont and Marylou Valiant. You have the right to remain silent—" Rick rattled off Arthur's rights.

Cynthia opened the passenger door as Arthur howled, "Call off your cats!"

Harry slid out the opened door. "Come on, girls!"

Mrs. Murphy took one last lethal whack for good measure, then leapt out followed by Pewter, who appeared twice her already impressive size.

Tucker and Fair, both limping, reached Harry at the same time. Fair grabbed Harry and held her close. He couldn't speak.

Harry began to shake. Curious how she had felt so little fear when she was in danger. Now it flooded over her. She hugged her ex-husband, then broke to rush to Miranda, being attended to by Herbie and Mim.

"Miranda, you could have been killed!" Tears rolled down Harry's cheeks. She stopped to scoop up the two cats, clutching them to her, repeatedly kissing their furry heads, then knelt down to kiss her sturdy corgi.

"Well, if he'd gotten out of this parking lot, you would have been killed," Miranda stated flatly, oblivious to her own heroism.

"I'd say two hellcats and Miranda saved your life." The Reverend Jones reached out to pet the cats.

"And Tucker. Brave dog." Harry again kissed a happy Tucker.

Arthur Tetrick sat bolt upright in his car. He'd never felt so much pain in his life, and being the self-centered man that he was, it did not occur to him that what he had inflicted upon his victims was much, much worse.

52

The whole crowd—Miranda, Fair, Cynthia, Rick, Big Mim, Little Marilyn, Jim, Susan, Herbie, Market Shiflett, Mrs. Murphy, Pewter, and Tucker—sat in the back of the post office the next day. Addie had come home from the hospital, but now Chark was in. She had the ambulance take her to Martha Jefferson Hospital to be with her brother; he would recover, but the bullet had shattered some bone.

Arthur had confessed to the murders of Marylou Valiant, Sargent Wilcox, a.k.a. Nigel Danforth, and Coty Lamont. As a lawyer he knew that after his behavior at the church he was dog meat, so he planned to throw himself on the mercy of the court with a guilty plea and thereby escape the death penalty.

Rick, who had interrogated Arthur, continued his story.

"—probably the only time Arthur ever acted out of passion, but once he killed Marylou Valiant, he had to get rid of the body. Coty and Sargent, through pure dumb luck, walked in on him as he was dragging her to his car. Sargent had been at Arthur's barn for only ten days, but he proved willing and flexible. He and Coty helped him bury Marylou in the last place anyone would ever look—Mim's barn. Sargent must have pocketed the St. Christopher's medal when no one was looking. Shortly after that Arthur gave up steeplechasing."

Mim chimed in, "I remember that. He said he couldn't go on without Marylou. It was her sport. He'd officiate but he'd run no more horses. What an actor he was."

"When Marylou disappeared, the two prime suspects were Arthur and Mickey Townsend for obvious reasons. We had no way of knowing whether Marylou was even dead, though. Technically we had no crime, we had no victim, we had a missing person," Rick said.

"And Arthur was a most conscientious executor of Marylou's will." Jim Sanburne hooked his fingers in his belt.

"Well, then, what happened to start this killing spree?" Fair stretched his bandaged leg out slowly. It felt better if he moved it around every now and then.

"Sargent came back," Cynthia said. "Wooed Addie. And stirred up Coty, who had been content up until then, to make more demands."

"Oh, that must have scared the bejesus out of Arthur," Herbie blurted out.

"Not as much as seeing Marylou's St. Christopher's medal around Addie's neck before the Colonial Cup," Cynthia said.

"He thought she knew?" Miranda questioned.

"He realized Sargent or Coty must have taken the medal. He feared Nigel—Sargent—had told Addie and that she would tell Rick after the race. Imagine his shock when he saw that royal blue medal just before she went out on the course," Rick said.

"I know how shocked I was to see it." Mim shook her head.

"Sargent and Coty were bleeding him heavily. He had no designs other than killing them. Addie upset the applecart," Cynthia added.

"What about Linda and Will? They're still missing."

Rick held up his palms, "Don't know. We have no idea if they're alive. Their absence is certainly not lamented and I doubt Arthur would need to kill them. I don't think they knew anything. We only know that sooner or later drug dealers sometimes get what they deserve."

As the group talked, Harry fed the cats and dog tidbits from the ham sandwiches Market had brought over.

"What was the significance of the queens?" Mim asked.

"Arthur said that was just meant to drive us all nuts. The bloody queen, he said and laughed in my face. Marylou was a bloody queen when she dumped him for Mickey. Arthur exploded . . . and strangled her."

"Addie is lucky to be alive," Miranda said softly. "Poor children. What they've been through."

"Yes." Mim reached in her purse for a handkerchief to dab her eyes.

Mrs. Murphy chimed in, *"Men like Arthur aren't accustomed to rejection."*

"Here, have some more ham." Miranda offered a piece to the cat since she interpreted the meows as requests for food.

"I bet he ran Mickey Townsend off the road that terrible rainy day—he was quietly going out of control." Miranda remembered that cold day.

Harry watched Pewter as she reached up and snagged half of a ham sandwich. "Market, we should share Pewter. What if I take her home with me every night, but she can work in the store during the day and work here, too?"

"Yes!" Pewter meowed.

Market laughed, "Think of the money I'll save."

"*Yeah, Pewter's a lion under the lard,*" Mrs. Murphy teased her friend.

The phone rang. Harry answered it. "Oh, hello, Mrs. Carpenter. You can? That's great. Let me give you my credit card number." Harry reached into her purse, pulled out a credit card, and read off her number.

"What are you buying?" Miranda demanded.

"L.L. Bean is making me a special pair of duck boots in my size, with twelve-inch uppers."

53

Poised on a hay bale, Mrs. Murphy waited. Pewter stayed inside with Harry. Mrs. Murphy rather liked having another cat around. Tucker didn't mind either.

There'd been so much commotion this weekend, she needed to be alone to collect her thoughts. She heard the squeaks from inside the hay bale. When an unsuspecting mouse darted out, with a jet-fast pounce Mrs. Murphy had her.

"Gotcha!"

The mouse stayed still under the cat's paws. "Make it fast. I don't want to suffer."

Mrs. Murphy carefully lifted the corner of her paw to behold those tiny obsidian eyes. She remembered the help of Mim's barn mice. "Oh, go on. I just wanted to prove to you that I'm faster than you."

"You aren't going to kill me?"

"No, but don't run around where Harry can see you."

"I won't." The tiny creature streaked back into the hay bale, and Mrs. Murphy heard excited squeals. Then she walked outside the barn and watched through the kitchen window. Harry was filling up her teapot, a task she performed at least twice a day. Mrs. Murphy was struck by how divine, how lovely, how unique such a mundane task could be. She purred, realizing how lucky she was, how lucky they all were to be alive on this crisp fall day.

Harry, glancing out of the kitchen window, observed Mrs. Murphy, tail to the vertical, come out of the barn.

The phone rang.

"Hello."

"Harry, it's Boom Boom. You were supposed to go with me to Lifeline last week, but considering all the excitement I didn't call. How about Monday at one o'clock?"

"Sure."

"I'll pick you up at the P.O."

"Fine."

"See you then. Bye-bye." Boom Boom signed off.

"Damn!" Harry hung up the phone. She looked out at Mrs. Murphy in the sunlight and thought how wonderful, how glorious, how relaxing it must be to be a cat.

Dear Highly Intelligent Feline:

Tired of the same old ball of string? Well, I've developed my own line of catnip toys, all tested by Pewter and me. Not that I love for Pewter to play with my little sockies, but if I don't let her, she shreds my manuscripts. You see how that is!

Just so the humans won't feel left out, I've designed a T-shirt for them.

If you'd like to see how creative I am, write to me and I'll send you a brochure.

Sneaky Pie's Flea Market
c/o American Artists, Inc.
P.O. Box 4671
Charlottesville, VA 22905

In felinity,

SNEAKY PIE BROWN

P.S. Dogs, get a cat to write for you!